Praise for **CAFÉ CON LYCHEE**

"With the most exquisitely picked ingredients—loveably cantankerous Theo, adorably awkward Gabi, delicious descriptions of treats, and relatable discoveries of love and sexuality—Emery Lee has yet again cooked up a world and characters I want to return to over and over!" —Jason June, author of *Jay's Gay Agenda* and *Out of the Blue*

"*Café Con Lychee* is as sweet as the baked goods and boba that fill up its pages, along with the adorable enemies-turned-lovers romance at its heart." —Adiba Jaigirdar, author of *The Henna Wars* and *Hani and Ishu's Guide to Fake Dating*

"Continuing to be *the* master of tropes, Emery Lee's food filled, beautifully multicultural, enemies-to-lovers *Café Con Lychee* is everything that I love about eir books: humorous, sassy, the perfect amount of stress that keeps me obsessively captivated, and so incredibly gay." —Jonny Garza Villa, author of *Fifteen Hundred Miles from the Sun* and *Ander and Santi Were Here*

"*Café Con Lychee* is the confection of sweetness and sweethearts we all need right now!" —Adam Sass, award-winning author of *Surrender Your Sons*

ALSO BY EMERY LEE
Meet Cute Diary

CAFÉ
con
LYCHEE

EMERY LEE

Quill Tree Books
An Imprint of HarperCollins Publishers

Quill Tree Books is an imprint of HarperCollins Publishers.

Café Con Lychee

Copyright © 2022 by Emery Lee

All rights reserved. Printed in the United States of America.
No part of this book may be used or reproduced in any manner
whatsoever without written permission except in the case of brief
quotations embodied in critical articles and reviews. For information
address HarperCollins Children's Books, a division of HarperCollins
Publishers, 195 Broadway, New York, NY 10007.

www.epicreads.com

ISBN 978-0-06-321027-1

Typography by Erin Fitzsimmons

22 23 24 25 26   PC/LSCH   10 9 8 7 6 5 4 3 2 1

First Edition

To my grandparents,
thank you for showing me how
beautiful love can be across cultural lines.

ONE
THEO

They say your life flashes before your eyes just before you die, but let me make something perfectly clear—whoever's in charge of that clip better not include a single fucking shot of Gabriel Moreno or I'm pressing charges.

It's already bad enough having to look up at him from the soccer field, grass stains so deep into my clothes I'll have to spend the next week getting them out. He's got that goofy grin on his face as he stammers out an apology like he doesn't run me over every other practice.

Actually, I think it's more than that by now.

"I'm so sorry, Theo," he says, holding out a hand to me.

I reluctantly take it because I know Coach is watching and I don't want another "fails to play nice with others" report.

That's just the way I am, I'm afraid—bad at school, bad at making friends, and really bad at playing nice with teammates who are quite possibly, singlehandedly, the reason our team hasn't won a single game in two years. Our motto is literally "Undefeated at being defeated." And I don't know, I guess it was naive of me to think that we could turn things around, really take junior year by storm and maybe earn me a couple of bonus points on my college apps so my parents would be a little less disappointed in me. I guess today's disaster is the universe telling me to stop dreaming too big.

"It won't happen again," Gabriel says.

Then we stare at each other with blank faces, because neither one of us believes that crap.

"All right!" Coach shouts, blowing his whistle. He really likes that whistle, like it's the one thing that keeps him feeling powerful even as he wastes his time coaching the worst soccer team in history. "Let's just start from the beginning, okay?"

Coach likes me since I'm the fastest kid on the team and one of three people who can actually aim, but sometimes I think he only sticks around because it makes him feel like less of a loser to see we're even more useless than he is. What other reason could he have for coaching a soccer team that never wins and wasting all his afternoons trying to make it good? But maybe he just appreciates not having to go home to an empty house since he and his wife got divorced last year.

When five o'clock finally rolls around, my back aches, either from the fall or carrying the weight of the entire team. Justin Cheng catches up with me on the way home.

The fortunate thing about living in a town that's barely ten square miles is that I live only about a mile from campus, so the walk isn't too bad. The real struggle is during winter, when the snow gets waist deep and you have to claw your way down the street. But considering it's mid-September, I don't mind. Of course, the goal would be to live somewhere like New York, where walking is practical and I wouldn't get stuck seeing Gabriel Moreno everywhere.

The neighborhood is mostly what you'd expect from white suburbia, and even though it's rush hour, there are barely any cars on the road. We have to pass the one familiar roundabout to get back to the shop, and everyone's doing their usual thing of stopping and waving people on before they go. My brother always drags me about how people won't be so nice if I ever get out of Vermont, but that's most of the charm. I wanna go somewhere people actually think like I do instead of all this picture-perfect greenery and maple creemees.

"You took that hit like a champ," Justin says.

I shrug. "Muscle memory."

Justin laughs like that's the funniest thing he's ever heard. We've been friends since second grade. As the only two East Asian kids in our class, it just kind of made sense for us to hang out together. I give him the boba hookup, and he reminds me how lucky I am that my parents don't disown me for being a solid B-minus student. Symbology, or something.

When we get to the shop, I find Mom wiping down the front counter, her shoulders hunched. It's been like that for the past few weeks—me walking in sometime around five to find the place emptier than the stands during one of our games and my mom scrubbing down the same sparkling stretch of counter. This time last year, there would've been at least a handful of customers standing in line to get a milk tea or something, but that was also before every ice cream, frozen yogurt, and dough-nut shop started selling them too.

And that doesn't even touch on our issue with the Morenos. Other ethnic shops have popped up from time to time, but considering the town is so white that most of them don't even know what mung bean is, they always flop in a year or two. Our shop and the Morenos' are the only two that have been able to stick it out, like maybe they're just different enough that people are willing to stop by both, but that also means we're in a constant game of tug-of-war to keep them from pulling too many customers away from us and taking us out altogether. Which is why, even if Gabriel wasn't the single biggest nuisance on the planet, I'd still hate his guts.

"Ah, Theo," Mom says, as if I don't get home at the same time every day, "you can help me count tips."

Mom never asks me to do things. It's always "you can do," like she's granting me the special privilege of being her servant.

"Hey, Mrs. Mori," Justin says. "Can you get me a taro bun and one of those cool sunset drinks?"

I can already feel the tension rolling off Mom before she says, "What's a sunset drink?"

"Oh, it's one of those teas with the cool colors," Justin says. "Hold up, I got you."

He slips his phone out of his pocket, probably pulling up

4

some Try Guys video or something. Finally, he holds the screen up to Mom's face, and she raises her lip. "What is that? That's not tea. Looks like a lava lamp."

"But everyone's been posting pictures of them!"

I lay a hand on Justin's shoulder and say, "I'm gonna go count tips," before stepping behind the counter.

Justin's voice floats back to me as he pleads his case, but he should know it's not worth the breath. My parents are traditional. Well, as traditional as a Chinese and Japanese couple really can be, I guess. They only believe in brand names, they never buy them at full price, and most importantly, they don't follow trends. If it's not carved into the stone of their recipe books, they won't make it. Except the boba thing, but I guess it's that old Chinese nature to steal a drink from Taiwan and claim it as our own.

Inside the office, the door closes a little too loudly behind me, but at least it blocks out the argument that's bound to come from the counter. Justin's gonna stand there begging for his weird rainbow drink, and Mom's never gonna budge. That's just the way they are.

Sliding into the desk chair, it's pretty clear to me I'm the most generous person in my family. I let Mom stick to her old Asian ways, I entertain Justin's quirks, and I even call this space an office even if it's really only a storage closet with a desk in it.

I pull out the little Spam tin safe Dad uses to store the tips from the day and start counting. Considering most of our customers are older Asian folk looking for the only authentic Asian pastries in town, we don't earn a whole lot in tips. It's fine, though, because I'm always in charge of counting them, which means no one bats an eye when a dollar or two goes missing.

The crinkled bills slide into my pocket as I jot down the total thus far. A couple of bucks won't mean a whole lot to my parents, but it'll make a huge difference for my future, so I ignore the little jolt to my nerves I get every time I close the safe and return it to the desk. We don't close till eight, but I doubt anyone will be in for the last couple of hours. I know my parents keep the shop open hoping we won't have to waste the buns and someone will come pick them up, but they usually end up in the trash.

When I step out of the office, it's to find that Justin has already left. With or without his order, I have no idea.

"How are the tips? Good?" Mom asks.

I nod, handing her the little pad with the total for the day. She looks a little sad as she reads it, but she doesn't say anything.

"I'm gonna head to my room and get working on some homework, if that's all right," I say.

"You never want to help," she says. "Thomas always used to help after school, but you waste your time playing soccer and now—"

"Okay, fine," I snap, my voice coming out louder than I mean it to. "You want help? What do you want me to do?"

Mom turns to me with a sharp look on her face, the angle of her eyebrows more than enough to tell me I've crossed another line by talking back to her like that. She'd never admit it, but she'd probably think higher of me if I'd killed a guy than she does because I can be a bit mouthy.

She eyes the store like she wants to take stock of how many customers we have before putting me in my place. There's no one here, though, and she seems to realize that pretty quickly, sighing as she says, "No, I don't want your help if you're going to talk to me like that. Go make sure you don't bring home any more bad grades."

We live above the shop in a little two-bedroom loft. I used to share my bedroom with my brother, Thomas, but he started college last summer and moved in with some guys I don't know or care to meet. It's not twenty minutes away, but I guess it's enough of an excuse for him to never really help out around the shop anymore or even check in to see if we're still alive.

Once my door is closed, I pull out the shoebox under my bed filled with ones and spare change and add today's earnings into it. Taking a couple dollars a day from the tip jar may not seem like a profitable business, but I started almost a year ago, and now the box is practically overflowing.

Most of the white kids at school brag about getting an allowance or getting paid to mow the lawn or selling nudes. I've spent most nights and weekends working in the shop since I was old enough to count to seven, but I never get paid for my time there, and I definitely don't get a damn allowance. So really, in the end, this money is only a small cut of what my parents owe me for all the hours I put in.

And when I graduate next year, it'll be my college fund,

since my parents never started one for me and have made it pretty clear since my ADHD diagnosis that they don't have high hopes for me in terms of higher education. I don't know how much I'll have by then, but hopefully enough to get out of Vermont, even if my grades won't get me in anywhere impressive. In the end, it's all about the freedom, not the schooling.

I just have to ignore the part of me that feels guilty every time I come back from school to see the shop mostly deserted. Sometimes traffic fluctuates, though, so I'm sure it's only a matter of time before people get sick of the Morenos' greasy snacks and watery coffee and come crawling back to us.

The thing is, all my parents really have is the shop. When they moved out to Vermont and put all their time into getting the place up and running, they basically lost all their old friends and never got around to making new ones. And now that Thomas lives across town and almost never comes around anymore, all they really do is work in the shop and nag me about my crappy grades and overall failure as a son. I think it gives them a sense of control to focus on how useless I am and try to make me into someone my grandparents would still invite to Christmas dinner.

But considering how much their grip on me tightened between Thomas going to school and the shop slowing down, I can only imagine what'll happen if they lose the shop altogether. There's no way they'll be able to look past me skipping town if they don't have something to distract them anymore.

There's a knock on my bedroom door, and I quickly shove

the shoebox back under my bed and plop down on my comforter before saying, "Come in."

Dad peeks his head in and looks around like he's not sure where to find me in the eight-foot space. I hadn't even realized he was home, but it makes sense, since neither of my parents really have a life outside the shop.

"Oh, Theo," he says, like he was expecting someone else. "Your mom talk to you about the shop?"

"No, what about it?"

He hesitates in the doorway for a minute before taking a step inside and stopping. "The Morenos are stealing our customers again. And with that new place opening up, we need a plan to win them back."

"Are you asking for my opinion?" I say.

Dad laughs, and I'm not surprised. It'd be a cold day in hell before my parents made a decision based on my advice. "We think you can promote the shop to your classmates. Remind them why our shop is still number one."

"My classmates aren't interested." They're really more of the basic, hipster-coffee-shop type anyway.

"You don't know if you don't try," Dad says. He reaches into his pocket and pulls out a stack of "graphic design is my passion" business cards. "Just try."

I reluctantly take the cards, looking over the tacky font, which reads *Golden Tea, Boba, and Bakery—If you don't like stale bread, try our bao instead!*

I raise an eyebrow. "Try our bao instead of *what*?"

"I've been standing outside Café Moreno, handing these out to customers," he says with a wink.

I roll my eyes, setting the cards aside until I can throw them out without Dad seeing.

He doesn't say anything else before he leaves my room, which is standard Dad. Our conversations are always pretty one-sided. I don't see the point in chatting with a brick wall.

TWO

GABI

Fridays are, inarguably, superior to all other days of the week. The junior-senior parking lot lies largely vacated, since Fridays are everybody's skip days, and since Coach predicted this when setting the schedule, there's mercifully no soccer practice.

But, best of all, the usual Friday foot traffic keeps my parents too busy with the shop to grill me on my afternoon plans. Sweet bliss.

Clearing the student lot, I take the sidewalk toward the line of three brick buildings that make up our school. The soccer field looms on my right, the baseball diamond to my left, and all my peers look zombified as they groan and stumble in, desperately trying to survive the end of the week.

My best friend, Melissa, sits on the brick stair lining leading up to the school building closest to the parking lot, earbuds in and head bobbing to the beat. She looks perfectly at home, like nothing can break her focus, but I know she's waiting for me like she does every morning. After all, I'm her *Kiki's Delivery Service*, except I only distribute breakfast and I had to exchange my broom for a used Corolla.

"Morning," I call, and she immediately glances up, like she didn't actually have anything playing. I tuck a low bow before extending a to-go cup and white paper bag out to her. "Your tostada y café, bitch."

She rolls her eyes but grins as she accepts the free food. And really, she can't complain, since I've been her resident no-delivery-fee Dasher since freshman year.

"I love coffee," she sings, which is the understatement of the decade. I've never seen anyone guzzle the stuff down quite like Meli, and she usually takes it black. I only managed to persuade her into trying my family's café con leche by lying about what the "leche" meant.

I plop down next to her, snatching the cup out of her hand to take a quick sip before passing it back. I've never been a huge coffee drinker, but I always steal sips of whatever Meli's drinking.

"Any updates on the float?"

She sighs, but I know it's all she really wants to talk about. Meli's the president of the Homecoming Committee, mostly because her art teacher recommended her last year, and she didn't know how to say no, but she's so engrossed in it, it's practically become her whole personality. She's always been a perfectionist, so even if she's not fond of a task, once it's assigned, she'll

12

make sure it's immaculate. I'm on the committee too—since she all but forced me to join—but I'm basically her lackey at this point, since school spirit and sports aren't exactly my forte.

I wait patiently as she pulls out her phone and brings up her homecoming Pinterest board. It's jam-packed with Meli-approved decor—some twists on the cliché Wonderland theme as ideas for the float, red and black decorations for the dance hall, even a formal dress that fits the theme with a buy link. We're still over a month away, but leave it to Meli to be ready so early.

Five minutes before class, we head into the hallway. The narrow space lined with metal lockers is already teeming with the students who actually showed up today. Meli passes me her phone to show me two different streamer colors that are pretty much the same. As I pass it back to her, it's with just enough time to witness my own untimely demise as I run into Theo Mori, who stands with a couple of the guys from the soccer team.

We manage to avoid the mint-green tiles, but I accidentally slam him into the lockers, a resounding clang echoing around us. I throw myself backward but slam into the lockers on the other side, given the hallway really only allows space for a couple of people at a time.

Now, three pairs of eyes who unmistakably hate me glare back as I stumble around an awkward apology.

But really, the worst of them is Theo. I mean, not that he's the worst person, but it sucks more pissing him off. Not only because he's the co-captain of the soccer team that I need to stay on to placate my parents, but also because he's gay. Well, more importantly, he's the only openly gay kid in our graduating class, and I guess a part of me always felt like we should be friends because of that, even if I'm still so deep in the closet, I'm half-draped in that horrendous Christmas sweater my tía bought me last year and probably can't ever come out. Also because of my parents.

I'm not sure how long I stand there before Meli finally twines her arm in mine and whisks me away from the hollow stares. And part of me wants to go back, swoop in, and channel some of that Keiynan Lonsdale swag as I lay out some super-suave explanation that makes all the guys forgive my blunder. Or maybe I'd just out myself. Probably the second one.

Meli ditches me outside my homeroom, and I quickly walk down the first aisle over to my assigned seat, waiting for Theo to take the one behind me that he's occupied since third grade. It's weird, like fate is constantly trying to make us dance together, but no matter what I do, I can't get past my two left feet.

After school, I have to attend a Homecoming meeting. Over the summer, we met every other week, but now that only a month remains until the big game, Meli's insisting we hold more frequent meetings, even if that interferes with my usual Friday plans.

I'm the last person there, which Meli says is because I run on "Latino time," which is ridiculous because I'm only like two minutes late. Vivi's already waiting for me, sitting in the wobbly desk near the window, and considering Vivi's almost always early, it's definitely not a Latinx-specific thing. Meli's just mean.

I slip into the desk next to Vivi and flash her a smile. We only started being friends after we both joined the Homecoming Committee at the end of last year, but she's cool. We both adore Kehlani—as any decent person should—and she's one of like three people in our school who'd actually tried an authentic Puerto Rican bread pudding before I brought the one my lita makes, so there's that. Really, the only reason we don't spend more time together is because she and Meli mesh like toothpaste and orange juice, which has only gotten worse as Meli's Homecoming tirade has progressed.

Vivi drops her voice low and says, "She's rampaging again."

I chuckle, and despite the fact that Melissa's half yelling at Jeff for making a mistake on the flyers that are supposed to go up tomorrow, she still shoots a glare in my direction. I roll my eyes. We all know she's overreacting. Sure, Homecoming is a pretty big celebration at our school, since we don't have a football team, so administration has been banking on our soccer team to showcase a "balanced academic lifestyle," but it's pretty inconsequential in the long run, and Meli will realize that sooner or later.

Vivi and I spend most of the meeting texting each other memes as Meli drones on about things that we've mostly covered already. I get Meli's irritation that incompetence on the committee seems to be running pretty high, but my mind is focused elsewhere as I scroll Instagram and stumble upon pictures of people holding weird rainbow-colored bubble tea drinks. It never occurred to me that the Moris might start branching out into something so aesthetic, but there's no way my parents will be happy about it. They hate the Moris and their shop enough as it is.

"Gabi."

I look up to find Meli standing over me, her lips pressed together.

"You didn't hear a word I said, did you?" she says.

I laugh awkwardly as I close the Instagram app and smile up at her. "Does bread pudding count as an apology?"

She rolls her eyes.

I glance around to find that most of the committee has moved on to individual tasks—laying out the schedules, planning the dance, organizing the decorations.

"Come on, Gabi," she says. "We're getting too close to Homecoming for you to be this spacey."

That definitely feels like an overstatement, given that my only two tasks as class liaison are making sure that the class reps have everything they need to get their floats together and providing snacks for our meetings. I stand up, placing a hand on Meli's shoulder and flashing her a smile.

"You should already know how this works, Meli. I'm always on your team."

And her face softens a little as I throw her own words back at her. She swats my hand away, but I can see a small smile pulling at the corners of her mouth. "Okay, fine, but don't disappoint me."

The true highlight of my day comes when the meeting lets out and I head to the back of campus, past the cafeteria, to our dance hall. Okay, I kid. It's the highlight of my week.

Ballet.

I've wanted to be a dancer since age six, but at age seven, my parents made it perfectly clear that dancing is for girls. Especially ballet. So I relinquished my dreams of pursuing it professionally, but when I took a dance elective last year, I actually became friends with our teacher, Lady—yes, that's her real name—and after I spilled my heart over her infamous rum cake, she offered to train me every Friday after school. It's like having my own fairy godmother, except, frankly, I look better in the tutu.

The only downfall to our arrangement is my awkward trek across campus, head bowed, doing my best to make sure no one spots me. Truthfully, they probably wouldn't even deduce my destination, but I also know the second word gets out that I do ballet, everyone will know I'm gay, and that means I can't risk anyone finding out. The only person I opened up to about any of this was Meli, but then, she's also the only person I felt comfortable enough coming out to.

Lady's already stretching against the barre when I arrive, and she flashes me a quick smile. I guess you could say I'm one of those teens who gets along better with adults. Parents love me;

my peers wish I'd choke on a papa rellena. Talking to Lady is nice, though, because she's only in her early twenties, she's the only Latinx teacher I've ever had, and she looks like she could still be in high school, so I can kind of pretend I actually fit in for once.

"Hurry up and get dressed," she says as her foot hits the mat. "I can't stay super late today."

"Oh?" I say. "Hot date tonight?"

She laughs. "I actually have a job interview. Namely, a Zoom interview."

I raise an eyebrow. "Interview for what?"

"A job that pays above minimum wage."

I freeze. "Wait. You're leaving the school?"

She shrugs. "I don't know yet. It's just an interview."

But that means she wants to. It means that her best-case scenario is the one where I lose my last chance at dancing.

"I—" My voice cracks. "Don't you like working here?"

"Of course I do, Gabi, but jobs aren't all about what you like," she says. "At the end of the day, sometimes being an adult means making a decision you don't like to get the things you need."

I don't know what to say. I understand sacrifice. I do. But—I mean—now what am I supposed to do?

She watches my face drop before shaking her head and flashing me a smile. "Don't worry so much, okay? I still don't know if they're going to offer me a position. And even if they offer, I may only take the position part-time. Focus on your craft and worry about the rest later, okay?"

I nod because I know it's what she wants, even if my head doesn't quite feel the same.

Over our last few meetings, we've been working on choreographing a dance together, which basically means she's been using me as a moving mannequin to help her plan the whole thing out, but I don't mind. When I was in her class last year, we had to memorize an original Lady dance piece and perform it for her as our final, and I loved every second of it, so it's kind of cool to be a part of that now.

The last segment of the dance isn't finalized yet, so we work through the bit before as she brainstorms ways to conclude it, but my headspace is all wrong. It's kind of ironic, given dance is my escape from all the world's anxieties, but here I am stumbling through each move as my fears become insurmountable and throw me off my feet.

It's only as I shoot for a cabriole, lose my balance, and stumble back into the barre that Lady suggests we take a break.

Passing me a water bottle, she says, "Don't overthink it, okay? Stay in the moment."

"I wasn't—"

Lady rolls her eyes. "Please, *you*? If you think about it, you'll overthink it." And I have to admit, it kind of stings that she knows me so well. "Anyway, you don't know what'll happen next, so let it happen naturally. It's the same with a performance, right? You have the skills and steps, and you just have to let it happen."

I let her words sit with me for a moment before nodding and

setting the water bottle down. "I'm ready to get back into it if you are," I say.

She smiles, motioning for me to join her.

And really, I feel so much better once I'm dancing. My whole body feels free as I fly through the moves, and even just getting the chance to suggest a plié here or a pirouette there feels like I'm finally getting a chance to live in a skin I'm proud of.

And I can't believe I might have to give it all up.

I get back to the café right after five. Normally, I'd be training until six, but well, Lady's interview cut everything short.

I hate going back to the shop after school, because Mom will usually already be off to her night classes, which means Dad's running the shop himself and is more likely to rope me in. I actually kind of like helping out in the kitchen, but let's just say customer service and I don't quite mesh. The problem is that I'm not allowed home alone even though I'm sixteen. Mom says I could get murdered or accidentally burn the house down or something. Sometimes, I think she's worried I'll sneak someone over to have sex, but that isn't in the cards for me. I guess no mom ever wants to admit that her son is just ugly.

Although, I guess she'd accept that sooner than she'd accept that I'm gay.

When I step into the shop, Dad's wiping down the counter, but it's not nearly as crowded as I feared it'd be. Actually, there's only some elderly woman sitting in the corner, sipping from a cup and reading a romance novel.

Dad raises an eyebrow as I enter, and says, "You're back early?"

I shrug. "Study session ended."

I hate lying to my parents, and not only because it makes me feel like a degenerate, and like Jesus is looking down, ready to smite me. I'm just a truly atrocious liar. I feel like I'm dangling a massive, neon *HE'S LYING* sign from the center of my chest.

But Dad doesn't react, like it never occurred to him that his overachieving nerd of a son might actually tell him an untruth.

The back-room door opens up, and Mom steps out, a clipboard in hand. "Pedro, you read this part?"

She freezes when she sees me, her eyes going wide. "Gabi, you're back early."

I try to keep my tone nonchalant as I slip my book bag off my shoulder. "I thought you had class."

Mom and I stare back at each other like she's struggling between admitting that she skipped and making up a lie. Either way, it's pretty hypocritical, since she'd skin me alive before condoning my playing hooky.

"Gabi, there's something we wanted to discuss with you," Dad says, letting Mom off the hook. It's not fair that they can team up like that. I need a partner in crime, stat.

"¿Qué pasó?"

Dad sighs and looks at Mom like he expects her to deal the final blow, which he probably does. Finally, she shakes her head and turns to me. "We're selling the shop," she says.

My eyes shoot wide. "I—wait—what—why?"

Mom sighs. "We got a good offer for it, and we really aren't in a place to refuse."

Which is definitely the first I'm hearing of any of this.

"What changed?" I ask.

"Your Mom and I," Dad says, "well, we always knew this wouldn't be permanent. It was just supposed to be long enough to get our feet on the ground, get a house, let your mom go back to school."

Mom's nodding along, but none of this makes sense. They've had the shop since before I was born. They said it was their first son, you know, before me. Now they're going to throw it all away?

"We aren't getting the same traffic we used to," Mom says, "and with my tuition, and you'll be going to college soon too—"

"I don't have to go to college," I say, and I mean it. I don't really have a whole lot of desire to go anyway. I'd assumed I'd take the shop once I was old enough.

Dad shakes his head. "Cállate, Gabi, of course you're going to college. We just have to be practical. Between those chinos stealing our business and that new fusion café—we'll get more money selling the shop than keeping it, so we really can't justify holding on to it anymore."

"Fusion café?" I say.

My mom sighs. "Gabi, you haven't been paying attention."

And yeah, that's not entirely untrue. But between Homecoming and soccer and dance, I don't really have a lot of free time like I used to, so the shop hasn't really been at the forefront of my mind.

My dad says, "The money we can get from selling . . . well, it will pay for your mother's nursing degree, and it's more practical I go back to real estate anyway."

And everyone loves being practical and making big adult decisions I'm not allowed to weigh in on, like being sixteen means I can't have any say or opinion on my own life. Like I'm a prop getting tossed around until some adult decides to hit the stop button.

"I know this is hard for you, mijo," Mom says. "I know how much you loved the shop as a kid, but this doesn't mean you have to stop baking."

I shake my head slowly, but all I can say is, "Is that what you're looking at right now? The contract? You were going to sell it before I even got home?"

And my parents look taken aback by the venom in my voice. I guess they are. I guess I kind of am too. I know better than to talk back to them, but this is a slap in the face. Not only did they not care how I felt about all of this, but they were going to sell away our family legacy without even conferring with me first.

My mom sighs and says, "We're not turning it in until Monday. We were going to discuss it with you this weekend."

A weekend. That's all I was going to get to say goodbye. I don't even realize there are tears building in my eyes until Mom comes over to me to wipe them away. Dad turns his face away. He always says men aren't supposed to cry, but I guess he'll let it slide this time as long as he doesn't have to see it.

But I don't know how to tell him it's only bound to get worse, that everything I've put my heart into is slowly slipping out of my hands and I have no idea how to slow the fall.

THREE
THEO

Saturday morning, I wake up to loud arguing rushing in from downstairs. It doesn't take much to figure that means Uncle Greg is in the shop. I'm pretty sure he had a different name before he left China, but now he's just Greg, and it's fitting, since he mostly acts like a douchey white guy whenever he comes around.

Uncle Greg's hated Dad since he and Mom first met in college. He made it clear Mom should've married a Chinese guy and gave her extra shit for taking a Japanese last name. He still comes around, though, so I guess that's better than Dad's family, who completely cut him off once he proposed to a Chinese girl.

I throw on a pair of jeans and a T-shirt before heading downstairs. Uncle Greg used to like me when I was young, mostly because I was an athlete, and he wanted me to win the Olympics or something. Ever since I came out, though, he's made it clear that Thomas is his favorite, and frankly, I don't give a shit. The last thing I care about is approval from a guy who spends most of his free time watching videos of girls who are barely legal on YouTube.

"Morning," I say.

Uncle Greg's shouting something at Mom in Mandarin, and Dad's got the world's best poker face on as he ignores both of them and rearranges the pastries in the fridge. Dad and I scored two tickets on the don't-speak-Chinese train, but even I can tell the conversation is a wreck from Uncle Greg's tone, and the way Mom is leaning away from him. Plus, I think Dad actually picked some up between all those soap operas he watches with Mom and the messy karaoke nights.

"Sup, Uncle Greg," I say, really just to draw his attention away from Mom.

He looks up at me grumpily, but Mom looks kind of relieved.

"Theo," he says. No, *Hi, nephew, how are you doing?* He used to start with a *You got a girlfriend yet?* But I guess now that he knows I'm gay, my love life isn't nearly as exciting for him.

"Greg," Dad says, like my distraction was exactly what he needed to get a word in, "if you want to talk numbers, we have the paperwork in the office."

Ah, the numbers. I guess that's what Uncle Greg's so upset about this morning.

Uncle Greg technically owns the shop. He bought the place fifteen years ago while my parents, Thomas, and infant me still lived in California. A few years later, he got tired of running the

25

place, so when Dad lost his job, we packed our bags and moved out to Vermont so my parents could run the shop in exchange for free housing upstairs. A win-win except now we answer to Uncle Greg, who's both the CEO and landlord. Plus, we live in Vermont. That's a major bummer.

"No need," Uncle Greg says. "I already know you don't do a good job, Masao. I've been paying your rent for how many years now?"

Dad just looks away and makes himself busy, and I envy his patience. Uncle Greg always comes in to complain and throw low digs at Dad, like his being Japanese single-handedly killed our customer base. And then there's the way he treats Mom, like she's some whiny kid who couldn't even pick a decent husband. God, I hate that guy. He probably voted for Trump.

"Greg," my mom says, "we gave you the payment you asked for at the beginning of the month."

"Which was less than last month," Uncle Greg says.

"Which was still more than you asked for."

"Should be higher. I can make more money on this place if I make a new store. No one wants to buy your silly drinks anymore, especially with the new competition."

I roll my eyes. Uncle Greg wouldn't be making shit if he converted the shop, because no one else would put up with him except Mom. We all know that.

But that's the dance he puts us through every month. Acting like he doesn't need us and we should all be bowing at his feet and begging him not to put us out when we're the ones keeping

his shop alive and earning him money. And it pretty much goes without saying that he's not actually going to kick us out, but he likes the power to know that he can, stringing Mom along and using her as his personal punching bag.

He stands there looking smug as he runs off something else in Chinese. He slaps a sheet of paper down on the counter in front of Mom, and her head jerks back in response. Dad steps over, peering over her shoulder to look at it, but neither of them say anything.

"So much possibility!" he says, and I don't know what he's actually talking about, but it's pretty clear he's being an asshole. I definitely won't miss him once I finally get to flee for college and never have to look back.

By the time Uncle Greg leaves, Mom looks deflated, and I want to cheer her up, but let's face it, I'm not built for cheering people up. Thomas is the son you go to if you need emotional support and advice. I'm just the son who runs his mouth too much and is best for tearing people down.

Dad passes Mom her favorite milk tea, probably at like 25 percent sweetness, since she says there's no greater crime than a milk tea that's too sweet. She spares him a small smile, but they both look vaguely miserable, and I feel like a major asshole eavesdropping on their visual conversation.

Finally, Mom looks up from her milk tea and says, "Greg is gonna take the shop."

"He's always spouting that shit. He doesn't mean it."

Mom gives me a narrow-eyed glare, but it's Dad who says,

"Watch your mouth, Theo."

I roll my eyes again. Even in these trying times, the most important thing is making sure I'm not spiraling into delinquency.

Then Mom looks directly at me as she says, "We haven't been making as many sales as we used to. Not as many customers, either. I don't know what we're doing wrong, but—"

"You haven't done anything wrong, June," Dad says. "That Puerto Rican shop has been ruining our business for years, and with that new café—"

But I don't even have to look at my mom to know she's shaking her head at that. Things don't just "happen" to her. Everything has to be someone's fault, so if we're suddenly losing ground to the Morenos, it must be hers.

"He says if we don't boost our sales by next month, he's going to convert the shop," she says. "And yes, he means that."

She holds up the little flyer Uncle Greg slammed onto the counter, and it looks like there's some sort of layout map on it, advertising a new day spa.

I snatch the paper away, staring blankly at the words *Luxury Day Spa* across the top. "What the hell? He can't be serious," I snap. "He wants to toss our shop to wash white people's feet?"

"Theo," Dad snaps again, "watch your mouth."

He places a hand over Mom's, but I tear my gaze away. I don't want to see the heartbroken looks on their faces as they think about losing the shop forever. I mean, God, I haven't even told them I'm planning on running away for college. What are

they gonna do once Uncle Greg takes the shop and then I fly off a year later? Especially after all the pretending-not-to-cry-in-the-bathroom Mom did after Thomas left.

If Uncle Greg takes the shop. It's not actually over yet. There's still plenty of time to boost sales and foot traffic and whatever else it is people use to judge if a business is doing well, right?

I shake my head, pushing out the sound of Dad whispering something softly to Mom. God, Uncle Greg is such a dick. I can't believe he would do this to them after everything, like they aren't literally here earning money for him day after day. Like we aren't literally his family.

And now I'm pissed at them for even caring. Why do they care about this shop anyway? They could get different jobs. Mom's good enough to be a professional chef, and Dad used to work in accounting. If they weren't so damn stubborn, they could move back to California and be happy far away from Uncle Greg's abuse.

But more than anyone, I'm pissed at the Morenos. I'm pissed that we have to compete with them in a town where only a quarter of the already pathetically small population cares about ethnic food. No, I'm pissed at Gabriel. It's like he was born to thwart me at every turn, like he's barreling over my parents' dreams like he barrels over me every practice.

Or maybe I don't even know who I'm pissed at anymore. I just know I'm furious, and if I don't take it out on someone, I'm going to burst.

And then that delayed processing kicks in as I suddenly realize what Dad said.

With that new café . . .

What new café?

"Theo?" Mom says.

I turn to look at her and instantly regret it. Her eyes are a little red, stress lines circling them. She motions for me to sit at one of the many vacant café tables, and after a deep sigh, I comply. She comes around the counter and sits across from me, Dad standing behind her.

"I know this must be hard for you," Mom says.

"Let Uncle Greg take the shop. I don't care."

My parents stare back at me wide-eyed, like they're not sure what kind of monster they've been raising. And hell, they're probably right. Thomas would probably be prepping some rally to move the town in support of our little shop, getting a Supreme Court judge to call and cancel Uncle Greg or something.

Mom says, "I know you don't love working at the shop, but this is our home. We've put everything we have into making it something special."

"Why?" I say. "The customers don't care. We haven't updated the menu in years, and half the time people ask for shit, we tell them we don't have it. We're a bunch of underpaid field hands so Uncle Greg can get rich without ever doing a day of work himself."

Mom looks like I've slapped her across the face, and Dad

looks—well, livid might be an understatement.

"Theo, we raised you better than this," Dad snaps.

And yeah, he's probably right about that too, but I do aim for disappointment, so at least I'm getting that part right.

"Go to your room," Dad says. "You're grounded."

"You mean you don't want my help with the shop?"

Neither of my parents seem to think my joke is very funny, and I can't really blame them. I tuck the chair under the table before racing up the stairs to my bedroom.

The one benefit of almost never getting grounded is that when my parents actually do decide to ground me, they have no idea how to do it properly. Sunday morning, they have me locked in my room, but my phone lies faceup on my comforter as I FaceTime Justin, and my laptop's propped open on my desk, bookmarking my search on this new café.

World Fusion Café.

After my thought that that's the literal worst name for a café ever, I've pulled up their menu, some pictures of their store, the works. And yeah, it's basically my worst nightmare. It's like if you took all the white people faves from my parents' shop and fused them with the Morenos' crappy food, like one of those weird Pokémon mashups.

"So you think your uncle's actually serious? About converting the shop?" Justin asks.

The truth is, I don't really know. A day ago, I would've said there was no way he'd actually take the shop and it was all just talk to stroke his ego and put Mom in her place for marrying a Japanese guy, but now, I'm not really sure it matters. "Either way, Mom's spooked."

"Ugh, that sucks," Justin says. "No more free boba."

I roll my eyes. Yeah, sucks Justin won't get free boba anymore, but the real problem is whether or not my parents are going to fall apart. Mom's stress level was already through the roof with all the crap Uncle Greg puts on her. Then there's the fact that Thomas is gonna be pissed when he finds out.

And then there's the issue of my guilt, which frankly, I didn't even realize I could feel anymore.

It's not like I've been standing outside chasing potential customers away with one of those tacky spinning signs or a sweaty costume.

But I have been stealing some of our tips for a while.

I never meant to hurt my parents. That needs to be out in the open first and foremost. I was just trying to improve my odds, build a future for myself, since they didn't start a college fund for me and kept saying my shitty grades and lack of organizational skills meant I'd never survive college at all.

But maybe it's my fault for having a shitty brain and being a crap student who can't get a full ride anywhere, unlike Thomas. Maybe it's my fault for not convincing my friends to hang out at our shop instead of the hipster coffee joint down the block. Maybe I should've been helping out more, washing dishes and learning how to make that matcha cheesecake.

The screen shakes as Justin steps up to the counter at the

World Fusion Café, his phone bouncing awkwardly in his shirt pocket and making me wanna hurl. The reception's pretty terrible, like this place doesn't even have Wi-Fi, which I guess is a point in our favor.

I considered scouting out the place myself, but I'm grounded, and I can't imagine anything worse than paying for their shitty food. So Justin volunteered, dragging his on-again, off-again, "not-girlfriend" Clara, but his camera angle sucks, and my screen is mostly full of the blue fabric of his shirt.

"Um, yeah, I'll get the sunset drink," he says, his voice broken up by static. "Oh, and the fish balls. And an order of croquettes. Oh, and the kimchi empanadas. Actually, and the—"

I tune him out as he orders half their menu, which frankly all sounds pretty horrifyingly disgusting. Kimchi empanadas? Guava taiyaki? And do I even want to know what chicharrón ramen means?

Justin gets his number and slips over to one of the booths, with Clara sliding in next to him. Honestly, the place is too big and too fancy to be a "café and bakery." The walls are lined with vintage photos and a world map made out of chalkboard scraps, and then there're the fancy wooden booths with plush pillows and little vases with a single flower in the middle.

"This place is sweet," Justin says, plucking his phone out of his pocket. He places it faceup on the table, and I get a glimpse of Justin's and Clara's faces.

I roll my eyes. "Focus on the mission, asshole."

Justin looks like a total goof, but at least Clara looks nice, her hair tied back in cornrows with little beads at the end and icy blue lipstick that would absolutely wash out anyone with paler skin. She's so out of his league. "I'm totally focused," he says. "And hungry. These two things can service us well."

I roll my eyes again.

Clara laughs, leaning into Justin's arm. "You're never gonna train him, Theo, so you might as well give up trying."

A white girl stops at the table and places a couple of little baskets in front of them. She's pretty, but she struggles over the word "takoyaki" as she puts it down.

"I know this is enemy territory," Justin says, "but you gotta admit this shit sounds pretty cool."

"I'm perfectly good with not having black beans in my fried rice, thanks," I say.

Justin's only response is a long, drawn-out moan as he bites into an empanada.

I cringe.

Look, I'll admit I may not be this place's target audience, since I've never been very fond of anything with the word "fusion" in it, but what the fuck does "world fusion" even mean, and why do they have to parade around some bastardization of my culture, like there aren't enough people doing that already?

"Okay, the empanadas are a seven out of ten," Justin says. "The croquettes get an eight. The fish balls are like five point five."

Clara pushes her little basket away and says, "The tostones get a four, if I'm being generous."

"So what you're saying is, it's mediocre?" I prompt.

Justin shrugs. "Yeah, mostly. The drink's pretty good."

Clara smiles. "Mostly just pretty, though."

Well, that's good at least. But why are people so into the place? Sure, they've got some wonky mixtures straight out of one of those BeanBoozled jelly-bean boxes, but why do people keep going back?

"You're stressing too much," Justin says. "You should come down here, and I'll buy you a milk tea. Lavender to chill you the fuck out. You don't even have to tell your parents."

But Justin has to realize this goes way deeper than my parents. As much as I hate working at the place, the shop is still important to my family. It's our legacy, the one thing we've laid down permanent roots with. We don't have all that intergenerational wealth white people take for granted and shit. The shop, our recipes, the relationships we've built with customers—that's all my family has.

"Why are people so into this place?" I groan.

"I don't know," Justin says. "A unique menu? And I guess the atmosphere is pretty cool, so maybe that too."

That's probably a good point. We haven't redecorated the café since Uncle Greg bought it. We're lacking that Instagrammable aesthetic people are probably looking for. We also haven't updated the menu in a while, but it's not like I can convince Mom and Dad to start making kimchi empanadas. Hell, they'd rather let the shop die than that, and I can't really blame them.

But what if we can shake things up just a little? It doesn't

35

even have to be anything spectacular. I just need enough of a distraction to lure people away from the fusion café and back to our shop. Then they'll remember our shit is so much better and never want to go back to this appropriative hellscape.

Clara's head whips to the side, her lips pressed together. "Uh, is that Gabriel Moreno?"

I freeze as Justin flips his phone camera around, catching sight of my worst nightmare standing in line with two girls I don't know all that well. Pretty sure Melissa is on the Homecoming Committee or something, but I've never had any classes with her, and she's always just struck me as one of those teacher's pet white girls I have no interest in talking to. The other girl I don't know by name, but she's one of those quiet ones who's always in the corner with a book or something, so I guess all together, this is just Gabriel's band of nerds.

God, why is he there? It's like everything I hate all rolled up into one room.

"Want me to go say hi?" Justin says.

Clara laughs, but I growl, and Justin bursts out into a fit of laughter.

"Why do you hate him again?" Clara asks, but frankly, the list is way too long to get into.

"He's a bootlicker and the enemy," I say.

Justin laughs again. "Are you really still bitter that he reported you for copying his homework in like fourth grade?"

"Do you understand the lecture I got over—you know what? Forget it. Just finish eating and get out of there," I say. "There are better places for you to waste your time."

Justin flips the camera around and says, "Oh, yes, definitely better places for us to waste our time."

Clara smirks. "I'd say so, yes."

And I gag, though at least this time, it's not because of the food.

FOUR
GABI

Sunday morning, I climb out of bed feeling antsy but determined. I start with some of the warm-up stretches I'd usually do with Lady, letting the blood flow through me as I work up the nerve to put my plan into action.

First position: Talk to my parents. No big deal.

My parents haven't left for the shop yet. Dad's preparing French toast for breakfast, and he's dancing to some Celia Cruz the way only dads really can. Mom says he used to dance a lot when he was younger—probably where I inherited that gene—but right now, I'm firmly convinced that's a lie they made up to keep me from figuring out I'm adopted.

"Buenas, Gabi, grab a plate," Dad says.

I reach into the cabinet and pull out one of my mom's inherited china plates to claim my breakfast. "You seem really happy for someone about to sell away our family legacy," I say.

Dad freezes, the lively music sounding hollow in the morning

38

ambience. He reaches for the old radio he's probably had since he was a kid and flips the music off before letting out a heavy sigh. "Dios mío, Gabi, can't we just have a nice breakfast today?"

"Sorry." There isn't really anything else to say. I have to tread carefully if I'm going to get my Puerto Rican parents to even hear me out.

Dad plops some French toast down on my plate, and I shuffle over to the living room. Mom's pretty strict about not eating on the furniture, but I sit down on the carpet, setting my plate on the coffee table before slathering my bread slices in syrup.

Mom comes down the stairs, hair already styled and dressed in a black pantsuit. She doesn't dress up for most occasions, but I guess she considers this one important. Go figure.

"Paperwork's almost done," she says, slipping up behind Dad in the kitchen. "Just needs your signature."

"Bueno. I'll get to it after breakfast."

Mom raises an eyebrow like she can't compute why he can't just put his plate aside for a second and sign it, but she finally shrugs, turning to find me seated on the floor. "What's got you down, mijo?"

And I can't even believe she's asking me that, like it isn't totally obvious.

I sigh, taking a bite of my French toast and chewing slowly before saying, "Meli's been working really hard preparing for Homecoming."

"Oh," my mom says, her voice hiccuping like she's completely caught off guard. "That's good, no?"

"I—yeah, it is, it's just . . . I'm supposed to be helping her, but I'm not really great at all that stuff, you know?" I say. "But everyone's been relying on me to bring the snacks to the meetings."

I see the light switch on behind my mom's eyes as she realizes what I'm doing. "Gabi—"

"I know, I know," I say. "It's just . . . you guys didn't really give me a lot of time, you know? And this is already such a big thing, and I feel like I'm letting everybody down and . . . I mean, isn't there a way we can keep the shop open? Just until Homecoming is over?"

My parents look at me, then at each other, then back at me. I can see a battle raging behind their eyes, but it's something. Like maybe they aren't entirely ready to get rid of the shop either.

Finally, Mom sighs and says, "I don't know, but I suppose we can . . . ask?"

Dad shakes his head slowly. "I guess we can try. Homecoming's not too far out."

"Thank you," I say, rushing up to my parents and hugging them. They both go stiff, and I know they're onto my trickery, but at the moment, I don't care. All that matters is that I buy myself more time. Keeping the shop open until Homecoming means I still have another month to figure out how to save it for good.

"So, I may have used you as an excuse for my parents to keep the shop."

Meli pauses as I pull up into the parking lot outside the

World Fusion Café, an eyebrow raised. "You did what?"

I shake my head. "I just asked them to keep it open until Homecoming. You know, so I can keep bringing snacks to the meetings."

Meli laughs, rolling her eyes. "They actually went for that?"

"I'm hoping maybe that means they're hesitating on selling too?"

Meli eyes me for a moment, and yeah, I know it may be a little too much wishful thinking, but I need something to keep me upbeat as I execute the next part of my plan.

Second position: espionage.

We need to figure out what's going on with this World Fusion place so we can work out a plan to keep my parents' shop afloat and convince them it's more profitable not to sell.

But frankly, even from the parking lot, I feel like a weed in a flower bed. Like some great, omniscient being is peering down at me, watching as I traverse a space I don't belong in, eagerly waiting to pluck me out or spray me with some chemical that'll make me wilt.

Which is part of why I told Meli to come with me, since she's always been the stronger personality in our relationship and can keep me from backing out like a coward. But she's also really bad at anything that requires emotional literacy, so she's just kind of staring at me as I grip the steering wheel to calm my breathing.

It kind of reminds me of when I first came out to her, the way she'd had to coax me into it, but could barely handle the conversation once I started getting all emotional and pivoted the whole conversation to gay celebrities or something. That's just the way she's always been. If you have a problem you need solving, Meli's your girl. If you need someone to hold on to while you cry? Well, that's what stuffed animals are for.

But when there was no one else I could trust with my sexuality, Meli was there for me without hesitation. *You should already know how this works, Gabi. I'm always on your team.* I think that means a lot more than being good with words.

And it also helps to make up for the fact that she's being kind of distant now as she answers another Homecoming email. I know she's trying to be supportive even if she's not the best at showing it, and I know that's also why she invited Vivi, even though I actively strive to keep the two of them separated. She figures if I have a backup, it won't be as big of a deal when she has to bail early. That's been her method since fifth grade.

As I finally get my breathing under control, we step out into the parking lot. Vivi's already waiting by the front, and she throws us an overenthusiastic wave as we approach. It's actually kind of nice having Meli and Vivi, since they're so opposite—Meli pretty emotionally unavailable but perfect for that no-nonsense, get-shit-done attitude, while Vivi tends to be excitable and all-in, even if it took her a little while to open up.

"I'm ready to stuff my face until I burst," Vivi says, and Meli just rolls her eyes.

I consider reminding her that we're technically on a reconnaissance mission, but I know they're both doing me a favor

42

just by being here, so I don't want to be a downer.

There are only a few people in line in front of us as we enter, which should be reassuring, but a group of eight enters behind us and a few more people come in behind them. Even in the days when our café was booming, we weren't *that* booming. After all, we always split our clientele with the Moris—who my dad calls the "retail equivalent of living next to a garbage dump," because all they do is lower the value of the businesses around them—but scanning the bustling tables, I already recognize some of our regulars. Regulars we haven't really seen in a while.

The menu's weird and I can barely read it. It's got this outrageous sketch in the background, like they were trying to detail the shapes of the continents, but they're all kind of wrong, and North America looks way too big. Then there's the weird sloping font, which only makes the actual contents of the menu harder to read. I don't actually know what bao even is. Or takoyaki, for that matter. And there are the twists on the familiar. Tres leches taiyaki? Taro bread pudding? And whose bright idea was it to put kimchi in an empanada?

Vivi twines her fingers through mine, and I realize it's because my hands are clenched into fists.

"It's okay," she says as she leans into me, her voice soft. "Don't be so mad."

But I don't know how to tell her I'm not mad—I'm scared. Sure, my parents always hated the Moris, saying they took some of our best customers when they opened shop down the street, but this is different. This isn't, *Aw man, we lost Heather with the good tips.* This is months of decreased sales and lower foot traffic. It's an overwhelming existential threat that's about to cost us the shop forever.

The cashier calls for the next customer, and Meli slips her phone into her pocket before stepping up and ordering. I pull my hand out of Vivi's before shoving both hands in my pockets. It was my idea to come here to scout, but obviously, it was a terrible one. I kind of just want to curl up in a corner and die.

"What can I get you?" the cashier asks.

But I freeze. Both because I'm so nervous I can't feel my thumbs, but also because he's kind of cute, and I can already feel a blush rising in my cheeks.

Before I can trip over myself and say something awkward, Vivi half pushes me aside and says, "He'll have the guava and cheese pastries and a café con leche. I'll take the guava smoothie and the bread pudding, please."

The cashier punches in the items, and Vivi hands over her card without even looking at me. Then she slings her arm through mine and starts dragging me toward a table.

"What was all that?" I ask.

She blushes. "Well, you seemed too nervous to order, so I did it for you. Plus, if this really is research, you have to try the stuff your parents' shop is known for. It's the only way to really compare."

"You didn't have to pay," I say.

She flashes a smile, but her eyes seem fixated on my shirt

44

collar. "You're already upset enough. Didn't seem fair to make you pay the enemy."

Despite ordering before us, Meli's just kind of hovering. She waits until Vivi shoves me into a booth to sit down across from us.

"Um, Meli, everything okay?" I ask.

"Yup, just busy," she says, eyes glued to her phone, but I'm not sure if it's because she's actually that swamped with Homecoming stuff or if she just doesn't really want to talk to Vivi.

A girl comes by with a tray, carefully laying out all our food before bouncing back toward the kitchen. I eye it warily, my stomach heavy. Is it worse if the food is good or bad? And what's my course of action after? Will this really make any difference in the grand scheme of—

"Oh my God, just eat it already," Vivi says around a big bite of bread pudding.

I sigh, picking up one of the pastelillos. They're weirdly shaped—super round, almost ball-like. I take a bite. Not disgusting, but certainly not great. I mean, they don't even taste that fresh, like maybe they were pre-frozen or something. And the guava's a little too chunky, the crust not flaky enough. Pretty disappointing.

Meli bites into a croquette, eyes still pointed toward her phone. She glances up just long enough to say, "Your parents' are better," before going back to whatever she's doing.

Vivi nods along. "Yeah. It's okay, but I don't get the hype."

And something about that hurts worse than if this shit

45

ended up being the best damn Caribbean food I'd ever had. I mean, really? It's not even good, but it was enough to draw all our customers away? What does that say about us? Or the future of the shop?

Vivi places a hand over mine. "Relax, okay? They're probably just all here because the place is new and has cool decor and stuff. They'll be back within a week."

And I really want to believe her, but there's a stone sitting in my stomach, grinding up my insides and weighing me down. I can't remember the last time I felt so hopeless.

FIVE

THEO

Sunday afternoon, I head to Justin's after he and Clara get done with . . . well, I don't really want to ask him what they were up to. The point is, I texted him saying, I've got a plan. You in? And like the loyal friend he's always been, he didn't even ask questions before agreeing. So after a quick trip to the grocery store, we're back at his house, ready to kick off my foolproof master plan to run the World Fusion Café out of business.

Justin's kitchen lies largely unused. His parents redid it five years ago, just before their marriage died and his dad moved to Florida. Now his mom pretty much avoids cooking at all costs, using his dad's child support checks to order takeout most nights and filling in the rest with freezer-section pizzas.

But the space is huge, full of granite countertops and updated appliances and unexplored hopes and dreams. I don't know what his parents had in mind when they set the place up, but now it's going to be our practice hub, the perfect place for us to run through recipe after recipe without having to worry about my parents finding out.

Justin huffs as we drop the grocery bags onto the floor. He lives only a couple of blocks from the grocery store, but the walk was pretty brutal with like, half our body weight in shit weighing us down. I sure hope this works, because if not, I wasted months of stolen tips for nothing.

"So now what, T?" he says.

"Let's get everything into the fridge, and then we can reevaluate."

I'm not entirely sure what I'm gonna make, but I've been helping my parents around the kitchen since I was seven. It's basically second nature.

"We need a new menu," I say. "Something trendy and popular to win the customers back. Only Mom and Dad can't know about it, because they'll be pissed if they find out."

"You want to run an underground café?" Justin asks.

And I shrug, but yeah, I guess that's kind of what I'm saying. It's not like I can bring new customers into the store with sunset drinks and fancy smoothies, because Mom and Dad will never approve of messing with our family recipes.

But I could convince them to let me run deliveries, right? Say we're just going to expand our customer base by bringing their food to them. Then I could add whatever clever concoctions will appeal to our customers, like a secret, traveling menu. That way I could lure them in with all the gimmicky stuff my parents refuse to sell, and once they're there for the trends, we can sell them the traditional stuff too and remind them why our food is better. Hell, if I can work out a way to bring it all to school, I can specifically target my classmates to move them away from World Fusion. Then the money could go back to Uncle Greg, and once everyone falls in love with our drinks again, they'll be racing back to our shop faster than all those Massholes doing a hundred on the freeway. Genius.

Justin's staring back at me with a look of concern, which probably isn't too surprising. There's practically steam coming out of my ears from how hard my mind is working, and I'm not exactly known for being the type of person invested in heavy thought.

Justin raises an eyebrow. "Do you really think sneaking around behind your parents' backs is the best way to go about this?"

I wave him off. I can't stop to consider the potential repercussions yet or they'll dampen my creative workflow.

Pulling my phone out of my pocket, I open the World Fusion Café Instagram page. They don't have that many posts, but they do have a hashtag in their bio. I follow it to all the posts their patrons have been laying out for the past couple of weeks. I figure I can start going through the popular stuff and go from there. I mean, if people care enough to share this shit on Instagram, it's gotta at least be eye-grabbing.

Justin peers over my shoulder as I scroll. Then he shouts, "Oh wait, go back!"

I jerk away from him. "Back to what?"

He snatches my phone out of my hand before scrolling up the list of post thumbnails and clicking on one. Some girl smiles goofily, her eyes crossed and her tongue stuck out. I imagine that's not the part that caught Justin's attention, though.

"How about this?" he says.

She's got a drink in her hand—light pink, faded near the top where the ice is probably melting, and little boba balls at the bottom. "It just looks like lemonade," I say.

"Bingo!" Justin says. "Pink lemonade. But what if we made blue lemonade? Or orange lemonade? Or gray lemonade?"

I legitimately can't imagine even my fad-driven classmates would want to try gray lemonade, but maybe he's onto something. I'm here trying to whip up some masterpiece, but I just have to get their attention, right? It doesn't even really matter what goes into it as long as it's exciting and I can convince a bunch of photo-hungry white kids to buy it. Easy.

"Okay," I say. "Let's get started."

Monday's the day I become firmly convinced that I died and went to hell. First, there's school, which frankly is pretty much a perpetual hellscape by design, but then we have a pop quiz in second period, and I get my grade in fifth to find I failed, which isn't unusual given my history, but I promised myself I was gonna do better this year, and I'm really not living up to that. I know my chances of going away for school shrink with every poor test score, but at this point I'm too overwhelmed to do much about it except ignore it and hope it goes away. Oh,

50

and hide the results from my parents, just to be safe.

After school, I go to soccer practice and get mowed over by Gabriel Moreno. Three times. It's not a new record, but it's definitely enough to have my teeth clenched.

And as practice dies down, Joey Amos says, "Anyone want to go to that World Fusion Café?"

I'm literally standing three feet away from him, and he says it casually, like it doesn't basically translate to fingernails on a chalkboard.

A few of the guys nod along, and I'm just frozen, because what the fuck am I supposed to say to that?

Finally, Justin chimes in with, "I went yesterday. It's nothing special."

Joey nods and says, "Yeah, I went this weekend. The food's whatever, but they've got boba tea and those cool Latin pastries. It's dope."

Clearly no one but Justin realizes I'm vibrating with rage at the moment. As Joey and the gang turn to leave, Justin shouts out a quick, "The boba's mushy, anyway!" because apparently he's the only loyal person I know.

"It's fucking ridiculous," I grumble. "They know it's not even good, and they're going anyway! Just because they have weird shit?"

Justin shrugs. "Guess they like the diversity?"

Which is ironic, because I looked it up, and the owners are definitely white. Apparently appropriated diversity is the only acceptable kind.

Justin and I made some pretty good strides the evening before in planning out our new shop ideas, but they're still not ready to go yet. I wrote up a list of some of our shop's bestsellers—the classic boba milk tea, the taro buns, the lychee snow—so I could try to come up with some new recipes that play off our fan favorites and make sure anything we add to the menu balances well with what we already have to work with, but all we really have in terms of new ideas thus far is funky-colored lemonades and a couple of mixed tea flavors. At this rate, I don't think we'll have anything ready to sell until the end of the week, and that means one more week of watching everyone around me act like major sellouts.

Justin claps a hand onto my shoulder and says, "Don't worry. The hype'll fade eventually."

Then a new voice cuts into the middle of our conversation, saying, "It's not just hype, though."

I turn to find Gabriel Moreno standing a few feet away from us, eyes wide as he stares back at us. Was he eavesdropping? Not that I was particularly quiet in my ranting, but still.

"Um, sorry," he says. "I mean, about running into you. Three times. Well, and about the shop."

"What about the shop?" Justin asks.

Gabriel just shrugs.

And God, I want to punch him in the face. Not just because he's annoying as shit, but also because I just really want to deck someone. And I don't like the way he's looking at me, like he knows every little thought that's been wiggling around inside my head and knows exactly how to make them all feel so much worse.

He sighs and says, "My parents' shop hasn't been doing so great since the Fusion Café opened. I take it yours isn't either?"

And I don't know where he got the nerve to ask that, but it's really boiling my blood.

I mean, does he really think I'll just show our weaknesses to the enemy?

Gabriel pauses, glancing down at his feet for a second before saying, "I—I'm not sure how we can compete with them, but maybe if we work together . . ."

And there it is. The explanation.

I roll my eyes, turning on my heel and stomping back to the locker room. I don't want to have this conversation with Gabriel fucking Moreno. It's not even a pride thing.

Okay, it's not *just* a pride thing. What can he even do, anyway? Our parents are rivals, we're sworn enemies, and the kid can barely stand on his own two feet. He's even more clueless than I realized if he really thinks I'd just give him my plan so he can steal it for his parents' shop. If only one shop is gonna stand a chance against World Fusion, it's gonna be ours. And once Justin and I get my plan into motion, even Gabriel Moreno and his crappy pastries won't be able to slow our shop's momentum.

I just have to keep my cool until then.

SIX

GABI

nsurprisingly, the week barrels forward with a lot of downward momentum. There's the shop, which I still don't know how to save, even though I've spent every night brainstorming plans. I don't know what Theo has going on, but with the way he and Justin have been plotting every day at practice, he's obviously onto something, and I wish I could say the same for myself. But even thinking about Theo and what he might be planning keeps taking me back to that moment on the field when he caught me eavesdropping on his conversation. It wasn't like I meant to do it, really. I was just kind of zoned out and then I overheard him talking about the one thing that's been drowning my mind for the past week.

But I also figured it wasn't worth justifying that to him, since he already hates my guts. Really, that was probably just one more excuse for him to solidify his aversion toward me.

While Meli started the week off casually reminding

everyone to get their Homecoming dance ideas in—apparently the Wonderland theme isn't specific enough, so we all have to work out micro-themes now—by Thursday morning, she's sending nudges into the group chat every couple of hours or so, like we don't all have lives. And then there's Vivi, who didn't really want to part ways after our Sunday afternoon café stop and has been super eager to hang out since, like maybe she sees how busy Meli is and thinks that means I have infinite free time to spend with her. And it's not like I don't *want* to hang out with her, but with everything going on, I only have like two brain cells left, so I really can't keep up with whatever's going on with her four sisters today.

Anyway, just before homeroom on Thursday, I head to the dance room to talk to Lady, both because I could use her advice on how to get into the next position of this "save my parents' shop" plan, but also because I'm hoping being in the dance room will chill me out. Dancing really is the most effective anxiety treatment, so even if I can't get into full ballet mode until Friday, a few minutes in my happy place should help.

But when I get there, I find the door locked and all the lights turned off. I send her a quick text asking where she is, but I can only wait a few minutes before I have to turn and head back to homeroom or risk being late.

And yeah, the trek back sucks. I've got a plan brewing in the back of my mind about offering a special weekend discount to get more customers in, but I don't know. It feels kind of half-assed, and considering I only have until Homecoming to prove to my parents that the shop is worth keeping, I feel like I need a hard-and-fast solution that'll really have people pouring in. And without Lady to give me advice, I kind of feel like I'm drowning.

So on to homeroom, one of my least favorite periods of the day. I mean, everyone looks and feels like a zombie in homeroom, but it also sucks because no one really has anything to do, which means zero distractions from the tension of sitting directly in front of Theo.

But as I step into the classroom, I find a flurry of activity, everyone cheering and waving their arms and who knows what else. It's like a whole mob of high school students has formed to kill the beast, but they're all crowded around my empty desk.

Well, I guess that's more of a coincidence. It looks more like they're swarming Theo.

"Excuse me," I mumble as I try to elbow my way to my desk, but no one's really listening. I claw my way through the crowd, finally getting a grip on the back of my chair and using it to pull myself the rest of the way through the swarming bodies.

What is going on?

"I want the secret milk tea!" the girl next to me shouts.

Then I hear Theo's voice waft out of the crowd. "No problem, Lilly. Sorry, guys. That's the last milk tea."

The crowd groans in some weird, collective exasperation.

I push my head through the crowd of shoulders, catching sight of Theo where he leans back in his seat, a big grin on his face. He's got some clipboard on his lap, and he's marking things off on it.

He looks up, his smile instantly melting away as his eyes land on me. And yeah, I should've expected that, but a jolt runs through me like a slap in the face.

"You still have buns left?" one of the guys to Theo's right asks.

He glances over, a retail smile popping back onto his face. "Absolutely. I'll add you to the list."

I itch to ask him what he's up to, but I know scratching will just turn this whole curiosity into a gaping, festering wound. That's just the way things are with Theo Mori. If you dare get too close, someone's going to get hurt.

Or maybe it's just me.

"What are you all doing? Get to your seats."

I jerk to attention as Ms. Kilburn, our homeroom teacher, strides into the room and kicks the doorstop out from under the door. She lives up to her name being one of the strictest—and frankly, just plain meanest—teachers on campus.

Some groans, some shuffling, some squeaking of chairs, and then everyone's back to their desks.

I turn my head slightly to catch a glimpse of Theo where he sits smugly in his seat. Our eyes lock, and he points a finger forward, his smirk falling into a glare.

When the bell rings, I swiftly cross to the door to cut him off. He scowls at me but doesn't say anything as he forcibly shoves me aside.

"Theo, wait!" I call.

"Fuck off."

"I—What were you doing back in homeroom?"

"Why does it matter?"

"Does it have something to do with the World Fusion Café?"

He stops walking, and a heavy weight of regret settles into my stomach. People swim through my peripheral vision as they make their way up the hallway, but they're blurred now as I zero in on Theo.

He turns around, eyes narrowed, and says, "What does it matter to you?"

"I—" I want to tell him that I recognize the emotions tearing through his chest. That I empathize with how infuriating the café is, the toll it's taking on our parents' businesses. I want to convince him that we could work together, be allies, maybe even be friends once we establish our common ground.

But all I do is stare, because Theo's face is telling me to get as far away as possible before he combusts and takes me down with him.

Yet, there's a voice in the back of my head saying this is my chance, my in, my one opportunity to hang out with this guy who may be the only person in our entire school who could actually understand me.

"I—Are you selling stuff?" He stares back at me blankly like I haven't even spoken, but my words fall like deadweight in the middle of the hallway. "Can I buy something?" I add to break the tension, but it resonates hollowly between us.

Then Theo takes a step closer to me, his voice low. "Don't tell anyone about this, you got that?"

But I'm not really sure what he means. Our entire class

seemed pretty in the know about it. Or does he mean administration? Does he seriously think I just eat lunch with the principal or something?

"I won't," I say. "I mean, I wouldn't do that. I'm not like that."

He shakes his head, taking a step back. Then he presses his lips together and says, "After school, before practice, I'll be outside the cafeteria. You know, if you want to buy something."

Then he whirls around and disappears down the hallway before I can promise him I'll be there too.

Between second and third period, I nearly bump into Lady in the hallway as she pulls me aside.

"Sorry, I had an interview this morning, so I got to school late," she says. "Everything okay?"

"Another interview?"

"Fingers crossed this one actually takes," she says, even though that's basically the worst-case scenario for me. "Anyway, what's up?"

And I'm not sure where to begin, both because there's so much going on, but also because I only have like five minutes to get to my next class.

"I—what do you do when you need to make a plan but everything's happening too fast?"

She raises an eyebrow at me, like she knows she missing a huge part of the equation, before saying, "Gabi, you're sixteen. Stop worrying about all these lofty plans and just live a little."

But she doesn't get it. Yeah, I'm a teenager, but that doesn't mean my life isn't important. It doesn't mean my actions don't have consequences. And it definitely doesn't mean that my parents always know what's best. They may not see it now, but I know they'll regret selling the shop if they go through with it, and I'll be the one stuck dealing with the fallout.

Lady's eyes soften as she watches me, like she can see the breakdown going on behind my eyes. "Okay, look," she says, "I can see whatever's happening is important to you, but you just need to take a breather and let things happen. You must have a friend you can talk to, right? Someone to help you get through all of it?"

But Meli's too busy at the moment, and Vivi and I just aren't close like that. I don't know how to open up to her about these kinds of things.

So all I have is Lady, and dance, and I'm about to lose those too.

"We can talk more tomorrow, okay? When we finish the dance?"

And I don't really feel up to waiting hopelessly until tomorrow, but before I can say anything else, she's heading in the opposite direction, most of the hallway already emptying out, so I hurry off to third period before I can get written up for being late.

I still have time before Homecoming. I still have time to work out a plan.

So here's hoping meeting Theo after school will inspire me.

SEVEN

THEO

Students aren't allowed to sell anything on campus. That's a super-basic rule since like, the age of the dinosaurs or something, but I've decided to ignore it. The hard part is finding somewhere to actually store everything, since it's not like I can just start baking in sixth period. Fortunately, Justin's my hookup on that. Well, kind of.

Clara's aunt works in the cafeteria, so I call in a favor to get everything packed away until the end of classes. We just slip it all in through the back before everyone starts arriving on campus. After the last bell, I meet Justin and Clara at Justin's locker before we head to the cafeteria.

"I hope this isn't a long-term plan of yours," Clara says. "My aunt'll kill me if she has to keep hiding stuff for us."

"Us" is an awkward word choice coming from her, especially since Justin doesn't even seem all that committed to her, but I'm not gonna tell her that. I just say, "If this goes right, we'll figure

something else out for the future."

Clara pushes open the cafeteria door, and we follow her inside, quickly slipping past the main hall toward the back room, where all the lunch ladies work. The space is pretty empty, since the last lunch period ended hours ago. She guides us back to the massive industrial refrigerator where our supply awaits us.

I was smart about it—woke up early to get cups of milk tea sealed, pastries baked, and everything tucked away into coolers. I couldn't add boba to the drinks, since it'd be soggy by now, so that's something to work out for the next trial, but I already sold out of most of my stock in homeroom. All I had to do was add "mystery" to the title and mention I'd be selling shit after school, and suddenly everyone was falling all over me. Foolproof plan.

Justin and Clara help me drag out the coolers, and there's already a small line of people waiting to pick up their orders. Sweet.

"I have the forms," I say, passing a stack of orders to Justin. "Just make sure everyone gets what I marked them off for."

Justin sighs but accepts the orders anyway and starts handing out drinks. I figured I should handle passing out buns, since I'm the only person who really knows what's in them.

"Damn, Theo," Clara says. "You're a hot commodity around here."

"I think most people are just here for his buns."

I look up to see Gabriel Moreno standing a few feet away,

an awkward smile on his face. I raise an eyebrow, my lip curling back as I say, "Is that supposed to be some kind of gay joke, asshole?"

His eyes go wide, a blush coloring his cheeks as he says, "I—what? No! I didn't—I was just—"

But I just ignore him. I've dealt with enough homophobic bigots in my time to know when someone means business, and clearly, Gabriel Moreno does not. It's still kind of annoying that he's here. I know I'm the one who told him I'd be here, but I was mostly just trying to shake him off.

"Just buy something and leave," I snap.

He stops stammering, staring back at me blankly for a second before saying, "Um, what do you have left?"

And frankly, not a whole lot. I think we've got two unreserved pork buns and a red bean bun. All the fancy-colored, weird-flavored messes got reserved early, and really, even the traditional stuff ran down once people realized we were out of the special stuff.

But I don't really want to talk about my buns with Gabriel Moreno. It's like answering the door for Jehovah's Witnesses—setting yourself up to fail.

I snatch the three buns out of the cooler and pass them to Clara, who eyes me a second before holding them out to Gabriel.

He looks them over for a moment before hesitantly accepting one and fishing around in his pocket for some cash. Once Clara finishes the sale, Gabriel turns to me and says, "Um, Theo, can we chat for a minute?"

And I don't even know why he's asking, when it's so obvious the answer is no. I've basically done everything I can to avoid this guy since the dawn of time. I mean, my parents literally taught me to steer clear of the Morenos before they even taught me how to wrap a dumpling.

But he flashes me this look that I can't stand. It's this puppy-eyed, twitchy-nosed kid-who-just-got-his-lollipop-kicked-out-of-his-hand frown that he always has on the soccer field. Like he's just so fucking pathetic that his very existence is filled with sadness and despair.

It's entirely possible that I'm just being dramatic, but when I glance at Clara, she has this look like she feels bad for him, and it just pisses me off more. Like, yeah, I cry when I watch those sad puppy videos too, but Gabriel's not actually a puppy abandoned by his owner. He's an upper-middle-class Vermont kid whose parents' business beats ours like ten months out of twelve. It's not my fault that emotionally, he's about as stable as a cheap Styrofoam cup. Yet, looking at him, I almost feel bad, like I always do on the field, like I'm somehow responsible for his inability to control his feet or his balance or the goddamn ball.

And suddenly I'm filled with the same helplessness I feel watching my parents get chewed apart by Uncle Greg. It's knowing that nobody's going to appreciate my help and I'll probably just keep disappointing everyone, but a twisting in my gut telling me I have to do it anyway until I'm an unchecked ball of guilt and rage without even knowing where it's coming from or what I can do to get rid of it.

With a huff I say, "Just make it quick."

He steps away from the crowd, and I follow him, but I swear to God, if he tries to lead me off campus or something, I'm going to scream. He goes to the other the side of the cafeteria— far enough that everyone's still within view but completely out of earshot—and says, "I, um, I'm sorry about the comment earlier."

"I literally don't care," I say. "If that's all, I have a business to get back to."

"Wait!"

I pause. His eyes are wide, like he just got caught doing something dirty, and he keeps wringing his hands like he can't keep them still. I really should tell him to go get a life, but I just stand there, eyebrow raised, until he speaks again.

"I—why are you selling snacks outside the cafeteria?"

I shrug. "Easy cash."

"For your parents?"

I roll my eyes, turning to leave, but he grabs hold of my wrist, his grip surprisingly firm given his scrawny build.

"You're competing with the World Fusion Café, right?" he says, his voice coming out in a breathy rush. "Trying to make up for your parents' losses by selling stuff at school, but it's not sustainable. I mean, one, you could get expelled if administration finds out, and two, there's no way to do it on a large scale. I mean, not really."

My eyes shoot wide. "Are you threatening me?"

"What? No!" he says, and he looks totally shocked, like the thought never even occurred to him, but let's be real. Boot-lickers gonna lick boots. Even if it *has* been years since he officially sold me out, I find it very hard to believe he'll let me get away with breaking such a huge rule when he and his friends are such teacher's pets. "I—well, I'm offering to help you. Asking to, I guess. And hoping you'll help me in return. Please."

The last word comes out like a whisper.

I shake my arm free, pulling it back, away from him. "Why would I want your help?"

He doesn't seem to have an answer to that, and frankly, I'm not sure why he dragged me here in the first place. I'm the one who came up with the new business model, and I'm the one who's going to make it work. I don't need Gabriel Moreno's help, and I definitely don't want it.

And then there's his desperate plea for me to help him. What does he really think is going to come out of this? I'm not some wise Asian elder trope here to guide his family out of poverty. If he wants to save his family business, maybe he should be making a plan instead of trying to mooch off mine.

He stares back at me, his eyes pleading that soft, pathetic Gabriel Moreno plea, and I turn on my heel, heading back to Clara and Justin. I don't know if he's going to try to steal my idea or report me to administration, but I'm gonna have to tread carefully from here on out.

EIGHT
GABI

Things with Theo didn't exactly go well. The voice in the back of my head tells me I'm a fool and a masochist, and that if I had any self-respect, I'd forget Theo even exists and move on with my life.

But then, the voice in the front of my head is saying he's a genius. Or, at the very least, he's onto something. Homeroom is eating out of the palm of his hand, and as I get changed for practice, everyone's talking about Theo's . . . bubble tea.

God, I wish I had half his confidence or at least some innovative idea. I only have until Homecoming to convince my parents the café is worth keeping, but all I've managed to do thus far is piss off Theo. Well, and fall even more behind, because while the public discussion is starting to shift from the World Fusion Café to the Moris' shop, it doesn't mean a whole lot if they aren't talking about ours.

I sigh, struggling to stay upright as I tie my cleats. It feels so wasteful to gear up for soccer practice when no one really wants me to be here anyway. I should be figuring out a way to save our shop, not floundering around on the grass making more and more enemies. And I don't know, even if the other guys treated me the way they treat Theo—or even just tolerated me since I could never handle all the attention they give him—I can't help but feel like playing soccer is so counterintuitive to who I am that I'm basically erasing a piece of myself every time I take the field.

But then, I guess that's why I'm doing it.

The locker room has mostly cleared out by the time I straighten up and make my way out to the field. I try not to focus too much on practice itself. Just get in and get out. Nothing serious.

We warm up and run through some drills. Then we form two teams to run a scrimmage, which is always super fun, since literally nobody wants me on their team. Theo and Joey get to choose the teams, and Theo's face looks about as miserable as I've ever seen it as he realizes that the last-choice pick will be on his team. It's me. I'm always the last player left over.

I try not to take it personally, since I probably wouldn't want me on my team either, and focus my thoughts on the shop again. Theo's not going to help me, but maybe I can follow his lead anyway?

But even if I manage to make some sales at school, will it really make any difference? Financially, it's not enough to carry the shop, and my parents have already stressed that we need to earn enough to justify my dad staying out of real estate and the burden on my mom with school. And frankly, we'll just end up in the same standstill with the Moris again, and I doubt that'll be profitable enough to compete with the offer my parents got, however much that actually was.

The team races across the field as they hunt down the ball, but I'm not even sure where it's at. It kind of seems like everyone's stumbling over each other more than they are actually accomplishing anything, but I guess I can't really talk when I'm barely paying attention to any of it.

Anger and disappointment and frustration wage a war inside me until I really wish there was a way to just swing a fist into my problems and force them away. I wish I was the type of person who could fight every obstacle and come out victorious instead of constantly feeling so helpless about everything.

Then the ball rolls to a stop in the grass in front of me, and some switch flips on in my brain.

I charge at the ball, a low shout building in my throat.

And then Theo's there, passing the ball over to Jeff, who's poised to take a shot.

But I can't stop my momentum.

Theo turns and catches sight of me, and his face falls as I barrel into him with reckless abandon.

Theo lets out a soft yelp as his arm lands underneath him in a vain attempt to catch himself.

Our bodies are lumped together, legs entangled, my face pressed into the crook of his arm. I'm kind of frozen by the contact, but also the utter shame that I'll have to face the moment I try to get up.

"Get off me!" he shouts.

I scramble away from him, trying to put some distance between us even before I get to my feet.

He huffs, dark hair falling into his face as he pulls himself into a sitting position and cradles his right wrist in his left hand. "What the fuck?" he says.

I shrug, forcing a small smile on my face to break the tension. "I guess I just got lost in the game."

"Yes, you definitely lost us the game," he grumbles, but I don't respond. I don't think there's anything I can say to make this better.

Coach comes over, a look of exhaustion and irritation on his face. "All right, up, you two. Shake it off."

I leap to my feet and watch as Theo leans down to push himself up, only to face-plant as his wrist gives out.

Crouching down, I hold a hand out to Theo, but he just scowls back at me. Coach steps around me and reaches a hand down, grabbing hold of Theo's left wrist and pulling him to his feet.

"Mori, why don't you go sit out for a while?" Coach says.

Theo looks like he'd rather stick his good wrist down a garbage disposal, but after one disgusted look in my direction, he nods and heads for the bleachers.

Coach tells us to continue on without Theo, but now on top of feeling useless and dejected, I feel guilty. Theo should be out on the field, not me.

"Yo, pay attention, Gabriella," Kris says, kicking the ball toward the goal.

But he misses. By a few yards. Everyone groans.

"Okay, let's just call it for the day," Coach shouts, finally accepting what the rest of us already know—there's really no point holding a practice without Theo. We all stick it out because there's no *I* in team or some other corny nonsense, but we really just stand around on the field waiting for Theo to try to win the game for us. Which, you know, is probably why we never win.

Justin jogs over to the bleachers and plops down next to Theo while the rest of the guys head back toward the locker room. Common sense tells me to go with them, but instead I cross to the bleachers, watching as Theo's and Justin's eyes land on me.

"I—um, I'm really sorry, Theo," I say. "Again. I—I'm sorry."

He looks about ready to punch me in the face, but his wrist is swollen pretty badly. Like, badly enough that a punch to the face would hurt him a hell of a lot more than it would hurt me.

"Fuck off, Moreno," he snaps.

I wince. "Is your wrist okay? It looks pretty gruesome."

He rolls his eyes. "It's fine. Go away."

Justin turns his attention to Theo's wrist for the first time, his eyes widening. "Shit, dude, that's like—that looks bad."

"It's whatever. My folks'll put Neosporin on it or something."

"I don't think so. We should get you to the emergency room."

"It's just a bruise!"

"It looks worse than a bruise," I say, flinching as both pairs of eyes fall on me again. "I—um, look, I have a car. I can drive you to the ER or something?"

Justin shakes his head. "Nah, better we go to the urgent care where my mom works."

"Whoa, whoa, freeze," Theo says. "I didn't agree to go anywhere with either of you."

Justin rolls his eyes, reaching for Theo's wrist. Upon contact, Theo hisses, drawing back, which makes Justin roll his eyes again. "Come on, we're going."

Theo shakes his head. "You can't force me."

Justin grabs hold of Theo's good wrist, yanking him off the bleachers and half dragging him toward the parking lot. "So, where are you parked?"

A half hour later, Justin and I sit in the waiting room of the local urgent care. Justin's mom came out to grab Theo a few minutes ago, and now we just sit in this increasingly awkward silence while he scrolls through something on his phone and I skim the plaques lining the wall. I feel like I should say something, but I figure Justin probably hates me as much as Theo does, and we both know it's my fault Theo's here.

And like, I know it's not serious, but I still feel guilty and have no idea how to make up for this.

It takes twenty minutes for Theo's parents to arrive. I can't remember actually seeing them in person before, but his mom looks irritated and his dad looks thoroughly concerned. Justin pulls them aside to recount what happened—hopefully leaving out that it's entirely my fault, and probably reassuring them that Theo's not like dead or anything.

Ten minutes later, Justin's mom returns with Theo. His wrist is bound in a thick black brace, but otherwise, he looks mostly unscathed.

"Just a sprained wrist," Justin's mom explains. "It should heal in a couple of weeks. I'm gonna have to recommend you sit out of practice until then."

Theo rolls his eyes but nods anyway.

"Pretty terrible timing," Mrs. Mori says. "You were supposed to start running deliveries today."

Theo shrugs. "I can still do deliveries."

"How are you going to carry everything with one arm?" Mrs. Mori presses. "You're going to hurt yourself or drop everything."

"I can help," I say, my mouth working at the speed of light and leaving my brain in the space dust.

Mrs. Mori turns to me, an eyebrow raised. "Who are you?"

Theo groans. "Just a friend from school."

I freeze, the word catching me off guard. I can't even fathom a world in which Theo and I are friends. He probably just said it to keep his parents from figuring out he was consorting with the enemy, but it leaves me jittery as I say, "Yeah, I, um, I drove Theo here. Because I have a car. So I could help with deliveries, I mean."

Theo shakes his head. "It's fine, Gabriel. I've got it."

Mr. Mori laughs. "Theo, accept the help if the boy wants to offer it. This is why your teachers think you're unfriendly."

Theo flushes, but he turns his head away, mumbling something I can't make out.

Mr. Mori turns to me with a smile and says, "Theo will happily take you up on your offer. Sorry we can't pay you."

I wave him off. "No worries. Really, I'm happy to help."

Mr. Mori drops me a wink and says, "I'll give you my number. You let us know if Theo is being a troublemaker, yeah?"

I catch sight of Justin shaking his head out of the corner of my eye, but I ignore it as Mr. Mori passes me a business card. I'm just going to help Theo to make up for hurting his wrist in the first place, and maybe, somewhere along the line, it'll help inspire a solution to help my parents' shop. What's the worst that could happen?

NINE
THEO

Friday morning, I consider faking the flu and staying in bed. You know, anything to not have to face Gabriel Moreno again. It's so fucking annoying that my parents agreed to having us work together. I can't say it's particularly out of character for them to make decisions for me, but this is a whole new level of low. And even bitching to them on the ride home and telling them that Gabriel is actually their rival's son did nothing to change their minds, considering that they have a complete inability to ever admit they may have been wrong about something.

When I get to school, Justin asks me how my wrist is doing, and I ignore him. Eventually, he'll get the hint that I see him as a traitor now. And hopefully that realization comes before the final bell, so he can apologize before I'm supposed to go to his place after school to work on new recipes.

And since Justin and I are supposed to be working on our

secret business after school, I had to spend all last night thinking about what to do with Gabriel. The "deliveries" were really just a cover to explain the surprise money from selling at school and the missing supplies, so it's not like I need his help driving around town dropping off boba. Honestly, even if I *was* running deliveries, I definitely wouldn't need his help. Not when the guy would be more likely to drive me into a river than actually be helpful. So now I have to find a way to keep him from reporting me to my parents for bad behavior while simultaneously keeping him out of the way so he can't break or sprain anything else. Honestly, just dealing with this guy is a full-time job.

When I get to homeroom, Gabriel's already sitting there, twiddling his thumbs or something. I bypass his desk before slipping into my own and dropping my book bag onto the floor. His back stiffens the second I sit down, like he's itching to talk to me, and it really pisses me off. This kid cannot take a hint.

He turns his head slightly, like he's trying to look at me, and I resist the urge to shove him away from me. He's only a text message or a trip to the principal's office away from blowing my whole operation at any moment, so I have to at least maintain enough civility that he feels inclined to keep quiet.

"Gabriel," I say.

He turns around, eyes wide.

"Justin and I are going to his place after school for work."

"I—" He pauses, glances downward for a second before saying, "I actually have something after school today."

76

I roll my eyes. "Too fucking bad. Cancel it. You're the one who offered to help, aren't you?"

A blush rises in his cheeks, but he just nods, ducking his head and turning away. It's only as my anger subsides that I realize what a crappy move that was on my part. I could've just let him go to his thing and been free for at least the afternoon.

Just great. He's got me so pissed off I can't even think straight.

"So," he says turning back to face me, "where should I meet you after school?"

"Actually," I say, an idea quickly building in my head, "you should go to the store. You have a car, right? You should pick up some stuff we'll need."

"Okay," he says. "What do you need?"

"I'll text you a list and Justin's address."

He nods.

Perfect. Now I just have to come up with some obnoxiously difficult list to keep him busy for a few hours while Justin and I get stuff done.

I completely forget why I'm pissed at Justin until I see him again in fourth period. He waves at me, which I just ignore as I slide into my seat. I can't even fake taking notes because I'm not allowed to use my right wrist, so I'm stuck staring forward, pretending I actually care what's being said and am just that interested in Mr. Monaghan's chalkboard scribbles.

Unsurprisingly, I knock out like ten minutes in. When the

bell rings, startling me awake, it takes me a second to remember exactly where I am and start getting my shit together.

And that second's all it takes for Justin to pop up at my desk, a glare on his face. "Yo, asshole, why are you ignoring me?"

I consider taking the whole cold-shoulder thing to the next level and just breezing past him like I don't even know he's there, but besides the fact that I'm shit at holding a grudge, I'd rather yell at him.

I turn to him, the angriest glare I can muster on my face. "You sold me out."

He raises an eyebrow. "I didn't tell your parents anything—"

"Not my parents," I snap. I drop my voice low in case any of the stragglers heading into the hallway are listening in. "Gabriel. I didn't want him to drive me to urgent care, and now I have to work with him and it's all your fault."

He rolls his eyes. "Jeez, Theo, I thought your wrist was broken! I was just trying to help."

And maybe he was just trying to be a good friend or something, but considering how badly things worked out for me, I'm not ready to brush it aside. I just throw my bag over my shoulder and head for the hallway. He follows behind loyally, only a step away. I say, "I didn't need your help, and now you've just gone and made things worse. This is what happens when you talk to the enemy!"

"Well, sorry," he says. "But for what it's worth, I think you're taking this whole thing too far anyway."

"Of course you would. You hate when I'm mad at you."

"Not that," Justin says. "The whole Gabriel Moreno thing. Like, yeah, I get it, the kid's annoying and your parents are rivals or whatever, but he just wanted to help you. It's not like he skinned your cat or something."

I whip toward Justin, eyes narrowed. "Are you seriously saying you don't realize that every time he tries to help with something, it just gets worse? Like now I have to spend my time babysitting instead of dealing with what should be my biggest problem this year. Not to mention!" I wave my sprained wrist in front of him for good measure.

Justin sighs a deep, hearty sigh like he's beyond done with my shit, but whatever. Of course it's easy for him to say, "Gabriel's not so bad!" because he doesn't have to deal with him. He's not the one with years of Gabriel-infused homeroom, with a goddamn sprained wrist, and a hell sentence adding to what's already the most obnoxious semester of my life.

I text Gabriel the most absurd shopping list I can think of just after sixth period. You know, hoping he then won't have the time to confront me about it.

Instead, he catches me after school just before Justin and I can make a break for it.

"You really need all this stuff?" he asks.

I shrug. "Yeah, we've got some really complicated recipes to dive into. It's not too much, is it?"

He looks a little nervous, but finally shakes his head and says, "No, I've got it. I'll meet you at Justin's later?"

I nod.

"Text me the address."

I nod again, waiting for him to leave so I can "forget" to send him the address. But he just kind of stands there waiting until I finally pull out my phone to text it to him.

When he gets the message, he skims it over and says, "Eesh, that's kind of far. Do you guys want me to drop you off before I go to the store?"

And yeah, the address is kind of far because it's a bullshit one. I figured it could buy us some peace time if he "gets lost" and only shows up when we're just about finished.

But now he's looking at me with those Gabriel doe eyes, like he's just so concerned about Justin and me walking the whole six miles out to whatever address I just sent him.

And it makes me vaguely nauseated—the pathetic, desperate look. Gabriel's not my problem. I don't owe him anything, and yeah, maybe he's trying to be helpful, but when has that ever actually worked in my favor?

Finally, I sigh and say, "It's not that far."

He looks sad as he says, "If you say so."

"Wait," I say, holding a hand out to him. "I meant, it's only like a mile away. I must have accidentally sent you the wrong address."

I take his phone from him, pretending I'm reading over the text to figure out which part I messed up, even though I already know. Finally, I say, "Oh, yeah, it should say Campbell Boulevard."

"Oh," Gabriel says, looking down at the text like he's not sure how I could've possibly typoed that.

"Anyway, bye!" I say, quickly steering Justin away so we can escape before Gabriel tries to call us back.

"Wow," Justin says. "You really tried to give him the wrong address."

I shrug. "I corrected it."

"Kind of a douchey move, since you already sent him on a wild-goose chase, don't you think?"

But honestly, I can't believe I corrected the address. That was so unnecessary. It's just something about Gabriel's ridiculous face that had me crumbling, like he's some baby I can't punch in the face, because who the fuck punches a baby? That's just messed up.

It doesn't take long to walk from school to Justin's house, and we make the whole trek in silence. I don't know if Justin assumes I'm still mad at him so he doesn't bother striking up a conversation, or if he just doesn't have anything valuable to say. Now that Gabriel's temporarily out of the picture, I'm stuck thinking about my own problems again, which, frankly, may just be worse than dealing with him.

I need to get out of this damn state, and that means I need to stop wasting time on Gabriel and start figuring out how to deal with Uncle Greg.

We kick off our shoes at the entryway before crossing through the living room to get to the kitchen. Justin's mom isn't home, and she probably won't be back until late. She's taken on so many extra shifts since her husband left that I'm not sure whether she desperately needs the money or just hates living in the house they set up together. Maybe both.

"So, what are we working on today?" Justin asks.

I sling my book bag onto the counter, ignoring the grimace Justin gives me. He's probably worried I'm spreading book-bag germs all over our cooking surfaces like some old Asian auntie, but we'll clean them anyway, so who cares?

Rifling through my stuff, I pull out the order forms. The main reason I printed them was to keep track of exactly how much of each item we made and make sure I didn't promise people shit we didn't have, but they're actually perfect little receipts for measuring what sold the best.

"All the weird stuff was gone almost immediately," I say, looking at the first set of orders. "Why the fuck?"

Justin shrugs. "Probably because it's limited edition."

I raise an eyebrow.

"You know, like a pair of sneakers or those weird vinyl figures. The value always skyrockets when people know they'll only have one chance to get it."

He's probably right about that. Actually, that might be one of the biggest weaknesses of our café—our menu never changes. Maybe people are just sick of our stuff, or maybe they realize it'll always be there if they want to come back for it.

You know, until it's not.

I make a note of that on the side of the order forms. "Okay, so we should make everything limited edition?"

"We need enough repeats to spread by word of mouth, but I think limited numbers are good," he says. "You know, so people really prioritize getting it. Don't miss out! You might not get another chance!"

"How do you know all this stuff?" I ask, considering Justin's never even had a job, let alone run a business.

He shrugs. "It's what they use in like every commercial ever. Do you not watch YouTube?"

"Only Netflix."

"You should try watching some ads every now and then."

"Why do you think I only watch Netflix?"

Justin chuckles, but I don't get what's so funny.

I turn my attention back to the order forms. Drinks did better than snacks, which is kind of weird to me, but I also wonder if they're just more recognizable. After all, a lot of people have been posting boba tea on their Instagrams lately. I should probably consider that.

"They're better for aesthetic photos," Justin says, peering over my shoulder.

I jerk away because I didn't hear him coming. "What's better for aesthetic photos?"

"Drinks? Like the buns are tasty and all, but they basically all look the same from the outside, and frankly, girls look a hell of a lot cuter with a straw against their lips than a mouth full of food."

I'm mostly following, except for the girls part. I mean, I've known I was gay since I was ten, so I never got the "sexy" girl selfie trends—the duck face, the weird squats, the thigh gap? Utter absurdity.

But he does have a point about the cups. They're bright, colorful, and people are always drawing them on kawaii-style stickers and stuff. They're recognizable and cute. Marketable. I can work with that.

"Okay, so drinks over food. We want most things to be limited edition, and we need cute packaging. Anything else?"

Justin throws his head back laughing, but I just raise an eyebrow, waiting for him to finish. Then he says, "Cute packaging. Let's be real for a second, Theo. Neither one of us is known for cute. I'm more a sexy athlete type and you're not that kind of gay."

I roll my eyes. "I can make nice cups. How hard can that really be?"

Justin starts laughing again.

"Okay, fine, we'll pause on the packaging. Let's just stick with the drinks for now."

"We should add boba," Justin says.

"Can't. It'll get soggy."

"Well, what about those juice pearls? Or like jellies or something?"

I nod, adding *toppings* to the corner of the page as well. Actually, we might even be able to make the boba work. We'd just need a way to add it into the cups just before they get delivered. So maybe a top that doesn't seal?

"Ugh, I'm starving," Justin says, pulling open the fridge to reveal that, unsurprisingly, there's not really anything in there. "Fuck. We should order takeout."

"We don't have time for that. We have work to do."

A shady grin creeps across his face, and I'm tempted to slap it off. "What?"

"We could ask Gabriel to pick something up."

I groan. "No, thank you. Besides, he shouldn't be back for a few hours."

But Justin's already reaching for my phone, typing in the same password I've used for everything since fourth grade, and scrolling for Gabriel's contact.

He picks up on the third ring, the sound of traffic and blowing AC behind him. "Theo?"

"It's Justin," Justin says, leaving the phone on the counter. "We're hungry. You wanna grab food?"

"Um, I can," Gabriel says, ever the awkward piece of shit. "What do you want?"

"Anything's fine. Just swing by Taco Bell or something."

"Ew, no," I say. "If we're getting food, we're getting food, not dog slop. Just go to that pasta place in the square."

Gabriel chuckles. "Okay, will do. I've got one more stop to get the new ladle, and then I'm done."

"Wait," I say, my voice coming out in a gasp. "You're done? Already? It's only been like an hour!"

"Yeah, I just went to some of the retailers my parents shop at. Pretty easy. Impressed?"

More like furious, but there's literally no way to admit that

that doesn't make me sound like a dick.

Wait, does that mean I *am* the dick?

"Sweet. Thanks, Gabriel!" Justin says before hanging up the phone. "I can't believe you hate that guy. So helpful."

Justin's words feel like a sharp jab in the side. *So helpful.* And maybe he is being helpful, and maybe he was just trying to help me, and maybe I did send him on a pointless scavenger hunt just to get him to stay the hell away from me, but it's not like I don't have reasons. I *have* reasons. He's the son of the enemy. He's a teacher's pet. He sucks at soccer, and he *sprained* my wrist.

But the more I repeat the reasons in my head, the worse they sound. Yeah, he pisses me off, but do I really spend all my time hating this kid because our parents work in the same industry and he's bad at sports? Or have I just been putting all my frustrations over my parents' shop and Uncle Greg and our piss-poor soccer team on him? Do I even know him enough to hate him?

"He's the SpongeBob in this situation, isn't he? And I'm the Squidward?"

Justin stares at me like I've just spoken the world's most profound haiku. "Oh shit. Wait, does that mean I'm Patrick? No, wait, Squilliam, right?"

I roll my eyes. Okay, I'm definitely overthinking this. New plan—I'm just not going to think about it. Perfect. I'll just never think about Gabriel Moreno again.

TEN

GABI

I get a *Hey, it's Justin!* text from an unsaved number, followed
by Justin's and Theo's orders, and I have to admit, it stings
a little.

Maybe Justin was just fed up from texting on Theo's phone
and thought it'd be easier to do it on his own.

Or maybe Theo hates me so much, just the thought of Justin
talking to me from his phone pissed him off.

I wish Lady were here so she could give me some advice on
how to navigate social interactions while I work on my penché.
It felt like swallowing nails to text her that I wouldn't be able to
make it after school today because I had "a work engagement,"
and as it stands, the lack of dance practice has had me building
up nervous energy until I feel like I'm gonna explode.

My trunk is full of stuff I'm not even sure how they'll use as
I pull out of the last shop and dial up the pasta place. I figure I
can call in the order to make pickup easier.

But my hand freezes over the call button. It's something Theo said, I guess. About how I finished too soon. Like maybe he'd rather I spent the extra twenty minutes waiting for the food to be done instead of diligently calling ahead.

I resist the urge to slam my head against my steering wheel. I'm sick of overthinking everything. Sick of hesitating before every decision because what if something that will probably never happen might happen.

Like what if I show up at Justin's place too early, and that's the last straw—the straw that makes Theo decide he can't even bear to look at me anymore, not that he really does now. What if showing up a half hour later gives him the chance to realize he does actually want me around, that maybe we could actually be friends?

God, and what if the place catches on fire while I'm sitting in my car pondering ridiculous what-if scenarios and now Theo and Justin both hate me because I didn't bring them anything to eat?

I finally settle on calling ahead. I'll just text Theo that I'm on my way back, and if he sounds like he'd rather die than see me, I'll wait in the car for twenty minutes. No big deal.

Ugh, unless the food gets cold.

I can't believe I didn't think that through.

The food ends up being ready by the time I arrive at the restaurant, so I throw it into the passenger seat and head straight for Justin's house.

When I knock on the door, Justin answers it and waves me

in. "Ditch your shoes," he says, taking the bag of food from me.

"Um, what about all the stuff in the trunk?"

"Oh," he says, pressing his lips together. "Um, I guess you can keep your shoes on while you load in?"

And just like that, he retreats to what I assume is the kitchen without another word. So I head back out to the car and proceed to make three trips to load in all the garbage they asked for. Once it's all in the entryway, I kick off my shoes and take three trips moving it all into the kitchen. On the first trip, I catch Theo standing in the kitchen, carefully balancing a measuring spoon as he adds stuff to a blender. He doesn't even look up at me as I drop the bags onto the wide wooden dining table, so I just head back out without a word.

Once everything's inside, I pause near the counter to catch my breath. Justin sits at the table, his mouth stuffed with pasta as sauce drips down his chin.

Theo's got the blender on, and the sharp screech of it tears through the kitchen as I shout, "Theo!"

He looks up at me like he heard me, but his face looks blank.

"What do I do with the cold stuff?" I ask.

Theo just shakes his head and mouths something that looks like "Can't hear you."

I scream a little louder, but he just shakes his head again, finally turning off the blender. "What did you say?"

"I said—" but before I can get the next word out, he starts the blender again, the noise drowning out anything I could try to say.

He stops it and shakes his head. "Sorry. You were saying?"

"I was asking—" and he starts it again.

As Theo hits the button again, the roar of the blender gives way to the sound of Justin's laughter as he says, "Fuck, Theo, that's such a dad joke."

Theo smirks, which is the closest I've ever seen to him smiling that it completely catches me off guard as he says, "So what did you want?"

"I—"

"He doesn't trust you now," Justin says, which is a way better explanation for my mind-mush than the real one.

Because Theo's smirk is . . .

. . . weirdly hot?

Even if I know it's not really a smile, and it's definitely not directed at me.

The smirk falls from his face, replaced with his usual scowl. "What do you want, Gabriel?"

"I—call me Gabi," I say.

Which isn't a weird thing to say, because all my friends and family call me Gabi, but why did I have to say it now?

Theo rolls his eyes. "Fine."

"Wait!" I say. "Um, the cold stuff. That I bought. Um, what do I do with it?"

Theo shrugs. "Stick it in the fridge?"

"Is there room?"

Theo laughs. "You tell me."

So I open the fridge, and yeah, it's virtually empty. The

freezer's got a few more items stacked in it, but it's pretty empty too. I start unpacking the milks and juices for the drinks before moving on to the jellies and pastes that can technically be put into the cabinets if there isn't enough room, and then I hear the blender switch on again.

Once the blender dies, Justin says, "Yo, Theo, you gonna eat or what?"

I can practically hear Theo roll his eyes. "When I'm done."

"Oh my God, dude, take a break."

"Not interested."

The blender starts again, and I can't help but feel a little bit jealous of the easygoing way Theo and Justin talk to each other. I've never had that kind of friendship with another guy. They always just sense something about me is off, and either make fun of me or steer clear.

But Theo's gay, and he has guy friends. No one sees anything wrong with him.

So maybe it's just me.

I move across the kitchen to stack the straws and cups on the counter.

"Hey, Gabi," Justin says. "You gonna eat or what?"

"I—"

"Okay, seriously, and you're gonna call *me* the dad?" Theo snaps, but it sounds less angry. More . . . playful? Definitely not a word I'd typically associate with Theo Mori.

"Someone's gotta keep you kids in line," Justin says before shoveling more pasta into his mouth.

I smile, closing the freezer and stepping over to the dining table. "I'll eat. Food is good."

"See? You hear that, Mori? Food is good!" Justin shouts.

Theo just starts the blender again.

Lady texts me while I eat, a quick Hope everything's okay! Don't stress yourself out overthinking everything. See you next week! And it's not like she really said anything she hasn't said before, but it still feels nice to read it.

True to his word, Theo does in fact agree to eat, but only after slapping three cups down on the table.

"So, about the deliveries," Theo says. "I think you've figured out we aren't actually delivering anything."

I nod. "I could actually deliver stuff, though. I mean, if you need me to."

"I have the shop phone here," Theo says, pulling a little Android out of his pocket and waving it at me, "just in case we actually get any delivery orders, but unsurprisingly, no one's called in. We're just using the deliveries as the cover story so my parents don't get suspicious. Our *real* plan is to run World Fusion Café out of business by out-weirding their weirdness."

I raise an eyebrow. "I don't get it."

"It's all novelty," Justin says. "People only go there because their shit is interesting, so Theo wants to spice up his own family menu enough that people will be swayed back to their shop and World Fusion will choke."

"That's a cool idea," I say, which really is an understatement.

It's a way cleverer idea than anything I could've come up with, and it instantly makes me feel bad for not having come up with something more proactive to help my own family shop. "Kind of diabolical, though."

"Exactly my personality," Theo says with a grin. "Anyway, we're making limited-edition menu items to sell at school."

"How does that help your parents' shop, though?" I ask. "Like, in the meantime?"

Theo shrugs. "A few extra sales to help keep them afloat, I guess. As long as it convinces people that we have more to offer than the enemy, that's the main goal. Oh, and I guess you should take a cut too."

I freeze. "Wait, really?"

"I mean, you're putting in a lot of time to help. It wouldn't be fair if you didn't get paid for it."

And really, I'd been too afraid to ask for any sort of pay, since I volunteered myself to help, and it feels kind of unbelievable that *Theo* offered himself. But despite the flood of warmth I'm feeling at being recognized, I also have to wonder if taking a portion of Theo's profits is counterintuitive.

Maybe I'm projecting because I know how desperate the situation is with my parents' shop, but I feel like selling after school won't be enough to bring in the kind of money we need, especially if we have to split the profits. It could take years for World Fusion Café to go under, even if Theo's plan actually works. If he wants to really boost sales, he needs to be working on a larger scale.

93

And maybe I'm being selfish by focusing on my parents' needs instead of his, especially since this is technically his operation, but with Homecoming creeping up on us in a few weeks, it doesn't seem worth taking things too slowly.

"What if you actually ran deliveries, but like . . . during school hours?" I say.

Justin laughs. "Shit, what I would pay for buns in second period!"

Theo just shakes his head. "Way too many issues. Like, we'd have to disrupt class, which no teacher would allow, and then we'd need to constantly have someone watching the food and making new stuff. We don't have time for that." He passes Justin a straw, then hands one off to me and says, "Taste."

Each drink is a swirl of two different colors, but I'm not really sure what's in them. Justin sticks his straw into the one closest to him and slurps loudly.

"Um, which one should I try?" I ask.

Theo shrugs, picking up his little pasta bowl. "All of them."

"But Justin's drinking the green one."

"So, wait till he's done and switch?" Theo says.

The words are simple enough, but something about them makes my muscles feel tight, a chill running up my spine. "You want us to drink out of the same cup?" I say.

And it's like my dad is standing in the corner of the kitchen watching us, because all I can think about is what he'd say if he had any idea about what I was doing.

Sharing drinks with some boy? What are you, his girlfriend?

Theo raises an eyebrow.

I shove the image of my dad out of my head, looking for words to get Theo's scrutinizing look off his face, but my mind is mush and words feel insurmountable. "I just—I mean, I'm not gay," I say.

And the room falls quiet, tension crawling up my throat like it wants to choke me, but I'm still alive, so maybe even *it* doesn't want to be associated with me now. Coward.

Justin's staring down at the table, like he legitimately can't even bear to look up from the wood.

But the most painful part is Theo. He doesn't even look mad for once. He just kind of looks resigned, like he should've expected some dehumanizing commentary like that to come out of my mouth.

I want to tell him that that's absurd. That I didn't mean it. That I *am* gay. I'm gay! That's why I said it! I just—I'm awkward, and I'm gay, and I didn't want to out myself, so now I'm acting like a clown! That's all!

But I can't speak. Hell, I'm paralyzed by the fear that if I say anything, he'll instantly realize that I'm gay. And I'll be outed. Then the whole school will know, and then my parents, and then I'll lose everything.

But is it worth that look on Theo's face? I'm honestly not sure.

Theo finally breaks the silence by saying, "Oh, right, sorry. I forgot straight men can't share drinks." He plucks the straw out of my hand and adds, "Wouldn't want you to catch my AIDS or something."

I flinch, but I can't think of anything to say as Theo turns away from me and crosses to the other side of the kitchen. I glance over at Justin, but I don't know what I'm looking for. He's got his eyes glued to his phone, like he's pretty sure I don't even exist.

And honestly, I kind of wish I didn't. That would probably make everyone's lives a lot easier.

When I get home, my parents are in the living room, watching a soccer game. Well, my dad's watching a soccer game. My mom's sitting on the couch clipping coupons and glancing up only when my dad starts screaming profanities at the TV.

"Gabi," she says as I close the door behind me. "Come join us, no?"

I nod, leaving my book bag by the door before making the trek over to the couch. My mom clears away some of the paper scraps next to her and pats the couch for me to come sit. My dad's in the recliner, but he's leaning on his knees, one leg bobbing up and down as he watches the game unfold.

"You missed half the game," my mom says, running a hand over my hair.

I won't ever tell them, but that's kind of a relief. I hate watching soccer with my parents—the constant reminder that that's what they want from me, but not something I can give them. "I was helping Theo Mori, remember?"

"Ay, yes, I remember," she says. "I don't understand why you want to help that boy anyway. That family causes us enough trouble. Just the other day, they were outside trying to steal our customers. No class, those Moris."

"I'm the reason he got hurt, Mami," I say, leaning back against the couch. I tell my parents everything. Well, mostly everything. It's just too hard keeping secrets from them, even if my biggest secret is also the one I can't ever tell them.

"Okay, but you always say he's mean to you in soccer, no?"

"Leave it alone," my dad says. "Men shouldn't be all sweet and sensitive like you women. He just needs to respect him, huh, Gabi?"

I nod, but I feel vaguely nauseous. "We respect each other," I say, though I know that's not entirely true, but it's not like I can explain the situation to my parents. "And he's a really good athlete. I—well, he has to sit out of practice while his wrist heals, so I thought I could at least help out."

My dad waves a hand like, *See! Told you everything was fine!* And my mom just rolls her eyes. They've always been like this, as far as I can remember. My dad doesn't believe in saying more than necessary. Talking too much? Being too soft? Showing too much emotion? Those are girl things. Men don't do those things.

Which is just part of why I never know the right words to say. If my dad had any idea how much thought I put into every line, he'd think I was acting too girly. Hell, everything about me would just be evidence that I'm gay. The only reason he doesn't suspect it yet is because he would never want to associate that with his own son.

And now I'm thinking about Theo again. About what I said.

Being gay isn't some sort of infectious disease. It's not something to be afraid of. Yet, just the thought of the word coming out of my mouth feels like a punch to the gut.

I clear my throat and say, "I'm pretty tired, and I have some homework to do, so I'm just gonna head to my room."

My mom looks at me for a moment before smiling and patting my shoulder. I get up, heading to my room and immediately putting on some music. The space isn't big enough for me to get lost in dancing like I would with Lady, but I try anyway, running through a toned-down version of the dance we've been working on together.

But the tight space makes it hard to clear my head, and as I approach the unfinished ending of the piece, I find the same thought swirling around in my head again and again.

How can I ever feel comfortable being me when I'm the thing my parents hate the most?

ELEVEN
THEO

Saturday morning, I wake up feeling weirdly empty. I mean, on the one hand, I should be happy because it's Saturday, and that means as long as I keep Gabi from coming to me, I'm pretty much free of him.

But on the other hand, I still can't shake what he said to me.

It's weird, I guess, because I never liked him, so this just proves that my original opinion was right and is basically the world's biggest I-told-you-so to Justin, but I still feel dirty. Partially because of what he said specifically, but also just knowing that I was actually trying to give him a chance. Almost like a reminder that I can't trust anyone, because they're all probably just waiting to let their bigotry loose.

I slide out of bed and head down to the café. It's pretty rare for breakfast to be held in our kitchen anymore. Why bother when I can just grab something from downstairs?

But this time around, I instantly regret it. My parents' eyes shoot to me as I reach the first floor.

"You're up late," my mom says.

I shrug. "Sorry?"

"You and that boy are supposed to be running deliveries," my mom says.

Oh, right. That would make sense, since we don't have school.

"I, um, told him to take the day off," I say. "You know, child labor laws."

My mom stares back at me for a beat too long. "Those laws don't apply here, because you don't get paid."

"Okay, well, he still needs a day off."

"Theo, you didn't chase him away, did you?" my dad asks.

I shake my head, but I wonder if something in my body language gives me away. I kind of hate the way he says it, though. It's not a question, but this resigned sort of blame. There's no, *What happened?* There's no, *Let's hear Theo's side of the story.* And I guess I already know that it doesn't matter what I say. I'm Theo, the problem child. Theo, the barely passing student on the failed soccer team who will never give my parents grandchildren because I had to go and turn out gay. Of course I'd chase everyone away. The only question is when.

As if the world decides to take advantage of my shitty mood by making everything even shittier, Uncle Greg comes in the door, a smirk on his face. "I see you made more sales this month."

I'm tempted to skirt around him, but there's a self-destructive

100

side of me that can't bear to leave without hearing what my parents have to say. I slip around the counter and grab a melon bread for breakfast, trying to make myself small in the corner as I pick it apart.

"Yes, we worked very hard," my mom says, but her eyes already look tired. "Theo started doing deliveries to bring in more customers."

Uncle Greg looks at me, but it's far from a friendly look. Does that count as a win? I'm not really sure at the moment.

"You've done a good job," he says, "but your numbers are still low. What are you doing next?"

My mom's face is blank, and God, what can I even say to that? Does he not realize we've been busting our asses just to shut him up? It's not even like he's going broke! We're still paying him!

"Greg," Dad says, "we have more sales now, and as people start ordering more deliveries—"

Uncle Greg shakes his head, his lip curling back. "Don't be ridiculous. You still don't make me enough money. How long you expect me to wait? You've already been working here over ten years and you still don't make anything."

He begins walking around the shop slowly, his eyes scanning everything from the plastic tabletops to the lucky cat clock hanging on the back wall. Then he turns back around, a grin creeping across his face. "This place would make a great spa, don't you think?"

My mom sighs, crossing her arms. "There's not even room for—"

"Oh, we'll make room."

I freeze, the melon bread hanging out of my mouth as Uncle Greg steps up to Mom and holds out his phone, scrolling through picture after picture. I can't see much from my corner of the shop, but Mom's back stiffens as he scrolls.

"See?" Uncle Greg says. "All the plans are coming together. I just need to get the loan processed with the bank."

"Do it then."

The words are out of my mouth before I can stop myself, all three pairs of eyes shooting in my direction like they just suddenly realized I'm there.

"What?" Uncle Greg says through clenched teeth.

"I said do it," I say, and it kind of feels like my mouth is working on its own, but between the Gabi thing and Uncle Greg's morning rampage, I don't really have any self-control left. "You wanna get a loan? Convert the shop? Good luck. We all know you can't do shit on your own or you wouldn't have needed my parents in the first place."

"Theo!" Mom shouts, but I don't care. I can't convince myself to care. My nerves are on fire, and she's lucky I'm not crossing the shop to deck Uncle Greg in the face.

"You better learn some respect, boy," Uncle Greg says before turning to my mom and spitting his words in her face. "You teach your boys to act like this?"

My mom bows her head, shaking it slowly. "Of course not. Thomas—"

But that's the last straw for me. I won't just stand here and listen to my mom rant about how much better of a son Thomas is than me when he's not even *here* to defend them while I take all this shit.

"Fuck Thomas!" I shout, turning and stomping back toward the hallway.

"Theo!" Dad calls out, stepping into my path. "What the hell is wrong with you?"

"You can't even handle your own son and I'm supposed to trust you with my shop?"

Dad reaches for me, but I push his hand away. I turn my face downward as I speed-walk toward the hallway. I don't care how they decide to punish me. I don't care if they ground me for a year or cancel my inheritance or toss me out into the wilderness to fend for myself.

But I'll be damned if I let them see me cry.

I don't know when Uncle Greg leaves, but when I finally come downstairs a few hours later, there's no sign of him left in the shop. I tell my parents I have schoolwork to do, and they don't question me or really say much of anything as I head out without my book bag. They might say something when I get home, but that's a problem for later.

I text Justin and tell him to tell Gabi to fuck off. Actually, I say something like, *Tell him I don't need him this weekend,* and Justin replies with, *Sure! No problem! And I'm really sorry. I should've listened to you,* which I just don't reply to. He was all over himself guilty when we cleaned up the day before, so I already know he's sorry, and just like I told him yesterday, it's not his fault that Gabi turned out to be a huge homophobe. Besides, talking about it just makes it more present, which makes it harder to get past. I just want to shove it down as deep as it'll go and never think about it again.

It's been a long time since I've just kind of walked through town like I had nowhere better to be. My weekends are usually pretty busy with the shop or school or friends, but now it feels like everything's kind of hollow, and I'm not needed anywhere.

It kind of reminds me of the way things were before I came out—before I felt sure of myself and really understood my place in the world. Back when I still kind of felt like I was just floating through empty space, waiting for answers that would piece everything together for me.

But now I'm back to being empty and have no idea what I'm even searching for.

I plop down on a wooden bench, pulling out my phone and just kind of hovering over it for a second. My first thought is that maybe I should call Thomas, see what he's up to, ask him if he wants to hang out for a bit. But really, it's been a while since I felt like I could call on him like that. Even before he started college, he just grew up a lot faster than me, I guess, and suddenly we reached this point where just talking to him became scolding after scolding about all the things I was doing wrong with my life.

I open Instagram, scrolling mindlessly to distract myself. Nothing on there is particularly interesting, but it makes me feel like I'm doing something even though I'm not really.

A picture of Thomas with his new roommates shows up on my timeline, and I close the app. I don't want to think about all the ways his life has improved since he stopped hanging around, all the ways he's living up to all my parents' hopes and dreams while I remain the family screwup.

By the time I pull myself off the bench and head back toward the café, my chest hurts more than my wrist.

My parents are behind the counter as usual, but my mom's face looks serious as she stands in the corner on her phone, speaking quickly but too quietly for me to hear. They both look up as I enter, flashing me these uncomfortable glances before they turn around and pretend to be working on something.

Finally, Dad looks up just long enough to say, "Theo, you're grounded. Go to your room."

And yeah, that's pretty predictable.

But whatever. I don't care.

I go straight to my room, closing the door behind me and pulling out my laptop to keep browsing through out-of-state colleges. I don't have the grades for most of them, but at this rate, I don't really care. I'll find some random community college in the middle of nowhere and rent out some old couple's basement if I have to.

I just know I can't stay here anymore.

TWELVE
GABI

Saturday morning, Justin texted me to let me know I should steer clear of Theo, and well, both of them. Because they both hate me, which I can't really blame them for.

So Sunday morning, I resolve to make things right, even though the thought of it makes my stomach hurt so badly, I spend the first thirty minutes of my morning hunched over on the toilet.

Anyway, I grab a quick breakfast, telling my parents I'm going to help the Moris again, even though I know there's a pretty good chance Theo'll turn me away. It's like Lady always says when I hesitate before a big move—if I think about it, I'll overthink it. Then I'll just say something inappropriate again and only make things worse, so I'm going for winging it and hoping that somehow works out in my favor.

The Moris' shop isn't open yet, since it's only nine a.m., but

Theo's parents are working when I knock on the door. I guess Theo's mom recognizes me, because she flashes me a smile before unlocking the door and letting me inside.

"It's so good to see you," she says, but I notice she doesn't say my name, like she doesn't actually know it. "You and Theo are running deliveries again today?"

I nod. "Yeah—well, I actually just wanted to talk to him about scheduling and what he wants me to do and stuff."

She smiles sweetly back at me. "Theo's upstairs. He wakes up late and doesn't like to be social."

That pretty much fits in perfectly with my image of Theo, but I didn't expect his mom to drag him like that, especially since she barely knows me.

"I'll get him," Mr. Mori says. "You stay here. Help yourself to some tea, yeah?"

I shake my head. "I'm not much of a tea drinker, but thank you."

Mr. Mori smiles at me before heading down a small hallway. I didn't even realize the Moris lived upstairs. It's a pretty small shop, extremely circular and built in an old brick building, but the building itself looks like three floors from the outside, so it makes sense that space would be used for something else.

Mrs. Mori pushes me into a seat before heading for the counter. "Do you like custard? Or red bean?"

I actually don't know what red bean is, but I just nod as she asks me all the foods I'll eat. She brings some buns over to me, and despite my complaints about not drinking tea, she brings a couple different pitchers over as well. "This is oolong, this is jasmine, and this is matcha."

"Um, thank you," I say.

She pushes the buns toward me and says, "Here. Eat. Take them home to your parents."

I nod because I don't know what else to say to that.

I hear footsteps coming down the long hallway and muffled chatter. Actually, it kind of sounds like muffled fighting. I hear Theo's voice drift in as he says, "I don't want to talk to him."

And then a hushed whisper as his dad says, "Theo, you have to be nice to people, especially people who want to help you. You embarrass us when you're mean to everyone."

And then they both come around the corner and all the animosity is gone, like they just stepped out onto live television.

"Ah, Gabi, Theo's happy you're here and ready to talk."

"You're overdoing it, Dad."

"Hush," Mr. Mori says, before half pushing Theo forward to talk to me. And honestly, I feel kind of bad taking advantage of the fact that Theo's parents are on my side, but I know there's no other way he'll talk to me, so I guess I'll take what I can get.

"I—Can we go outside?" I ask.

I wait for Theo to object—for his parents to hound him more until he finally agrees—but he just sighs deeply before nodding and leading the way out to the street.

It's still pretty early on a Sunday, so there aren't too many people out. Across town, there's a farmers' market, and a lot of people are heavy churchgoers, but in this pocket, people sleep in.

"What?" Theo says.

I turn to look at him to find his eyes narrowed at me. I wait for the door to fall shut behind us before I say, "About the other day—"

"Look, Gabi," he says, "I don't want to talk to you. I only agreed to this shit to shut my parents up, so please just pretend we're having a nice discussion, then go."

And maybe I should after everything, but I can't deal with the look he's giving me. Hell, I can't deal with the look he gave me the other day, the way it was clear my words were eating him up inside. I know he pretends he's impervious to everything, but all it took were those couple seconds the other day to make it undoubtedly clear that he isn't.

Which means I have to make it right.

"I'm sorry," I say.

"You really think there's something you can say that'll make up for that?"

And no, not really. Actually, I hadn't thought my apology through at all, just for the sake of not overthinking it, but now I'm just stuck. What can I say to make it clear that I don't actually hate Theo or gay people or gay Theo?

And then the words just tumble out of my mouth. "I'm gay."

And, wow, that's—well, that's the first time I've ever just said it out loud like that, but somehow, it doesn't feel nearly as dirty or terrifying as I thought it would. It actually feels kind of . . . liberating? Like it's pulled this massive weight off my chest.

Even when I first came out to Meli, I wasn't able to just say it. I bumbled around my words like always, and she put the pieces together, but something about Theo just coaxed the words right out of me, maybe because he was the first person I knew could actually understand.

"That's a pretty pathetic attempt to make me not mad."

"I—what? No! I'm serious. I'm gay. I—I only said what I said because I was worried you'd find out and I didn't want to get outed, but then I hurt you and—"

He doesn't say anything at first, but something in his eyes shifts, like he's actually hearing what I'm saying, like he actually, for the first time, gets me.

And there's something electric in it, like suddenly the Earth's poles have realigned to bring us closer together. Like suddenly there's complete clarity in the air, and for the first time in my life, someone is actually seeing me for who I am.

Then he says, "I didn't suspect you were gay, you know. This was completely unnecessary."

I nod, but I can't even deny the relief bubbling in my chest. "I've been so afraid of people finding out for so long that sometimes I just—panic, even if I shouldn't."

He shakes his head. "So if you don't want people to know, why tell me?"

Because I trust you. And I realize that it's true, even if I don't say it out loud. Theo's always been cold to me, but there's something in his eyes that tells me he wouldn't sell me out. He'll keep my secret.

I say, "I could tell what I said hurt you, and I—well, I didn't want to hurt you. And I didn't want you to think I was a homophobe."

He looks up at his parents' shop, his eyes catching on something, but when I turn to see it, he grabs my arm and pulls me back to him, saying, "You wanna go for a walk?"

And I nod, because I can't imagine a better way to spend my Sunday.

Theo walks like we're on a mission, but we aren't really going anywhere. He turns down the corner street the shop sits off, and within two blocks, the river's rising out in front of us, the riotous water colliding against the stones that emerge from the shore. The crashing sound washes out the silence between us, and I'm whisked back into Justin's kitchen, Theo drowning out my words with the blender.

He feels like a different person now, more withdrawn as he walks, none of that cocky humor written across his face.

When he finally turns to me, his eyes look heavy. "So your parents are homophobic, huh?"

It feels like a weird way to start the conversation, but I just nod.

"Sorry, that sucks."

"Your parents were supportive when you came out?" I ask, but it sounds more like an accusation than a question. Why can't my voice just fluctuate the right way for once instead of constantly painting me like an asshole?

But Theo doesn't seem put off by it. He just shrugs, kicking a stray rock out of his path. It skitters into a drain, the sound of its landing lost under the roar of the river.

"They're alright," he says, which almost sounds worse than if he'd said they told him to take a hike. "They try, you know? I give them credit for that."

I can't really argue with that, given my parents can't even hear the word "gay" without going into a fit. "I like your parents. They're nice."

He raises an eyebrow. "Is that your request to trade?"

I smile but shake my head. "No. I mean, I love my parents, even if—"

"Even if they can't love you," he says.

But it doesn't sound like an accusation or even a question. It sounds like resignation and familiarity, like somehow, despite being from totally different worlds, he understands exactly what I mean.

"My parents love me," I say, my voice finally agreeing with me.

And Theo nods, but his eyes look kind of far away. "Conditionally, though, right? Like as long as you keep doing what they ask, they love you."

And I don't know if that's true. I don't know what my parents will say when I eventually come out. *If* I eventually come out. I don't know if their love for me is predicated on my being straight, but sometimes I think it might be.

I can see the thoughts floating behind Theo's eyes. He's not really asking about my parents. He's talking about his own.

I say, "Do you feel that way sometimes?"

He shrugs, but it's less flippant than usual, more desperate, like he knows words won't do enough. He stares down at the ground and says, "My parents got over me being gay, but I think it's because I was already a pretty major disappointment."

And I laugh, but Theo's eyes still look serious. Popular, athletic, clever Theo?

"I think your parents are proud of you," I say. He turns to me with an incredulous brow. "I'm serious. I mean, my parents would kill to have a son who's good at soccer."

He rolls his eyes. "My parents couldn't care less about sports. They want a college-bound son riding a full scholarship and dating some brilliant science girl. Like my brother, Thomas, I guess."

"Well," I say, "if they already have Thomas, it doesn't sound like that's what they need at all. It sounds more like they need Theo."

Theo turns around and flashes me this dorky grin that I never thought I'd see on his face. Then he says, "You sound like a Disney movie. I should've known you were gay."

And I'm not sure if that's supposed to be a drag or something, but frankly it's one of the sweetest compliments I've ever received.

"We should head back," Theo says, but I don't want to leave yet. It feels like, for the first time in my life, I actually have someone I can talk to about . . . well, everything, and the thought of losing that hits me like a punch to the chest.

"I—is there something you have to do?"

"I'm grounded, so I probably shouldn't stay gone too long," Theo says through gritted teeth.

"Grounded? Really?"

"My family's complicated."

"And they still let you talk to me?"

"My parents would never make a big deal with someone else around," he says. "There's no bigger offense than making a scene."

His voice sounds kind of wistful, but I don't pry. It just seems too invasive at this point.

And Theo looks back at me like he's staring straight through sheer curtains. "It's okay, Gabi," he says. "We have all week to annoy each other."

I chuckle, but I guess a part of me worries that the second Theo's back in his element, I'll be completely inconsequential to him.

Then Theo says, "That reminds me. I'm gonna have to tell Justin you aren't actually a homophobic prick."

And a spark of fear flashes through me. "I—um—don't tell him I'm gay. Please. I don't want anyone else to know."

Theo stares back at me a second before nodding. "Yeah, don't worry. I won't out you."

Relief rushes out of me on a breath that's a little too warm against the chilly Vermont air. Summer really is fleeting, and that means Homecoming is almost here.

And I'm running out of time to save my parents' shop.

But Theo gives me this look that's equal parts reassuring and heart-stopping, and maybe that's just his way of saying that my secret is safe with him, but the voice in the back of my head is finally shutting up, and I feel like everything might just be okay.

THIRTEEN
THEO

When I get back from my walk with Gabi, my parents actually don't chew me out for disappearing, which is nice. Mom seems like she's in a pretty good mood as she stands behind the counter with her phone to her ear, and despite lecturing me earlier for constantly getting into fights and scaring everyone away, Dad smiles at me as I enter.

Considering I was literally grounded just yesterday for talking back to Uncle Greg, it all comes as a surprise, but I guess I can't really complain.

"What's going on?" I ask, though I'm not entirely sure I want to know.

"Thomas called," Dad says, placing a hand on my shoulder. "Your mom is talking to him right now."

And I can't quite explain it, but I feel bile rising in the back of my throat. *That's* why they're so upbeat? Because my brother who bailed on them and rarely ever calls is checking in?

Thomas hasn't been by in a month, since he's always so "busy" with "school" and his "internship," but I bet he's just out getting wasted and fucking white girls and doesn't want to get caught. That would better fit my idea of the college life.

And I can't believe they're really just sitting around waiting for him to call, like he's some celebrity we have to be grateful just to hear from. He's a shitty son, and a shitty brother, and I cannot even put into words how fed up I am with them treating him like some fucking savior. Just the fact that they have to be excited to get a phone call from him should say enough.

Mom turns to me and says, "Theo, come say hi to Thomas."

I just roll my eyes, turning on my heel. "I'm not feeling well. Just tell him I said hi."

And it's kind of weird, I guess, because a long time ago, I would never have needed to go through my parents to say hi to my own damn brother. Even though we weren't that close when he left, the level at which I've been ghosted is way worse than I expected, but whatever, I don't care.

And the last thing I'm gonna do is pretend I'm excited to hear from him. He doesn't give a shit about us, so I don't give a shit about him either.

I pause on my way to the hallway, waiting for one of my parents to call me back and lecture me about not wanting to talk to my brother. But they're both so engrossed in the call that I guess they didn't even notice what I said. Just one more reminder that no matter what I do, I'll always be the son nobody wanted or needed.

●●●

On Monday, I get to fourth period to find Justin angrily scribbling away at something in his notebook. Ordinarily, we'd hang out in the morning before homeroom, but I way overslept my alarm and got in maybe six seconds before the late bell.

He doesn't look up until I lean over his desk and slap my hands down against it, startling him back. "Busy, are you?" I say.

Justin groans. "I just have a shit ton of work to do." Then he looks at me like he just realized I'm me and says, "Oh, shit, man, I'm really sorry about Gabi. That shit was so messed up."

"It's fine," I say. "I mean, Gabi and I worked it out. We're good."

Justin's face does this weird scrunching motion, and I wonder if maybe I should've braced him for impact. "So you're friends with a homophobe now?"

"He's not a homophobe," I say. "It was just a big misunderstanding."

Justin rolls his eyes. "I mean, whatever, it's your life, but I never thought I'd hear *the* Theo Mori stand up for Gabriel Moreno."

And, actually, yeah, I can't argue with that. I never really thought I'd be standing on my own two feet defending Gabi either. And really, he's still annoying, whiny and pathetic, absolutely terrible at soccer, but something about him coming out to me makes him feel like—I don't know—a real person? Does that make me an asshole?

I guess something about hearing that he has actual problems and isn't just crying about dirt all the time makes me feel like

I could stand to be a little nicer to him. Like maybe I've been redirecting all my anger at other things to this kid who just kind of annoyed me, and who maybe doesn't even really annoy me all that much anymore. And then, maybe that's what Justin meant all along, and I really am Squidward in this situation.

God, Reddit would have a field day with me.

"Dude, you okay?" Justin asks, waving a hand in front of my face.

I just nod. I highly doubt being an asshole is actually terminal, so I guess I'll be fine.

"In that case, leave me alone. I have work to do," Justin says.

So I just roll my eyes before sliding into my desk.

Soccer practice used to be the best part of my school day. You know, as long as I could ignore Gabi and avoid any major injuries from his shitty game play. But as everyone heads out to the field, I get benched because I'm now a liability or something.

The worst part is I don't even have anywhere else to go. After practice, we're heading back to Justin's to prep our stock for tomorrow's "deliveries," so I'm just here, soaking up unwanted sunlight and revisiting all our menu plans that I've already visited like a hundred times over.

I look out at the field as the guys run some plays, and actually, it's more painful than I ever noticed from the thick of things. There's Gabi, speeding across the grass like a tractor with two wheels blown out, but despite being the messiest player, he's definitely not the only one with two left feet.

Actually, most of the team looks like a stampeding herd,

like they aren't actually sure where they're going, but everyone's moving so they gotta do it too. I feel kind of bad taking all my rage out on Gabi, when the only person on the field who can't be labeled a crime against humanity is Justin, who's actually just sitting in the goal on his phone, since he's not worried the ball will make it to his side of the field. He's probably right.

I guess this confirms that I really was directing all my hatred at Gabi just because of the shitty situation between our parents, and it sends a spike of pain through my chest that almost makes me topple over. It's guilt, but namely the "I've been called on my bullshit and can't deny it any longer" kind that feels vaguely like a sharp stab between the ribs. God, I hate how much these things affect me, but it takes everything I have to shift my focus away from the twisting feeling in my gut over to what's happening on the field.

Coach blows his whistle and calls everyone to attention. Looks like he wants them to run that last play again, but I'm starting to wonder what the point of it all is.

I guess everyone on the team has strengths. You know, somewhere. But we also have a policy of "no student left behind," so it's not like they were chosen because they're good. They're just—well, they just wanted to play.

And maybe some one-on-one sessions could help them get the basics down—how to kick a ball, how to run without tripping, how to find the big white globe in the middle of a sea of grass—but Coach doesn't have time for that, and I'm not sure anyone else really does either.

Homecoming's not even a month away, and there's no way

we'll win the game, even if we're up against the literal worst team in the league to boost our odds. And really, I shouldn't be disappointed given everything, but I guess a part of me was hoping we'd actually win a game this season. Like maybe my parents would see some value in sports if there was actual success behind it, not just me dodging my own teammates and bringing home urgent care bills.

But then, maybe this is all my fault since I'm too injured to practice, and even when I'm at my best, I'm still not enough to make us win.

The team comes into the bleachers for a water break, and Justin plops down next to me, but he doesn't even seem to be sweating. "You sure you can't play with a sprained wrist?" he asks.

I shrug because I would if Coach hadn't said there's no way in hell. As it stands, I should be good to go about a week before the game, which is probably what Coach is banking on, since I'm our only—however slim—hope at winning.

Gabi steps up toward us but stops a few feet away, like he's not sure what to say. He really is painfully awkward. I don't know if he's worried I'll flip out on him, or he's just not sure what he wants, but seeing him sends another spike of guilt through my chest as I remember how shitty I've been. I try to shove the pain down and roll my eyes, waving him over.

He smiles, stepping over and saying, "Sorry you can't be part of practice."

"I might actually be the lucky one," I say. "You guys suck."

Gabi laughs, but Justin just rolls his eyes.

Actually, Justin's whole body language has stiffened since Gabi showed up, like our chat earlier wasn't enough to wash the stain of Gabi's word vomit away.

"So," I say, hoping to cut into the tension, "I basically have our plans laid out for tomorrow. All that's left is making stuff."

Coach blows his whistle and throws in an, "Okay, break time's over. Get back to work!" for good measure.

Gabi winces, like he can't imagine anything worse than heading back out to that field, and really, it shouldn't surprise me. He definitely plays like he doesn't want to be there, but now I'm wondering if that really is why he plays so badly. Like soccer is his beard, and he forces himself to groom it every day even if he'd rather just shave it off and be free.

The pain in my chest starts to subside as the pieces come together and I realize that may actually be the case. As I watch the team return to the field, watch the way everyone goes floundering after the ball again, I have to wonder if maybe Gabi *could* be a decent player. Or at least, decent compared to the rest of the team, so still pretty bad, but better. If his weaknesses as a player really are more mental than physical, that means he's a work in progress that actually might not take that long to fix.

Maybe when it comes to playing soccer, it's just the same as when he tries to talk to people—he's so caught up in looking the part that he's missing all the steps that go into making it convincing.

We'll have to change that.

FOURTEEN
GABI

After practice, I gather my things and pick up my phone to find I've got a few missed messages: one from Meli asking if I can meet up to talk Homecoming and one from Vivi asking what I'm up to. I text Meli back with a, *Sorry, I have to work. Tomorrow, maybe?* and leave Vivi on read for now. It doesn't seem all that pressing.

We hit the showers, and then we head to the parking lot.

"Do you really drive to school every day?" Theo asks.

I nod. "Should I not?"

"The exercise might be good for you."

I probably should've expected the dig at my nonexistent soccer skills, but at least Theo still seems lighthearted and joking as opposed to actually calling me out.

I pop the trunk, and we all throw our stuff in before climbing into the car. Justin calls shotgun, which only disappoints me a little, and then we're off, driving the mile back to Justin's place.

We pull into his driveway, and Justin leaps out, swinging around to the rear of the car and knocking on the trunk until I pop it.

"Oh, Gabi," Theo says, and I freeze, my hand halfway to the door. I meet his eye in the rearview, and he flashes me a smile that stops me cold, my heart pounding in my chest. "Remind me to give you your cut later."

"My cut?" I repeat.

He rolls his eyes. "We already talked about this, didn't we?"

He throws open the car door and steps out, but I just sit there frozen because I'd kind of figured that deal was over after I royally insulted him like five seconds after he'd offered it.

I say, "I—I don't just want to mooch off you."

He turns back to look at me with an eyebrow raised but doesn't speak.

The truth is, I already felt kind of guilty agreeing to a share of the profits the other day in Justin's kitchen because this really is Theo's operation, and I don't want to sabotage his parents by cutting into their earnings. But I also can't pretend Homecoming isn't looming ever closer even as I still haven't quite found a solution.

Finally, I say, "I know you agreed to pay me because I'm helping you out, but I feel like I should contribute something more. Like maybe we could include some of my parents' stuff too? So I'm not just stealing from you?"

He pauses, leaning against the car door. "Like a joint venture?"

And I'm waiting for him to say that he can't stand the thought of having an official partnership with me, that just letting my family's food be on the same menu with his is against his religion, and I'm sure to fuck everything up. But finally, he just smiles and says, "If you're up for it."

He turns, slamming the door behind him and heading for the trunk.

But I'm still frozen, because my brain is struggling to process just how beautiful his smile was and figure out what it'll take to see it again.

Theo's the king of the kitchen, and it only takes about five minutes of Justin fooling around for him to act on it. He puts Justin on boba duty, which doesn't seem like a particularly arduous task until Justin spends the next couple hours huffing over a boiling pot, occasionally screaming, "They're too soft again!"

I was a little worried he wouldn't have anything valuable for me to do, but he takes up a director role, dictating what needs to happen next and letting me be his arms, since he only has one good one at the moment.

"When do we open our own shop?" Justin jokes before Theo sends him right back to overseeing the boba.

And then, before I know it, my mind is straying to a little bakery straight out of *Miraculous Ladybug*, the three of us dancing through the kitchen in French maid costumes. I leap gracefully from the counter, and Theo twirls me around before—

—uh, no, I'm definitely not daydreaming about musical numbers and kissing Theo, because that might be weird.

"Gabi!" Theo snaps, drawing me back into the room. "Hello?"

"Uh, sorry," I say. "What did you need?"

Theo rolls his eyes. "I said your phone's been buzzing non-stop."

"Oh," I say, plucking my phone off the counter. He's right, of course. I missed three messages from Vivi—all videos I don't have time to watch right now—and three texts from Meli:

> Seriously, you keep missing all the meetings. This is ridiculous. You better show up to the next one.
>
> You're good tomorrow, right? We can do tomorrow?
>
> Ugh, wait, you have soccer practice, right? So tomorrow at six?
>
> Answer me, bitch!!

I text her back, confirming I'll be present, before silencing my phone and setting it back on the counter.

"I wonder if you're right," Theo says, his voice low as he mixes some ingredients in a big bowl.

"Right about what?" I ask.

"The scale. Maybe we need to think bigger." He looks up, but his eyes look kind of far away as he stares past me. "I'm trying to work it out, but it's too hard to make it practical."

There's a sadness in his voice, and I hate that it's there. Okay, and more than that, I hate knowing that I put it there. That I had to go and crush his dreams by suggesting his idea wasn't good enough.

"Chill, man," Justin says, and I suddenly remember it's not

just Theo and me alone in Justin's kitchen. "It's a new idea, and we're just starting. It'll improve with time."

And Theo nods, but he doesn't look like he took it to heart. I'm slowly realizing there's a lot that goes on his head that I have no real access to, but God, I wish I could pry the door open even just an inch.

I consider telling them that I'm kind of working on a tight deadline, but I hate the thought of adding to Theo's distress. Well, I guess he might not care that much, since it's not like he has a stake in my parents' business, but knowing he's already got a lot going on, I'd rather just handle it myself.

Or at least work out a viable plan for how to improve our operation before I add it to his plate.

"Oh," I say, shifting the attention away from Theo's misery and onto me. "Um, my friend wants to work on some Homecoming stuff tomorrow, so I won't be able to help. I hope that's okay."

"Yeah, it doesn't matter," Theo says, which stings a lot. I can't say I expected him to cry about it, but I expected him to at least chastise me about bailing. I can't imagine what would hurt more than him just saying he doesn't actually need me at all.

I want to say something else, but I can't. I just quietly bring everything Theo asks for, while hoping that maybe my silence will make him feel like something's missing, at least a little bit.

Tuesday morning, Lady stops me on the way to homeroom.

"Don't be mad," she says.

"Mad?"

"I got the job."

"Oh."

Nobody's really paying any attention to us as they all rush to beat the bell, but it kind of feels like the world is zooming in just a little too close. Like everyone's waiting to see my reaction to this inevitable catastrophe I'd been naive enough to hope wouldn't occur.

"It'll only be part-time for a little while, so I'll still be here on occasion and someone else will handle the classes I can't make until they hire someone new—"

"But it's gonna be full-time later, right?" I say. "So we won't be practicing together anymore."

Lady looks back at me sadly for a moment before finally shaking her head. "I'm sorry, but this doesn't mean you have to give up dancing. You're great at it, and you'll keep getting better the more you practice."

I nod, but we both know it doesn't matter. We both know that without Lady, I don't have any way to keep going without my parents finding out, and that means there's no room for ballet in my future.

"You should get to class," she says, "but we'll still meet up on Friday, yeah? One last hoorah?"

I nod again, but my heart's not really in it.

The rest of the day pretty much blurs by in a stupor until I get out of soccer practice and head off to find Meli. Mrs. Berkley's AP Bio classroom also doubles as the Homecoming Committee's office. Sports aren't all that popular at our school, but the soccer season is pretty big news since administration has been working on improving the community's perception of our athletic department. As far as school spirit goes, people don't put a whole lot of energy into the games, considering we never win, but the parade and the dance and all the festivities are the biggest campus events we have. So, basically, Homecoming is God, which means for the next month, Mrs. Berkley will clear out of her classroom at the last bell so we can do what needs to be done.

Meli's got a whole mess of paper spread out over the desk and lab tables, and I cringe a little, thinking about how wasteful all that is.

"God, Gabi, what took you so long?" she asks.

She passes me an updated Homecoming prep schedule, but I just fold it up and slip it into one of my book-bag pockets. She'll have a new schedule in a few days and another one a few days after that. And while I kind of want to talk to her about Lady and dance and the hollow feeling in my chest, she's on a mission, which means she doesn't have time to be my friend right now.

"Only two people have turned in their ideas for the float," she says.

"I thought you were designing the junior float."

"I was, but Mr. Finnigan said I was taking too much control and needed to leave space for the rest of the class to contribute. But guess what? They're already fucking me over."

I don't bother responding, because I know she's not really

looking for an answer. It's always been weird to me how Meli can be so passionate about things she doesn't even really care about. Once Homecoming's over, she'll act like the whole thing was a waste of time she didn't even want to work on, but right now? It's everything.

And then I think of Theo but try to shake the thought out of my head. I shouldn't be so caught up in him, but I kind of am. I know there's not really any value in it. I'm probably just fixated on him because he's gay, and now he knows I'm gay and without ballet and Meli, he's basically the only thing in my life that doesn't feel miserable and hopeless. It has nothing to do with his voice or that smile or how cute he looks when he's determined.

I don't have a crush on Theo Mori.

Because that would be the world's biggest mistake, because I already know he'll never see me that way, if he even tolerates me.

"Gabi!" Meli snaps, and I jump to attention. "Fuck! This is serious! Can you pay attention for a second?"

"Sorry," I mumble, though I should probably defend myself, considering I didn't even want to be part of the Homecoming Committee and I'm literally only here to not be a monumentally terrible friend.

"I'm gonna get us badges to get out of class. The whole committee. I'll warn the teachers that I may have to pull some people, depending on what's going on and have Jeff collect everyone's schedules so I don't have to hunt you all down."

I raise an eyebrow. "That seems a bit excessive, don't you think?"

"No! We have less than three weeks left to perfect everything and we've barely even started on the Queen of Hearts decorations for the dance. We can't keep squeezing in work between everyone's hobbies."

I roll my eyes. Of course she'd call soccer and literal work "hobbies" while acting like Homecoming is the end of the world. I really hate Meli when she's like this, and I really hate getting strung along for pointless stuff. I mean, it's junior year—the year our grades are most important and when we have to be stressing about SATs and everything—and all Meli cares about is Homecoming.

But I guess there's a pro to being able to get out of class whenever I want to, right? I mean, that was one of Theo's biggest issues when I first mentioned an in-school delivery service. Well, besides the whole "it completely violates school policy" thing, but as long as we don't get caught, we'll be fine.

And really, who's going to report Theo Mori when he's our only chance of winning the Homecoming game?

Meli's already rattling off something else, so I just kind of push the thought aside for now. I just have to work out the logistics to make sure everything can really flow.

Well, and get Theo on my side, which I suppose is the real challenge.

When Friday rolls around, I'm antsy to get my brewing business plans together, but I still have one major flaw I need to rectify: our base of operations.

I report to my final dance practice with Lady, hoping that

going through the motions with her one last time will help bring me the clarity I need. We still haven't finished the dance we were choreographing, and I guess now we never will. Or I guess she'll just finish it without me. Either way, it feels too bittersweet, like I'll be leaving a part of myself behind when I exit the dance room for the last time.

So when Lady says our time is up, I ask her if we can keep going just for another ten minutes. Then I stretch it to twenty, and finally, I'm so exhausted I could practically pass out, but she just shakes her head at me and says, "We have to clean up."

So we do, even though every muscle in my body protests as we move the barres away and wipe them all down.

It makes me sad to think I'll never really be back in this room. The barres will sit idle, collecting dust until a new teacher decides to pull them out again. And even then, who will make use of this space like Lady? Who will instill a love of dance in the next round of students who pick up this elective just to kill time and grab an easy A?

And then a thought races into my head so fast, I barely have time to grasp it.

"Lady?" I say.

She looks up, a water bottle in hand and eyebrow raised. "What?"

"Is anyone going to be using this room while you're gone?" I ask. "I mean, I know you said someone is picking up your classes, but you're typically the only one who uses this room, right?"

She shrugs. "Yeah, I think they said they'll be holding the classes in the gym until they get a new dance teacher. Why?"

"I—I guess I was just wondering if maybe I could borrow it? For a project?" I say.

"A project?"

I know I've earned the incredulous look on her face, but I just say, "Um, Homecoming stuff."

She looks at me again like she's trying to figure me out before sighing. And I don't know what conclusion she's drawn, but finally, she says, "As long as you can work around my schedule, I don't mind. I'll need the room for last period, and Tuesday and Thursday after school, so just make sure you clear out by then, and it's fine."

"Thank you!"

She smiles sadly at me, and I feel kind of bad. She's probably only agreeing to it because she feels guilty for leaving me high and dry, but if this is the thing that makes all the difference in saving my family's shop, I'll take it.

I know I can't fix everything, but if it takes losing one dream to save another, I guess that's a trade I'm willing to make.

FIFTEEN
THEO

The week blows by in a mess of sleepless nights and overeager customers. Everyone seems to be really loving the new additions to our menu, but I have to admit that I'm beyond exhausted just trying to keep up. All I can do is hope that it's enough to keep the store going, and that we somehow magically stumble onto a less draining process, because I'm one milk tea away from throwing myself into Lake Champlain.

Anyway, Saturday morning, I'm just about to head out when Uncle Greg shows up to lecture my parents again. We're not exactly on speaking terms given what happened last time, but just the sight of his face sends me into a rage, and I know I need to get out of the shop before I do something I'll regret.

I text Justin, but he just responds with: Sorry, busy. Text you later!

So I end up texting Gabi instead. You busy?

He responds almost immediately. **Nothing I can't get out of. What's up?**

I stand out on the sidewalk, people flying by in cars or on bikes, and I can't even find the words to make my thoughts make sense.

I sigh, shoving my phone into my pocket. What am I doing? Gabi and I aren't friends. We don't even really like each other. We're just two game pieces that got pushed closer and closer together until we forgot how to move on our own.

So how pathetic does it make me that I kind of wish he were here right now? That I feel like his goofiness might actually be enough to drain away some of my sadness?

I slip my phone out again and type: **Are you at home?**

It takes a minute of staring and a deep breath for me to actually press send.

Then a second later, the response comes back. **At the shop, why?**

Do you want to take a walk with me?

Just a sec!

I sit down on the curb, and sure enough, a few minutes later, Gabi turns the corner, a dorky smile on his face as he jogs up to me, waving an arm in the air. "Theo!"

I roll my eyes. "I can see you, asshole. You don't have to wave."

He pauses, mouth gaping, and says, "Uh, sorry."

I get to my feet and dust myself off. Something in my chest feels a little lighter upon seeing him, but I would never tell him that.

"Everything okay?" he says.

I shrug. "I just wanted to get away for a bit. Walk with me?"

He nods, but he doesn't move until I start walking. He falls into step beside me, but he doesn't break the silence, like he's afraid anything he says will shatter the truce wall between us.

And honestly, I don't really have anything to say. I could vent about my uncle, but now that Gabi's here, I don't even want to think about it. I want to carve out this imaginary space where the real world can't reach me. At least for a little while.

"It's a nice day out," Gabi says finally.

"You're making small talk about the weather?"

"I—well, to be honest, I don't really know what you like to talk about, since you're usually just yelling at me."

I laugh, but his face still looks dead serious. It's not like he's wrong, obviously, because a few weeks ago, I would've offered to scrub the locker room toilets down if it meant not spending an hour with Gabriel Moreno, but I don't know. I guess I felt like we were past that. I mean, at least somewhat. He came out to me. He must not think I'm a total asshole, right?

But I guess I can't blame him if he does.

"We can talk about anything," I say. "I kind of just want a distraction."

He stares back at me kind of blankly for a moment before saying, "Did you know axolotls can regrow limbs?"

I blink once. "Ax-of-what-nows?"

"Axolotls? They're amphibians."

Bold of him to assume I know what amphibians are. He

136

laughs, sliding his phone out of his pocket and pulling up Google images.

Huh. So I guess axolitters are these little pink things with billowy gills and constant smiles? Kinda creepy, but in an endearing way, I guess?

"Anyway, they can regrow limbs. Like how lizards can regrow tails, but like . . . much cooler."

"Why are you telling me this?" I ask.

He shrugs. "You said you wanted a distraction."

"I did say that, but I didn't think you'd dive into the weirdest fact you know."

He sighs. "That's not the weirdest fact I know, but I digress."

I laugh, and he looks me like I just grew a new limb, but come on! What a loser! I told him I wanted a distraction from my life problems, so he went into random facts about axamanders like that's what I meant.

And he said it all with that Gabi puppy-dog look, with that ridiculous pouty lip and those big brown eyes.

And I guess it was a pretty decent distraction, since it completely derailed my train of thought, but I can't believe this is how his mind works. Like what's going on in there, pushing all the cogs around to make him say these random things? I feel like I need to invest in a logbook for Random Gabi Thoughts or something.

"Anyway," he says, dropping his voice low, "I don't know what's going on in your life, but if you want to talk, I'm open to listening."

My first instinct is to snap that if I wanted to talk, I'd talk to Justin, but then, he was too busy to respond, and it's kind of weird to feel like I can only talk to one person, right? It's not like I don't have other friends—they're just all the casual type of friends you chat with about homework or practice, but never anything important.

And it's weird because I'm not even sure Gabi is a friend, but I feel more like I can talk to him than any of the other guys on the team.

So maybe we are friends? Or maybe we're something else? And what does it say about me that I can't figure out the difference?

I groan, dragging a hand across my face. "Do you ever actually feel better after ranting?"

He pauses, his eyes darting to the ground. "Don't you?"

I shake my head. "Nah. I just feel angrier."

"Maybe you're stoking the flames instead of putting them out."

I laugh, my voice whistling through my lungs on weak breaths. "God, what the fuck does that even mean?"

He shrugs. "Well, sometimes when you vent, people egg you on, you know? Tell you how shitty the other person is, and then before you know it, everyone's dragging someone and being furious. But sometimes you vent, and the other person just tells you that your feelings are valid, and then you start processing how to move on."

And, I don't know, maybe what he's saying makes some kind

of sense, but it also sounds kind of empty to me. Isn't that what friends are supposed to do? Tell you that you're right while you tear apart the person who wronged you? Isn't that supposed to make you feel better?

"Let's try it," he says.

"I—okay, fine. So what do I do?"

He smiles. "Tell me what's bothering you."

I look out at all the people rushing by around us, and it feels pointless. Not even hopeless, really, but inconsequential, like I'm some kid crying 'cause I scraped my knee while a tsunami rains down on the world. Everyone's got problems. Only I'd sit here and act like the world is ending because my uncle's an asshole.

Then I look back at Gabi, where he's smiling at me like he has all the time in the world to just sit and listen to what I have to say.

And that opens up something in me.

"My uncle treats my parents like shit. He hates that my dad's Japanese, and that my mom had the nerve to marry him, and that my brother and I exist. He owns the café, and he's using his power over them to torture them, and I just can't take it anymore. That's why I was trying to save the shop—to earn enough money to get him off their backs. And I don't know, I guess I don't want to stay in Vermont forever, you know? I want to go away for school and branch out, but I can't do that because I'm stuck taking care of my parents."

"Will it make a difference?" Gabi asks.

139

"Will what?"

"Earning more money? Will your parents be free of your uncle if they earn more money?"

And it's such a ridiculous question, because that's literally what he's been hurling at them every month, but something on Gabi's face feels like he's got some info that I don't. "What do you mean?"

"I mean, it sounds like your uncle'll screw with your parents whether he feels they're doing well or not, right?"

"Maybe," I say. "I mean, yeah, I guess, but what else can I do?"

"Maybe nothing?" he says, and I just stare blankly back at him. He laughs, looking down at his feet. "I mean, maybe it's not your job to fix your parents or your uncle. Maybe you're putting all that weight on yourself 'cause you're scared of leaving, and you're punishing yourself for wanting to."

"What are you, my shrink?"

Gabi laughs, but a blush rises in his cheeks. "I'm not judging you."

"I know," I say, and he looks up, eyes wide. "Keep going, I guess."

He smiles. "I understand why you feel the way you do, and I think it's a perfectly reasonable way to feel, and what you're doing is admirable. I just—I see the way it's taking its toll on you, Theo, and I think you deserve a break. You can't be solely responsible for your parents."

"Maybe not, but I still have to try."

He nods, crossing his arms. "My parents' shop isn't doing

great either. With another offer on the table, they don't think it's worth putting in the time anymore. And I get it, financially speaking, but the shop means a lot to me and—well, I don't want to lose it, so I understand. It feels like you're being crushed, right? But also pulled in two."

I nod, though I probably wouldn't have worded it that way. Gabi's tone kind of says it all, low and just a little wobbly, like he's having trouble keeping himself steady. I know what that feels like.

"I—I don't know how to fix it all," Gabi says, "but I think I might have an idea to earn a little more money. If you trust me?"

I nod again. I mean, what else can I do? I wouldn't have called him if I felt like I had another option.

But I have to admit, he was right about one thing for sure—I don't feel angry. At least, not like I normally would after laying all my problems out. I feel seen, like I've finally been granted the understanding of another person.

"Gabi," I say.

He flashes me a smile. "Yeah?"

"Thank you for listening. And—I guess, if there's something I can do to help you with your parents' shop, let me know?"

I force a smile onto my face, but I'm sure it's jagged and awkward and potentially a little painful to look at.

And Gabi goes stiff like the hideousness of my forced smile just shook him to his core.

But after a moment, he blinks, and smiles back, and there's

something open and sincere in the curve of his lips. Like a promise, that whatever comes next—no matter how messy or unpredictable or potentially painful—we're in this together. And I can't say that's what I came looking for when I left the café this morning, but somehow, it feels like Gabriel Moreno found a way to give me exactly what I needed.

Monday morning, I wake up to a text from Justin telling me to pack light for the day. I stop by his place on the way to school to grab stock, and he gives me the rundown about how he and Clara "didn't break up" because they "weren't dating," but basically they're at that point where they stop talking to each other for a week. Normally, I wouldn't bat an eye, but this means we have to limit our stock to what can fit in a mini fridge that Justin drags behind him, with plans to store it in the locker room until the end of the day.

We don't have a lot of time to grab stuff, and I'm a little annoyed we put so much time into making stock we won't even be able to bring, but I make sure to focus on the mixed-milk teas and bright-colored cakes, since that stuff sells better anyway.

The irony of the situation hits me when Justin and I meet up again outside the cafeteria to hand out everyone's orders. The fact that Gabi and I had that conversation about bigger plans on Saturday just to turn around on Monday and find we're basically downsizing the business. And people are still ordering, but I think the sparkle is starting to wear off, because we actually end up with leftovers, which is just another strike against Gabi's reassurances.

Speaking of which, Gabi's not here, which is extra weird. Like even if he decided to bail on us, which he never does, he should at least be hanging out long enough for soccer practice.

"Maybe he found something better to do with his time," Justin says.

Justin still hasn't gotten over the homophobic comment, which is actually kind of flattering, since he's taking up arms over me, but really fucking annoying in this case because Gabi's not homophobic, and I'm stuck in the middle of them. And, of course, Justin's extra sulky now that Clara's out of the picture for a few days. He always gets salty when he hasn't had sex in a while.

Justin drags the mini fridge back toward the locker room, since I can't do a whole lot to support its weight.

"Fucking Gabriel Moreno couldn't even help carry the damn thing," he grumbles, and I have to admit I agree. Where the hell is he?

"Hey, guys!"

I look up to see Gabi running toward us, but not from the direction of the gym. Actually, he's not even dressed for practice yet, so what happened?

Justin just rolls his eyes and keeps dragging the fridge as Gabi finally catches up to us and tries to catch his breath.

"Where have you been?" I ask.

Gabi smiles, throwing an arm around my shoulders. I'm

not sure where he got the confidence, but it's not nearly as uncomfortable as I thought it'd be. "I found a solution to our problems."

I raise an eyebrow.

Then he digs into his back pocket and pulls out a whole wad of cash. I mean bills, stacked, all wrapped up with a hair band.

"What the fuck?" I say.

Gabi smiles, pressing it into my hand. "I did a test run for in-class deliveries and it went great!"

Justin's stopped hauling the fridge, his eyes wide and his mouth gaping. I think I look a little more composed, but I feel three times as shocked.

"How?" is all I manage.

"I got a special hookup. It's a whole thing, but I'll explain tomorrow. I've got to go. I've got Homecoming stuff to do!"

"But what about practice?" I ask.

"Tomorrow!" he shouts, but he's already doing a quick backward jog back toward the classroom buildings.

"Aren't you at least going to help me carry this thing?" Justin calls out.

But Gabi's out of earshot, his retreating back disappearing into the crowd of dispersing students. "Guess not," I say.

Justin just lets out a huff and a series of low grumbles as he grabs the fridge again and starts walking.

SIXTEEN
GABI

I spend Monday night getting everything together.

The badges Meli finally gave the Homecoming Committee on Friday basically work as the ultimate get-out-of-class-free cards. So after taking the weekend to set up our online shop, I used Monday to test-run our new delivery system, opening up only for limited orders so I can manage it all myself. And with Lady granting me use of the dance room, we now have a base of operations to get everything stored and packaged until the orders come in, and we can pull people out of class to deliver their orders.

Voilà! We're in business.

Tuesday morning, I ask Theo and Justin to meet me on campus a little early so we have time to run over our game plan. By the time I find them standing outside the main school building, Justin already looks run-down, and Theo's idly scrolling through his phone.

"Morning!" I say.

Theo looks up at me and smiles, but Justin just narrows his eyes. "You better have a good reason for dragging us here."

I smile, reaching into my bag to pull out the newly minted badges. I was careful to leave them on the top of the biggest pocket so they'd be in easy reach.

One balanced on each palm, I hold them out to the guys, who just stare back at me blankly.

Finally, Theo says, "You're not forcing us to join the Homecoming Committee, are you?"

I shake my head. "No, not at all. These badges are our key to getting out of class so we can run deliveries."

Theo raises an eyebrow. "Like *during* class?"

I nod. "That's what I did yesterday, and we got a ton of interest. It's great, because it lets people order when they're the hungriest and have the least impulse control. I even set up a website so they can order out of what we have in stock, and then we'll get a notification and can deliver it to their class, just tell the teacher we need to speak to them real quick for Homecoming business. I also set up a chat, so we can discuss who will accept which orders and—"

"Okay, wait, slow down," Justin says, arms crossed. "When did we decide we were running deliveries during class? I thought Theo said that was too messy. Not to mention entirely against school rules."

"Well, yeah," I say, my voice low, "but Theo and I were talking this weekend and—"

"Oh, so now you guys are just making plans without me?"

Theo rolls his eyes. "No, we're not making plans without you, because we didn't agree on anything. Gabi just said he had an idea."

"And I did, and it worked," I say. "You wanted to expand our reach, and I did."

"Our?" Justin says.

"Theo and I agreed to make this a joint venture."

Justin looks at Theo with narrowed eyes, like he's just now being clued in, but he doesn't say anything about it, instead turning back to me and saying, "You can't be serious. We could get expelled if we get caught."

And I know Justin's never going to have my back, since he's basically hated me since that day back in his kitchen, but I turn to Theo, hoping maybe he'll be just as excited about this as I am. "You seem like the type of person who's down to take risks."

Theo stares back at me for a moment, then shrugs. "Maybe, but you certainly don't."

And a few weeks ago, he would've been right about that, but somewhere between befriending Theo and losing my dream of dancing, I realized I couldn't afford to be scared all the time. "Look, if you guys don't want to do the deliveries, I'll let it drop, but people are really hype about this, and I think it'll be even more sustainable than before. It's not like they'll have alternatives to our stuff."

Theo looks a little hesitant, but there's also a sort of

determination in his eyes, like my words are really getting to him. Justin's another story. He looks more like he wants to punch me in the face than consider what I'm saying.

But it doesn't matter. Justin can hate me all he wants. I just need Theo on my side.

Finally, Theo nods and says, "Okay, we'll give it a shot. I don't want to pass up the opportunity, especially not after you worked so hard."

I smile as Theo takes his badge before Justin groans and takes his.

"So," Theo says, "how does this work?"

I pull up the website on my phone. "People place orders here. I'll add your phone numbers so you'll get text alerts when an order's placed. Then you just message the group to say you want to take the order, and then use the pass to leave class. Most of the teachers will approve you. Then grab the delivery item from the dance room, head to the appropriate classroom, and ask to speak to whoever placed the order. Just say it's Homecoming stuff. Then take them out to the hall and hand them their delivery."

Theo nods along, but Justin looks like he'd rather be anywhere else. Whatever. I won't let him get in the way of my high.

The first bell rings as I slip my phone back into my pocket. "I already loaded stock onto the website, so it'll stop accepting orders when we run out."

"Sounds good," Theo says. Just before I can head to class, he grabs my wrist and says, "And Gabi? Thank you. For all of this. I—I appreciate it."

I can't remember the last time I smiled as wide as I'm smiling right now, but even as I get to first period, my cheeks still burn from the stretched muscles. But I'm not worried about that. It's the good kind of pain.

By the time lunch rolls around, we've already gotten fifteen delivery requests. Justin seemed pretty eager to run them, so I guess he doesn't hate the plan as much as he pretended to. Either way, I grab my lunch and beeline for the dance room. I've got a freezer from my parents plugged into an outlet in the corner and a couple desks lined against the wall for prepping orders.

Theo shows up a few minutes after me, his eyes widening as he takes note of the setup. "Wow, you did all this?"

I shrug, trying to keep it nonchalant, but I can already feel the heat rising in my cheeks. "I want us to be successful, you know? We just have to make sure to hide everything before last period."

Theo nods. "It's kind of funny how much all this is helping my parents' shop, yet they'd probably die if they found out we were selling our stuff together."

"Because our families are rivals?"

"More that they don't like change."

"Is that why you're so desperate to leave?"

And a few different emotions race across Theo's face—shock, disgust, a resigned sort of acceptance. "I don't know," he says. "I just know that if I stick around, my life is always going to be about being what they want me to be. I just want to know who I am, without all their meddling."

"I think I have a pretty good idea of who you are," I say.

He raises an eyebrow. "Right. Theo the asshole. Theo the C student—"

I shake my head, my voice coming out as a rush. "No! Nothing like that."

He just stares back at me, and I turn around so I can stare at the barre against the far wall. It's easier to lock eyes with the metal beam where all my dreams failed to bloom than it is to look at Theo, because Theo's real, present, current.

And in a way, he's just as much of a pipe dream as ballet—I know it'll never happen, yet I keep dancing with these ideas in my head, letting my heart get lost in potential that barely exists.

"You're smart, Theo. Like, really, really smart. Clever." God, I sound like a children's special. I close my eyes, pushing the image of his face out of my head, trying to pretend I'm somewhere else, and I'm standing over some wishing well, confessing my inner thoughts where he'll never have to hear them. "You're brilliant, and not in the getting-through-high-school way. In the real way, like you could take over the world someday if you wanted to. And you're athletic and passionate, but more important, you're a leader. People don't follow you because they're scared of you. They do it because you have this fire that's impossible to resist, and all it takes is one glimpse of it to know just how powerful it really is."

I freeze as warmth circles my wrist. I turn to find Theo's

fingers wrapped around my skin, his eyes meeting mine, but they're different. Soft. Vulnerable.

Then he smiles and says, "That's a nice observation. Too bad it's all bullshit."

"It's not—"

But he cuts me off, bringing a finger up to my lips. And now we're standing inches apart, our faces close, like at any second, either one of us could close the space separating us, separating our lips, and turn the whole world upside down.

Then the door to the dance room flies open, and we jerk apart like some hurricane winds have gusted between us. Justin walks in, a scowl on his face as he says, "Fuck precal. Fuck it to hell."

"Take it you got your grade back," Theo says, recovering almost instantly.

And just like that, the bubble we were in pops, and the space becomes flooded with noise and stress and reality. But this wasn't just a daydream. I really did almost kiss Theo Mori, and even as the world rushes in, and we get back to work, my mind keeps fluttering around that instant, wondering what would've happened if I'd just taken one more step and leapt.

SEVENTEEN
THEO

By the time soccer practice comes around, my legs are already tired from running deliveries. We got a whole bunch of orders just before last period, so many that I basically only got back into the classroom a few minutes before the final bell rang and had to leave Justin to clean everything up for the day. It's kind of wild how easily every teacher lets us blow class now that we have the Homecoming badges. It feels like we're royalty, completely untouchable and unstoppable.

And something about that has me thinking about what Gabi said back in the dance room. I don't know if I was caught in the high of our success or the fact that he was the first person to ever lay such high praise on me, but I can't stop thinking about it.

Then there's whatever didn't happen while we were in there. Or am I just making the whole thing up? Because for a moment there, it felt like maybe he was going to—no, I'm probably making it up.

I don't even know how I would feel about it if I wasn't making it up.

I hit the gym and get changed into my soccer uniform. We're getting pretty close to the Homecoming game, and I'm still annoyed that I can't practice with the rest of the guys, but I think the blame has shifted in my head. I'm not annoyed at Gabi, not really. I'm annoyed at myself—at my fucking wrist for taking weeks instead of days to heal, at my own uselessness, and the fact that I'm not good enough to carry the team.

"Hey," Gabi says, stepping out of a stall behind me. He always changes in the stalls, which I never really paid attention to before. I wonder if that's part of his gotta-stay-in-the-closet mentality.

"I didn't realize you'd actually be around today. No Homecoming stuff?" I ask.

Gabi winces. "Truth be told, I'd rather be here than dealing with Homecoming, but I promised a friend I'd help."

My ego gets a bit of a kick out of that. I know how much Gabi hates soccer, so if he actually enjoys practice now, it must be because of me.

Or maybe he's just saying that he hates Homecoming that much. I may have jumped to conclusions on that one.

"Anyway," he says, "I think I'm getting better at this balancing thing, which is good, since we have to worry about our sales too."

"And better at the talking thing," I say.

He tilts his head like a confused puppy.

153

"You know, because you can actually form a sentence now."

He blushes. "Oh, right, yeah. I guess you're a bit less intimidating now that I know you."

Wait, what does that mean?

"Time for another miserable practice," he says with a smile. "I'll give you the log-in for the site dashboard if you wanna look at the numbers?"

My brain isn't even following what he's talking about, but I just nod as I hold open the door and we head out to the field. "You're getting better, you know. At playing."

Gabi rolls his eyes. "You don't have to try to make me feel better."

But I actually mean it. It's like my not being on the field means he no longer has a target to run into, so he can actually focus on keeping his feet on the ground. Definitely an improvement.

"If you want more help leading up to the big game, I can coach you," I say. I played around with the idea a bit before feeling comfortable saying it. It'll be a hell of a commitment to try to save Gabi's soccer skills, but I feel a huge spike of guilt about not doing anything to help if I can.

He turns to me, an eyebrow raised. "You really want to spend more time with me?"

I shrug. "We spend most of our time together anyway. Besides, I miss being involved."

He smiles, and it's kind of cute, which has me turning my attention to where the team is starting to gather on the field.

Their uniforms are all grass-stained, so it's a good thing we've got new ones coming in next week.

"I'd love that," Gabi says, and I turn my face back to his, a smile tugging at my lips.

"Good." I reach into my bag and pull out a quick training schedule I wrote up for him in my free time. It's not too hardcore, since we barely have the time as it is, but I think it'll help him get at least a little bit better.

I pass it to him and he takes it slowly, his eyes going wide as he looks it over.

"I—you already planned it all out?" he says.

"I ended up getting super into it as I thought it over last night. It's not a big deal, but I just figured if we work on a few weak points, we can hopefully get you ready in time."

He nods enthusiastically. "Thanks, Theo!"

I just shrug again.

"Oh, let me show you the log-in."

He grabs his phone out of his bag, navigating the webpage that I guess connects to our online store. I struggle to pay attention as he lays everything out for me.

Finally, Gabi sends me off on my own so he can join the team and I head to the bleachers. Everyone lines up to run their drills, and I just kind of sit on the cold metal, staring down at my phone like I actually care what's on the screen.

I tell myself the distraction is the big game—I'm so worked up over not being able to practice and not being ready when I finally get on the field. It's a whole mess.

But I know the game isn't the thing that's got my heartbeat speeding up, and I'm not entirely sure what to make of that.

After practice, Gabi gets called away to a last-minute Homecoming meeting and while I go to Justin's to work on shop stuff, Justin's too busy studying for a test for us to really get anything done. I get home just after eight, and I hit the shop expecting it to be entirely deserted, since our post–seven o'clock traffic has all but completely dried up. Instead, I find my mom standing behind the counter as she wipes it down and Thomas sitting at the table under the window. He waves at me as I walk in, but I just roll my eyes.

My mom starts detailing something, but I can't follow along very well since she's speaking Mandarin. But of course, golden boy Thomas follows perfectly, even throwing in the perfect response before they both start laughing.

"How was school, Theo?" my mom asks, which is weird, because she hardly ever asks.

I shrug. "Fine."

"Mom told me you're doing deliveries for the shop now, huh?" Thomas says. "That's pretty cool."

I shrug again. "It's fine."

"It was all Theo's idea," my mom says. "He came home one day and said he knew how to make the shop more money, and just like that, he did it! And the best part is, we can close early because no one comes in after five, so we save money that way too."

I . . . wait. Is she praising me? I don't think she's ever done that before.

"Sweet!" Thomas says. "I knew you'd eventually put that big brain of yours to work."

Ah, there it is. The backhanded compliment. Those are usually my mom's specialty, but I guess Thomas inherited those jeans, although I'm surprised they fit him since my mom's barely five feet tall.

It's kind of awkward standing there in the shop, the tension filling the room. Well, for *me* anyway. I imagine golden boy Thomas is blissfully unaware that anyone could ever actually hate him.

"I, um, I'm gonna go do some homework and then go to bed," I say.

"You don't want dinner?" my mom says.

"I'll find something in the kitchen."

My mom and Thomas go back to whatever they were talking about, neither of them even seeming to notice as I head upstairs, but I guess that's kind of always been my role in the family. They'll notice me when I'm needed, maybe send a few words my way, but at the end of the day, I'll never be a major player. I'm just a sub-in when there's no one else to fill the part.

"I think we can add boba now," Gabi says. "I mean, if you think that'll help boost sales."

It's Wednesday afternoon in Justin's kitchen, and it's the first chance we've had to really regroup and go through our menu since we were all too busy Tuesday after practice.

And wow, people were pissed. So many people stopped me during homeroom to ask what period the site would be up by that it was starting to draw teacher attention, and I had to promise new stuff on Thursday to get people to back down.

I guess it's kind of cool that we're this popular, and we're definitely starting to bring in more money, which is good for my parents, but wow. The pressure is on, and now it feels like there's even more people in my life for me to disappoint.

So now we're racing to figure out how to please the student body and make good on the promise I gave everyone in my morning rush. Justin's got his face half-glued to his phone, but Gabi's looking at me readily as he takes note of what we should work on next.

"We can make it, but it needs to be kept separate," I say.

He nods. "Yeah, I think that'll be fine, since we have a base of operations now. Actually, my parents have a portable burner they basically never use. I'll snatch that and then we can just make the boba at school."

That thought had never even occurred to me, but once again, here's Gabi with the cool ideas and smarts to make them happen. As proud as I was about the ideas I'd come up with, I have to admit we never would've gotten anywhere legit without Gabi. It hurts my ego a little, but it's worth the extra cash.

"I was also thinking about adding café con leche to the menu," Gabi says. "It's one of the top sellers at my parents' café, and I think it'll be a great morning incentive, especially if we take it off the menu by noon."

"Smart," I say. "Can the website handle that?"

He shrugs. "I'll just mark it as out of stock at lunchtime."

I nod. "Okay, cool. Just make sure you separate that from the teas, so people don't try to add toppings."

"Could they?"

"Could they what?"

"Add toppings?"

"I guess if it's iced coffee, but it'd still be pretty fucking weird."

"But that's the goal, isn't it?" Gabi says. "Make something so innovative they can't get it anywhere else? Like my drinks and your . . . toppings."

Justin looks up from his phone then, just in time to see me awkwardly staring at the floor while Gabi blushes furiously. "What's going on?"

"Uh, nothing, we're just talking about fusing drinks," I say to save Gabi the awkward confrontation. Well, and the mess of trying to avoid outing himself, since he's already proved he's not great at that.

Gabi nods, eyes wide. "Right, right, I just thought it'd be something they can't do anywhere else . . . you know, café con leche but with boba or lychee jelly or—"

"Café con lychee?" I say with a laugh, and then both our eyes shoot wide at the same time.

It's like our brains have somehow synced over the Wi-Fi as we both say, "That's brilliant!"

And for a moment, it's like time stops as we stare at each other, both of us caught up in this little pocket of humor and knowing it's corny and shitty and we should break out of it, but neither of us really wanting to. It's like the moment everything slams into me, and I realize how much things have changed between us in such a short time, how much lighter I feel standing in this kitchen with him than I ever have with anyone else.

It's this perfect little inside joke between me and the last person I ever thought I'd want to share an inside joke with.

Well, and Justin, who just rolls his eyes and says, "Okay, well, you don't really need me here then, right?"

I raise an eyebrow. "Somewhere to be?"

"Yeah, I have some stuff I really should be taking care of. You guys can stay, though, if you want."

"No, it's fine," Gabi says. "We can go back to my place. My parents won't mind."

I expect Justin to say we're better off here with a big open kitchen to ourselves, but he just shrugs and heads out of the kitchen with his face glued to his phone again, which feels a little cold, all things considered. Gabi and I quickly grab our things and any ingredients we'll need before seeing ourselves out.

We load our stuff into Gabi's car in silence. I feel kind of bad that Justin kicked us out and now we have to lug everything over to Gabi's place. I mean, I know it's not my fault, since I don't control Justin, but I still feel bad, like I set us up to fail.

I slip into the passenger seat and turn to Gabi as he sets

music to play from his phone.

"Sorry Justin's being so rude lately," I say.

Gabi laughs, mounting his phone on the magnet stand before switching the car into reverse. "I figure that's my fault after I said all that shit. Guess I permanently tainted his image of me."

"It's not you," I say. "He always gets super bitchy when he and Clara break up, even if they do it all the time."

"Clara?"

"Yeah," I say. "She was helping us with the orders when she and Justin were still together. They've kind of been this on-and-off couple since freshman year."

Gabi stares intently at the road for a little while, which seems totally excessive, since there's basically no one around. Finally, he says, "Do you know why they broke up?"

"Not a clue. Probably something petty. Usually is with Justin. Why?"

He shrugs, but his face still looks kind of concentrated. Then he says, "I guess I was wondering if we could do something to help get them back together."

I laugh, tugging mindlessly at the seat belt. "No offense, but I'm not interested in interfering in my best friend's love life."

"Not interference per se," he says, "just a nudge in the right direction. I mean, he's our friend. If it's really tearing him up inside, we should help, right?"

But that would probably piss Justin off. He's not the type of person to be chill with people meddling, especially not in things involving Clara, who he claims to not really have feelings for.

"Just leave it alone," I say. "We have enough stuff to worry about without potentially driving Justin away."

Gabi nods, but something on his face tells me he hasn't completely given up on the idea, like he's formulating a secret plan as we speak.

EIGHTEEN
GABI

When we get back to the house, only my dad is home. It's late enough that the shop is closed for the day and my mom's off at night classes, but still early enough that my dad hasn't started on dinner yet, and he gives me a weird, eyebrow-raised look as Theo and I enter.

"Thought you were working tonight, Gabi," he says.

"We are," I say. "Is it okay if we use the kitchen? We just need to put together some drinks for Theo's parents."

My dad sighs. "You're gonna make stuff and let it sit in the fridge overnight?" he says, then shakes his head. "The Moris really don't know how to run a business, huh?"

I glance at Theo, but he looks pretty unaffected. I chuckle awkwardly in an attempt to defuse the tension and repeat, "Can we use the kitchen?"

My dad shrugs and waves us off. "Fine, fine."

I motion Theo to the kitchen so we can get away before

things get messy. We unload our stuff and get to work, but the air is silent, and my brain runs through all these scenarios about Theo hating me now that my dad insulted his parents.

But finally, Theo says, "We should try to finish early so we can squeeze in some soccer practice tomorrow before school."

My hand freezes over the faucet as I turn to face him. "You're not mad?" I say.

"Mad about what?"

But now I'm worried that if I explain it, he'll just realize he should've been mad all along. "Um, nothing," I say.

We work in silence, and I desperately want to break it, but I'm terrified to try. Usually, at Justin's, everything flows easily, but being at home has my whole body on high alert again. What if I say the wrong thing or steer the conversation the wrong way, and my dad overhears, and suddenly he's grilling me on my sexuality? Or worse, telling me I shouldn't spend time with Theo anymore.

"Okay," Theo says as he tallies up our finished products, "I think we're almost done. We can just leave the toppings off the menu in the morning until we can make them at lunch."

"We don't have to practice tomorrow," I say. "I mean, if you'd rather make the toppings."

Theo smirks. "Gabi, you're not getting out of soccer practice, okay? This is for the good of our school."

I roll my eyes, but I'm feeling a little bit breathless suddenly.

My dad enters the kitchen and takes a quick look around before turning to me and saying, "Gabi, you boys almost done?

164

I want to make dinner before your mom gets home."

"Yup, almost done," I say.

My dad nods. "Bueno, don't want to spend too much time with the enemy."

Theo still seems unbothered as we start cleaning up, but something about my dad's comment gets under my skin, and before I can think better of it, I blurt out, "Theo's teaching me how to play soccer. Or, how to play *well*, I guess. 'Cause I know how to play, even though I suck at it."

My dad's eyes widen, and I have to wonder what's going through his head in that moment before he finally says, "Really?"

And the word itself doesn't say a whole lot, but his tone completely catches me off guard. I can't remember the last time I heard him sound so . . . hopeful? Relieved?

My dad turns to Theo, a smile on his face as he says, "Theo, you're good at soccer?"

Theo shrugs, and to the untrained eye, it's super nonchalant, but I can tell there's some tension in his shoulders as the focus of the conversation shifts to him. "I, yeah, I'm alright."

"He's the best player on the team," I say. "By far."

Theo chuckles. "Not that that's saying much."

"He offered to coach me," I continue. "He's got this whole training plan worked out too."

I know I'm laying it on a little too hard, but if there's one way to win my father over, it's to sell him on sports. If he thinks Theo's saving me from a life spent dancing and watching sappy movies or something, he'll adore him instantly.

Finally, my dad says, "Thank you for doing that, Theo. Gabi can use all the help he can get."

"Oh, it's nothing, Mr. Moreno," Theo says.

My dad smiles. "Call me Pedro. Hey, Theo, you want to stay for dinner?"

"I—" Theo glances to me like he's looking for my approval, so I just nod. "I, sure, I'd love to."

"You can tell me all about this plan you have for Gabi," my dad says. "You know, he's got just the right build for soccer, I always tell him. He's just gotta apply himself instead of wasting his time with silly things. Planning a Homecoming dance? It's not good to get wrapped up in that girly stuff, huh?"

Theo nods, but he looks incredibly uncomfortable, and I feel kind of bad putting him on the spot, but this is the fastest my dad has taken to any of my friends, so I'm kind of relieved.

Then again, it could just be that Theo's the first boy friend I've ever brought home. *Guy* friend. Friend who is a guy. Because Theo is *not* my boyfriend and my dad would kill me if he was.

"Gabi?"

I jolt as my dad shocks me out of my racing thoughts. "Yeah?" I say.

"Make some rice, okay?"

"I—"

"I can make the rice," Theo volunteers. "I mean, I make rice all the time. It's no big deal."

My dad beams, and I have to admit, it stings a little. "Look how helpful he is, Gabi. You're trained well, huh, Theo?"

Theo shrugs. "I just help my parents out sometimes."

My dad laughs. "An athlete *and* a cook. You really do it all!"

I push down the rush of jealousy that bubbles up in my chest. After all, this is what I wanted. Theo is getting along with my dad, and that means I don't have to worry about my dad telling me to stay away from him or blowing our operation. This is good.

I just wish it wasn't *quite* so good.

Or at least, I wish Theo wasn't.

Because the last thing I need is for him to remind my parents of everything they actually wanted in a son before they got stuck with me.

Thursday morning, I hit the field an hour before school starts to squeeze some practice in.

I expect to find Theo in his soccer uniform or at the very least his gym clothes, but he's just dressed like he's ready to head to class.

"Kinda well-dressed for soccer practice, don't you think?" I say.

He raises an eyebrow. "Well, I'm not the one practicing, so it doesn't really matter."

He's got a couple of soccer balls lined up on the grass in front of the empty goal. I set my book bag down on the bleachers. "So?"

He smiles, leading me over to his field setup. "You just have to kick the ball."

I cock my head. "That's it?"

"Considering how bad you are at it?"

I blush, pushing last night's dinner out of my head. It was mostly uneventful, but my dad's continuous praising of Theo—while subsequently dragging me—continued well after my mom came home and even after Theo left and I helped clean up the kitchen. And I guess it shouldn't be a big deal considering we're a Caribbean family and dragging each other is basically our first love language, but I guess it stings all the more because I know some amount of it is actually real. My parents can joke all they want about how terrible I am at soccer, but when I know it's all steeped in how much they wish I could be someone else, it kind of feels like they're just repeatedly kicking a bruise.

"You're pretty fast as long as you can stay upright, so right now, I just want to work on your aim. You don't even have to worry about shooting a goal. I just want you to kick the ball."

I look up at Theo and nod. Now's not the time to dwell on my insecurities. He's putting all this effort into coaching me, which means I need to do my best.

Theo steps behind me, placing his left hand on my shoulder and slowly dragging me back a few yards away from the first ball, but my mind is going blank just from the proximity.

"Okay," he says. "Start here. Give yourself a running start and take aim."

He steps away from me—like way away, like he doesn't want to get hit—and flashes me a grin. Okay. Showtime.

I stare at the ball where it sits idly in the grass. This should be easy.

Taking in a deep breath, I sprint for it, swinging my leg out with enough force to drive the ball straight into the goal.

My foot goes right over it and comes back down right on the round surface, knocking my feet out from under me. My back slams against the grass, and the sound of Theo's laughter encompasses me as my cheeks burn red.

Then Theo's standing over me, holding his good arm out to help me to my feet. I take his hand, mumbling an apology as he helps me right myself.

"That's pretty much what I expected, but with a little extra flair."

I sigh. "Okay, yeah, my ball handling sucks." I freeze, turning my face up to meet his eyes. He doesn't seem to have heard anything awkward in what I said, but my cheeks are still red, and my lip quivers a bit as I take a step away from him.

"You should try again," Theo says, "and this time, don't focus so much on the driving force. Just focus on where you want your foot to land."

And that makes sense, but all I can focus on is Theo, how close he is, the way his hand felt against my shoulder.

I shake myself out, my hands, my legs, my head, hoping to knock some Theo thoughts loose. And then I prep myself again, ready to take aim this time, to really impress him.

And as I barrel forward, I remember the sound of Theo's laugh, and suddenly I'm slipping, my back colliding with the grass again.

"Shit, you okay?" Theo asks, and then he's leaning over me again, a wince on his face.

I nod. "Yeah, not so bad down here."

He smiles, but instead of helping me up, he just sits next to me in the grass. "You sure you want to commit to this?"

And really, no, I'm not. I hate soccer. I hate sports, excluding dance, and I hate being up this early in the morning to do things I hate.

But I also hate letting people down, and there're so many I have to worry about—my parents, Coach, Theo. And I doubt I'll ever be good at the game, but if I don't even try? Isn't that just a big fuck-you in their faces?

"I'm sorry," I say. "I know I'm a lost cause."

He shrugs. "I mean, you're shitty, sure, but I wouldn't say a lost cause. I guess your heart just doesn't really seem to be in it."

Which is fair, since it's not.

"Something on your mind?" Theo asks.

I laugh. "Everything. Our sales, Homecoming—" But I won't add his name to the list, because that's just way too awkward. I don't want to think about him that way, even if that's exactly the way I've been thinking about him since this whole collaboration started.

I'm not in love with Theo Mori.

I'm not.

"This is all for your parents," he says, but he's not asking a question. I guess I'm just that obvious. "It's awful that they don't support you in being who you are."

I shake my head. "They're not bad parents, they're just—" But I don't know what words I'm looking for. Ignorant?

Confused? It feels weird making excuses for them. They should be the ones who know what's going on, who are mature enough to accept me even if I'm not what they expected. I shouldn't be the one educating them.

When I was a kid, my parents were everything—my heroes, my role models. But now they're just the people keeping my prison doors locked.

Or maybe they're both, and that's what makes things so hard.

"I'm not judging," Theo says. "I don't want you to think that I hate them or anything, because I don't. I barely know them. I just see how they're making you feel, and—well, I think if they saw how much they're hurting you, they'd want to do things differently. Or at least, they should. You don't treat people you love that way."

"I want to be a dancer," I say, and Theo turns to me, eyebrows raised. I don't know why I'm back to spewing random crap, but it feels good to actually say it with pride and not like it's some dirty secret to keep hidden under my bed. "I started taking lessons, but I can't tell my parents. They think dancing is for girls."

Theo laughs at that. "You can't confine a whole sport to one gender and then insist everyone's straight."

That gets a chuckle out of me. "I hadn't thought of it that way."

"Of course you wouldn't," Theo says, getting to his feet. "You spend so much time trying to hide the fact that you're gay that you never consider the good parts."

He doesn't say it with any animosity, but it still makes me feel kind of guilty because he's right. I've never considered an upside to being gay. It's just been shrouded in shame. "Good parts?"

He shrugs. "Yeah, like being able to weed out shitty friends easily. Or not having to worry about your parents demanding grandkids. Being able to wear colors without worrying you might be seen as not entirely straight. Or makeup."

And it sounds fun, but I could never. Just the thought of those things has me quivering.

Theo turns to me and grabs my hand. "You spend so much time worrying about what other people want you to be that you never have time to be yourself. Sure, I care what people think, but I'm not gonna let it define me. I'm a screwup, and I'm proud."

"You're not a screwup," I say, my voice soft. "You're iconic."

His left hand comes up along the side of my face, the tips of his fingers gently tickling my cheek, and it feels like my skin is on fire as he brushes it. His face gets closer to mine, and the space between us is dwindling.

I'm about to close the distance myself when he jerks back, eyes wide, hand instantly dropping mine. "I—I'm sorry, I shouldn't have—"

And my heart crashes in my chest, a thread of pain lacing itself through my muscles. "I—no—it's okay," I say.

But it's not okay. I feel like I just got walked to the edge of a

172

cliff to find I was the only one ready to jump.

I look down at my phone, my eyes widening as they land on the time. "I, well, I should go. Um, shower," I say.

Theo nods, but he doesn't say anything else to me as I gather my things and scurry off toward the locker room.

NINETEEN
THEO

Gabi rushes off like his life depends on it, and a part of me is offended, but I guess I also can't blame him.

I'm not entirely sure how to explain it, but something has been a kinda off between us lately. I guess it started with dinner with his parents, when he was acting all awkward. At first I thought it was just that awkward thing that happens whenever you meet someone's parents for the first time, but I guess the more over-the-top his dad got about the whole soccer thing, the more out of place I felt. Well, that, and the praise was a little weird, considering I barely know the guy.

But as I head to homeroom, I'm wondering if maybe it has more to do with whatever happened in the dance room the other day. And I guess what just happened on the field. The first one was easier to brush off as my reading too much into it, but the second feels pretty damning.

Somewhere in all the baked goods and caffeine, I think I

caught feelings for Gabriel Moreno.

Fuck.

When I get to homeroom, Gabi isn't there, and I tell myself it's no big deal, because he's probably just showering. Then I tell myself that I don't care, because I don't have feelings for him so it doesn't matter, and a part of me almost believes it.

Who am I kidding? No, I don't.

Anyway, I try to hyper-focus on my history notes in preparation for the quiz later, but I can't, which isn't a surprise, since there's nothing less exciting than history notes. But I also hate how painfully aware I am of each second that passes by without Gabi showing up.

Then, finally, he races into the room just as the bell rings, slipping into his seat as he tries to catch his breath.

"What the hell? Where were you?" I say.

He looks at me a bit sheepishly, then just shrugs and says, "Nowhere important. Homecoming stuff."

And I raise an eyebrow in response, but he doesn't explain any further, so I just turn back to my notes like I actually care to read them over. But if all this was just some elaborate scheme to avoid me, the last thing I'm going to do is let him know that it bothered me.

My useless brain cannot focus on a single fucking thing, and it is *all* his fault.

It's not even like I'm caught up in some Gabi daydream or something. I just can't actually focus on any one thing because every time I try, something else gets in the way. Like oh, what time is it? Five past nine? Well, Gabi was five minutes late today, so . . . Shut the fuck up, brain!

Anyway, I give up on the whole "school" thing by second period, so I just sit in the back of the classroom scrolling through Instagram with the sound off. I'm deep into all those randomly suggested posts after fully exhausting my own feed when a text notification pops up at the top of the screen from Mom.

Make sure you're home by 7. We need to talk.

And literally in no world is "we need to talk" not super concerning, but I just clear the notification, since I know she'll lose her shit if she realizes I'm texting back in class. Getting home a little earlier shouldn't be a big deal, so I'll just worry about it later. I'm sure I won't forget.

"Excuse me."

The sound of Melissa's voice shocks me out of my empty scrolling, and I nearly drop my phone. Then I realize she's standing at the front of the classroom, talking to Mr. Page, not me.

"Is it okay if I talk to Mark for a second?" she says, pulling out her little Homecoming badge and flashing it like a cop or something. "Homecoming stuff."

Mr. Page looks mildly annoyed, but he just sighs and nods, and Mark gets up and exits the room with her to deal with I don't even know what stuff.

I only realize I'm holding my breath once she's gone and it rushes out of me. It's not like she should recognize me or have any idea what Gabi and I are up to, but there was definitely a part of me that thought for sure we'd be caught the second she walked in.

Most of the Homecoming Committee already knows about the deliveries. I talked to Jeff about it during practice one day, and he said they're all cool with it, since it means they can order whatever they want to. Even the people who aren't placing orders aren't narcs, so whatever. No big deal.

But Melissa's a different story. I didn't even need to see her swinging her badge like a cop or a hall monitor with way too much power to know she's probably our biggest concern with this whole thing. She's always been a teacher's pet—literally reporting-people-for-overusing-the-hall-passes level—so if she catches us, we're dead.

Gabi said she spends most of her time doing Homecoming stuff, but even with all the extra privileges, I doubt she's never in class. I look down at my phone, quickly shooting off a text to him asking if he knows her class schedule.

It's definitely not a foolproof plan for avoiding her, but if we can skirt around making any deliveries to her classes, that might help us steer clear for a while. None of this will really matter after Homecoming.

Oh, crap.

I completely forgot about Homecoming.

Because while these little badges have been the perfect trick for getting our sales up during school, the second Homecoming is over, there's no way we'll be able to get out of class.

So what the hell are we supposed to do then?

TWENTY
GABI

I know I told Theo I wouldn't get involved in Justin's love life—and the voice in the back of my head still says I shouldn't—but I feel like I've already caused Justin so much grief, I owe it to him to at least try. Plus, as long as he's in a shitty mood, our café operation is in jeopardy, and with the Homecoming deadline growing ever closer, I really can't risk that.

So, after Theo left last night, I went ahead and dug up Clara. She wasn't particularly hard to find, and given her last name, her homeroom is pretty close to mine, which made stopping by earlier to figure out what her fifth period is pretty easy.

The bigger problem is that the number of orders we receive is so ridiculous that by third period I'm worried we won't have enough stock left for me to bring something to Clara in fifth. I end up putting in a fake order for a matcha cheesecake just so it won't sell out by lunchtime.

Really, the trick to the romance is in the presentation. Or at least, that's what I would want if someone was trying to woo me. So I head to the Homecoming office and get some ribbon to tie a nice little bow around the cake wrapper and type up a cute little note that I print and tie to the side. It just has a quick apology with a sprinkling of cute, romantic words that I wish Theo had written for me . . . um, well, cute words anyway.

The problem is, I'm so caught up in prepping Clara's surprise that I completely miss my chance to see Theo during lunch. I don't know, maybe I'm naive for thinking that we would talk about what happened on the field and suddenly everything would fall into place and we'd be wrapped up in each other's arms, but I also hate knowing that we left it like that. Like what am I supposed to do now? When he texted earlier, I thought maybe he was as hung up on all this as I am, but once I sent him Meli's schedule, that was about it. Guess I'm just the pathetic one here.

I report to fifth period just long enough for attendance to get taken, then dismiss myself to "take care of some Homecoming stuff." I really should thank Meli for the badges, because they're basically magic.

Fortunately, Clara gave me the right classroom, and a quick, "Can I speak to Clara about Homecoming?" has her sprung from class without a whole lot of hassle.

"You have something for me?" she says, an eyebrow raised. She's really pretty, but something about her feels a little too unreachable, like she knows just how pretty she is and she'll wield it like a weapon. Maybe that's just Justin's type. Personally, I prefer the kind of cockiness that isn't so impenetrable.

Stop thinking about Theo and focus.

"Um, yeah," I say, reaching into my bag and pulling out the little takeout box. She opens it up, a smile gliding across her face as she eyes the note and pulls it out. I watch her eyes flit back and forth across the page. Finally, she folds it up, slips it into her pocket, and says, "Thanks."

"Um, you're welcome."

She doesn't say anything else before heading back into class, but I'll just assume the mission was successful, since she didn't start yelling at me. Either way, I won't know for sure until I see Justin after school.

By the time the school day ends, my legs are exhausted, and I'm torn between feeling relieved that I get to skip soccer practice and dreading going to the Homecoming meeting, which considering how much I need to keep my badge, I can't exactly bail on.

The main Homecoming team is in the office when I arrive. Actually, they're all kind of in the thick of a fight, so I just scoot along the edge of the room to find a place to stand away from all that.

Vivi leans against the wall, phone in hand. I sidle up next to her and say, "What's going on?"

She shrugs. "Melissa's full-blown militant, since we only have a couple weeks left."

She's not entirely wrong about that, but I do feel the obligation to defend my best friend's honor or something. "She's just trying to keep everything together. It's a lot of pressure."

"It's a high school parade no one will remember next year. She needs therapy."

I save my *It's high school. We all need therapy* retort because Meli's just noticed I'm here, and now she's glaring at me.

"Why the hell are you so late?" she snaps.

"Sorry," I say, even though I'm really not that late.

Vivi whistles like she's just seen my life flash before her eyes, before dismissing herself to go run an errand. So much for team solidarity.

"This is ridiculous, Gabi. Either you're committed, or you're not."

Which, again, super ironic since she dragged me into all this in the first place, but I just shut my mouth and nod, because if we're gonna get into a fight like that, the last thing I want is to do it in front of all these spectators.

Relief washes over me as I finally escape the Homecoming meeting. I don't even bother saying anything to Meli on the way out. It's not worth it.

I beeline for the parking lot so I can get to Justin's place. I have enough to worry about without stressing over Meli's chosen fixation. It's only as I'm pulling into Justin's driveway that I remember I was supposed to meet up with Vivi, so I text her a quick, *Sorry, something came up*, before slipping out of the car and heading to Justin's front door.

Theo lets me in, a familiar look of annoyance on his face. Basically the same look he always gave me whenever I stepped out onto the field, but this time he closes the door behind me, rolls his eyes, and drops his voice low to say, "Justin's giving me a migraine."

It's not really the kind of comment that warrants a smile, but I can't help it. It's nice knowing his annoyance isn't with me. "What happened?"

"I guess he and Clara made up, and now he's being obnoxious as hell."

Oh, okay. So a little bit because of me.

We step back into the kitchen, where Justin stands hunched over his phone, eyes practically in heart shape as he stares at it longingly.

Theo says, "Gabi's here!" in the most dramatically sarcastic tone I've ever heard from him, but Justin doesn't even blink as he throws me a lazy wave.

Theo turns back to me and raises his eyebrows in a *you see what I mean* expression.

I chuckle.

"Anyway," Theo says, "let's get to the important stuff. We've got a few new recipes to test out. Oh, and a question to answer. How do we make all this work once we can't use the Homecoming badges anymore?"

"I—what? Why can't we use the badges?" I ask.

"I mean, it's almost Homecoming, and once it's over, we're shit out of luck."

"Oh."

In all the chaos, I've kind of lost track of time, but he's right. It's almost Homecoming, and that means my deadline to save our café is almost here. We're almost out of time.

"My parents are selling our shop after Homecoming, so I guess it doesn't really matter for me," I say.

Theo winces, eyes falling to the floor. "Oh, sorry."

Even Justin peeks up from his phone now that I've dropped a bomb in the middle of his kitchen.

I shrug. "It's fine. You're right, though. I don't know how we could maintain an operation like this without the Homecoming badges, so I guess that's our deadline to make everything work."

Theo nods. "I mean, we're generating a lot of revenue. People love what we're churning out. I know it might be a stretch, but that should count for something, right?"

I nod. "Yeah, it's definitely a bit of a stretch. I was hoping we'd be earning a lot more, and that our popularity at school would convince people to frequent the shops outside, but maybe my parents will reconsider selling when they see how much we've done so far. Is that what you're going to do with your parents?"

Theo just laughs. "Hell no. They'll never consider changing the menu or anything, but I've earned enough to keep us afloat for a little while. I can hold on to some of it, and give it to them slowly and just pretend I'm still running deliveries until we figure out a way to work around the Homecoming badges."

Theo freezes, and I stare back at him, eyes wide but not connecting why he looks so flustered until he shakes his head and says, "I mean, me. I. I mean, until *I* figure out a way to work around the Homecoming badges. That's obviously not your problem, once you convince your parents not to sell."

And it's weird seeing Theo look flustered, hearing the quiver in his voice as he stares down at his socks. I mean, this is the untouchable Theo Mori, the same guy I've always looked up to but been too intimidated to even carry on a conversation with, and now we're standing here in Justin's kitchen, and he's looking all flushed and nervous and all I can think about is the way we almost kissed a little while ago, but I just couldn't make it happen.

Finally, I say, "No, 'we' is good. I mean, I'm still down to help, even if my parents do sell the shop. I wouldn't just bail on you."

Theo looks up, a small smile teasing his lips. "Implying I can't handle it on my own."

"I—what? No! I just meant, I mean . . . If you want my help, you have it. 'Cause we're friends now. Right?"

The words hang between us for a moment, and my heart pounds in my chest as I wait for him to say that I'm in way over my head, that we're not and will never be friends, that all this was just a means to an end, and he's so thrilled to finally get away from me.

He smirks, crossing his arms. "Relax, Gabi, it was a joke."

He shrugs. "Yeah, I guess we're friends now. The apocalypse is upon us."

Justin laughs, slipping his phone into his back pocket. "Did Theo Mori just admit to a lapse in judgment?"

Theo rolls his eyes. "I don't even know what you mean by that, but whatever, we have work to do."

Theo tells me to grab the sugar out of the pantry, but my hands shake as I reach for it. I can't explain it, but it's like my nerves are on fire, every part of me too excited to sit still. I want to run through a field of flowers dressed like Julie Andrews in *A Sound of Music* and sing until I collapse.

For the first time in my life, I feel perfectly at home with a group of other guys.

Theo and Justin are my friends.

I lose track of time as we buzz around the kitchen prepping all our food and drinks for the next day. There's something almost magical in the way I can get completely lost in all this with Theo and Justin, like for a short period of time, nothing else really matters and I'm just floating on air.

Once everything's packed up and ready to go, I head back to my car and actually pull out my phone for the first time since getting to Justin's place. I've got a whole bunch of missed calls from Vivi, and a couple of angry texts.

I lay my head against my steering wheel. I can't say I usually feel particularly drained after working with Theo and Justin, but my muscles ache, like I really just want to go home and take a nap. But then, maybe I'm just a coward.

A knock on my window nearly scares me out of my skin, and I smack my head on my steering wheel, accidentally hitting my car horn.

A swell of angelic laughter surrounds my car, and I look up to find Theo losing it on the other side of my window. It hits me that I've never heard him laugh like that before, but it's kind of unfortunate that he's laughing at me.

I roll my window down and say, "What?"

He wipes tears from his eyes, the laughter still on his face. "You okay? You look like you're about to drive into a river."

"That's kind of morbid, isn't it?"

Theo rolls his eyes.

"I've been absorbed in work and I guess one of my friends is taking it pretty terribly."

"Oh, ouch, sorry," Theo says. "You can share these with them if you want."

He holds out a Styrofoam takeout container and passes it to me. I eye it for a moment before setting it on the passenger seat. "What is it?" I ask.

"Just some pastries. I realized we don't have enough of the individual packaging to bring them tomorrow, so I was gonna say you might as well bring them to your family."

I grin. "You're becoming your mom."

Theo's eyes widen for a moment, and then he smiles. "Yeah, I guess it was bound to happen eventually. Anyway, good luck with your friends. Text me if it gets too heated. I can pretend

I got hit by a motorcycle and need you to come save me or something."

I laugh, but my chest feels warm. "Thank you."

Theo flashes me a smile that almost stops my heart right there in Justin's driveway. "You're welcome."

TWENTY-ONE
THEO

Once Gabi pulls out of the driveway, I head back into Justin's house. It's getting kind of late, so we need to get to cleaning fast if I'm going to get home before my parents get suspicious. I mean, Justin's so googly-eyed over Clara right now that I could probably skip out on the cleaning and be home free, but I'm in a good mood, so I guess I'll take one for the team.

Justin sits on one of the barstools, eyes locked onto his phone screen. I really don't get it. I mean, I get being into someone, but I don't get how Justin can go from "Clara's not important, whatever" to not being able to so much as blink because he's worried he'll miss a text from her. And it's all kind of ridiculous anyway, since their not-relationship has always been pretty much confined to the physical realm of things.

I reach under the sink and pull out some cleaning spray before chasing down the paper towels. I figure I can dance around, cleaning just about everything, and then when the kitchen's all but done, I can bitch that Justin isn't helping enough and guilt him into doing the dishes.

But cleaning in silence kind of sucks, especially because it's not like my brain is good at being idle. I can't stop thinking about the deadline Gabi mentioned for his parents' shop, and then the way his eyes lit up like a freaking Christmas tree when I mentioned us working together even after that, and the way that that would have pissed me off a month ago, but now it feels almost endearing.

I groan, balling up the paper towel I've been using and throwing it at Justin's head. He doesn't even look up as it bounces off his forehead and lands on the counter.

He holds out the paper towel to me, his eyes still glued to his phone. "I think you dropped this."

"Put your phone away for a second, asshole. We've got cleaning to do."

"I spent all afternoon helping you, and now I'm busy."

I step around the island and pluck his phone out of his hands. He gives me a glare that could wilt a weaker man, but as it stands, it just kind of pisses me off.

"What the fuck?" he says.

"Yeah, back at you. I get it. You're super into your girlfriend. So help me get this place cleaned up, and then I'll be out of your hair, and you can go back to jerking off."

Justin glowers, taking a step forward and shoving me back against the dishwasher so he can snatch his phone out of my

189

hands. "You know, it's really shitty how you drag me into your problems and then expect me to just drop everything for you."

I raise an eyebrow. "Wait, so you have a problem with *me* now?"

"Yeah, actually, I kind of do," Justin says. "I'm sick of living in Theo's World. I have my own shit to do."

The words hit me like a punch to the gut, but what pisses me off the most is that he's totally wrong.

It's not "Theo's World." I don't make him do anything. It took everything I had to even ask for his help in the first place, and he was just helping me because he's a halfway decent friend. Or at least, I thought he was.

Justin turns back to his phone, typing up I don't even know what, and I throw the paper towel away before storming out of the kitchen. Whatever. If Justin wants this mess cleaned up, he can do it himself.

When I get back to the shop just after eight, neither of my parents are around, but Thomas is sweeping the floor, his phone on the counter struggling to blast some pop punk band. Thomas looks up as I enter, lips pressed together.

"You're late," he says.

My stomach drops as I remember the text Mom sent me in second period. The whole thing completely slipped my mind, and now I feel both guilty as hell for trusting my ridiculously unreliable memory not to screw me over and annoyed that I'm gonna get hit with some lecture from Thomas.

"Mom and Dad are gonna be pissed," he says as he turns the music down.

I roll my eyes. "That's not really a development."

Something about the way my own family treats me feels so much worse after spending time with Gabi's parents. I mean, it was kind of weird having his dad falling all over me, but for a moment there, it kind of felt like I was the Thomas. Like my talents were appreciated and people actually wanted me around.

Thomas smirks at me, swinging the broom around to rest it against the counter. "So where have you been? Please tell me you haven't been hooking up with some guy in a drive-in theater."

I roll my eyes again. There are a few reasons why Thomas and I just don't really mesh. There's the fact that he's everything my parents want me to be, and then there's the fact that we have nothing in common. He's big on the brainy stuff, thinks soccer is a waste of time, and only watches indie films or shit shot before 1989.

Well, all that, and he's just kind of a drag to talk to.

"I think Mom's worried about you," he says. "You know, not that she'd ever say that, but she keeps talking about you being gone all the time."

"So, what, she asked you to grill me and figure out what I'm up to?" I say.

He rolls his eyes. "No, I just thought I'd ask because you're always really hard on them, so I hoped maybe you'd open up to me."

"*I'm* hard on *them*?" I snap, all my previous irritation with him rising to the surface. "That's a joke, right? They're the parents, the ones who set the rules and act like I'm some freaking demon because I don't fit their perfect mold. It's not like there's anything I can do to change that."

Thomas lets out a deep sigh, leaning against the counter. "Okay, so they're not perfect, but they're still your parents, and they're trying."

But that's the thing, isn't it? Everyone's trying. Everyone's doing their best. But for some reason, I'm expected to give everyone the benefit of the doubt through every screwup or misstep, but no one ever does the same for me. Not Justin, not my parents, and sure as hell not Thomas.

"I think it'd mean a lot to Mom if you just talk to her sometimes, you know?" Thomas says. "I mean, with everything going on, I think she's just worried, and you're not exactly helping."

"Okay, so what are you doing then?" I snap, and I know I should bite my tongue, but I can't. "How are you helping? You show up once a month and sweep a floor and think that fixes things? You don't get to tell me I'm not doing enough when you're barely ever around."

Thomas stares back at me like he can't believe I would say something like that to him, and maybe he can't. I never would have before he went to college. I'm not an animal. I was raised to respect my elders and all that jazz.

I just don't see the point of it anymore. I'm sick of extending respect to people who will never do the same for me. I'm sick of being told day in and day out that I have to carry the weight of everyone around me, let it beat me down and crush me into something I don't even recognize, but that even after all that, I'm still not doing enough. Because I'll never be enough. I'll always be stupid, useless, not-straight Theo—the worthless son, the one who takes up too much space without putting any of it to good use.

I head for the stairs, only stopping as Thomas says, "Theo, wait."

We stand in silence for a moment.

Then he says, "Be nice to Mom, okay? She's going through a lot."

I roll my eyes. "Aren't we all."

TWENTY-TWO
GABI

I pull into my driveway and freeze. Vivi's sitting in front of my house, an angry scowl on her face, her phone in her hand. It's weird to see her there since she's only been over like once before, and I can't really figure out why she'd just show up out of the blue. I look down at my phone to check, and of course, she's called me three times on my drive home alone.

I groan, putting my car into park and grabbing the pastries Theo handed off to me before heading to the door. Vivi doesn't even give me a chance to say hello before she hits me with, "Seriously, Gabi? What, you can't answer the phone now?"

"I was driving," I say.

"For four hours?"

I think about what I should say next but end up not saying anything at all. Even though she's the one who turned up uninvited, I know any words that come out of my mouth will only incriminate me further, and I've got enough going on without picking a fight over this. Instead, I pass the Styrofoam container to her and say, "I'm sorry. These are for you."

She raises an eyebrow. "I don't know what kind of game you're playing—"

"I'm not, okay?" I say. "I've just been working a lot."

"Working on what?"

"For my parents," I say. "And helping Theo Mori."

She gets this look in her eye that I can't quite place, but it makes my blood run cold. It feels like a question, one I know I can't answer—*What's going on with you and Theo?*

But the problem isn't just that I don't really know what's going on between Theo and me, though I really don't. It's just that I can't be honest with Vivi without coming out to her, and I'm not ready to do that yet. I mean, we're friends, but we're not that close.

Vivi accepts the pastries, popping open the top to take a good look at them. She looks like she has something important on the tip of her tongue, but finally, she just looks away and says, "Meli's really pissing me off," she says. "Sorry if I took that out on you."

I let out a deep sigh, though I guess I shouldn't be that relieved that she's pissed at my best friend. But then, I guess Meli's kind of pissing me off too.

I sit down on the front porch and pat the space next to me. "Want to talk about it?"

Vivi eyes me warily for a moment before nodding. "You better not report any of this to her."

I laugh. "I won't. I promise. Honestly, she's been kind of getting on my nerves a bit too. I mean, I love her, but she's been super intense with this Homecoming stuff, and it's kind of draining."

"Yeah, it's infuriating," Vivi says, sitting down next to me. "I mean, who does she think she is? And like, who really gives a shit about Homecoming? I only agreed to help plan it because I can use it for my college applications."

I nod. "Yeah, I mean, I agreed to help because Meli's my best friend, but if I knew she'd be acting like this, I probably wouldn't have agreed."

But then, things wouldn't be going so great with Theo and the shop if I hadn't, so maybe I got lucky. I just wish things could stop falling apart all at once. Either I have to deal with the shop or I have to deal with Meli, not both.

Vivi's nodding, a furious glare drawing her eyebrows together. She pulls out a little egg tart and shoves it into her mouth. "I half wish we could just tank Homecoming and be free of it. You know, and then Meli can feel shitty about how mean she's been."

I laugh but shake my head. "The whole school will lose it if we tanked Homecoming. I mean, we're almost there, you know? Might as well just tough it out until we hit the finish line."

Vivi rolls her eyes. "God, ever the optimist, eh, Gabi?"

And I don't know why she says it like it's such a bad thing, but yeah, I am an optimist. Because at the end of the day, there are so many things that are out of my control, and if I give up hope that things will be okay . . . well, I won't really have anything left.

I let Vivi rant for an hour before I say I should probably tell my parents I'm still alive, and she says she has homework to do anyway. My parents sit in the living room watching TV, and I casually plop down next to my mom on the couch.

She gives me the side-eye and says, "Gabi, it's late. Where have you been?"

I shrug and say, "The front porch with Vivi."

She gives me another look before letting out a sigh and saying, "Next time, let us know when you get home."

My dad laughs, turning to me as the TV cuts to a commercial break. "Give him some space. He's not doing anything dangerous, right, mijo?"

I nod. "Yeah, just Homecoming stuff and work."

"You're spending an awful lot of time with that boy," my mom says. "I know you're just trying to be helpful, but . . ."

"But what?" I say, even though I'm pretty sure I don't want to hear the answer.

My dad shakes his head. "Your mother's just worried you're spending so much time with the enemy, but if that's what it takes to win the big game, there's nothing wrong with a little sacrifice."

I sigh, but I don't really know what to say, since I'm pretty sure we're gonna lose the game either way.

"Besides," my dad says, and for one blissful second, I'm relieved that he isn't forcing me to speak, until he says, "It's good you're hanging out with a boy for once. We don't want people getting the wrong impression."

My mom nods, but there's fury building in my chest, and before I can stop myself, I'm saying, "Wrong impression about what?"

"Ay, relax, Gabi," my mom says. "We're just saying that when you spend all your time talking to girls, people start to think things."

"Who cares what they think?" I say. "Why does it matter?" I don't know why my voice sounds so angry. Usually, I'm good at keeping quiet whenever my parents say ignorant stuff, but something about the way they're speaking really has my blood boiling.

Finally, my dad sighs and says, "I just think you've worked really hard to build your reputation. You have good grades, you're on the Homecoming Committee, you play soccer—If people get the wrong idea about you . . ."

"What idea?" I say. "That I hang out with girls? That's a bad thing?"

"Ay, cariño, we just don't want people thinking you're gay, okay?" my mom says, and my blood runs cold.

Of course I knew that was what they meant, but hearing the words spoken sends a sharp pain lancing through my chest.

I stand up, shoving my hands into my pockets. "I have homework to do."

I expect them to call me back as I head to my room, but neither of them say a thing as I slam the door behind me. Yeah, they'll probably be furious about me slamming the door, but right now, I don't care. Nothing they do to me can hurt worse than the pain in my chest.

Friday morning, I meet Meli in front of the school, and she immediately throws a death glare my way. Like, cold as ice, could cut glass, I don't even think this coffee I brought her will make a difference kind of death glare.

I greet her with an awkward, "Hey, Meli, what's up?"

"Don't give me that bullshit," she says. "You're a dirty traitor."

"I—wait, what did I do?"

"Don't fuck with me, Gabi. The Homecoming badges are a privilege that I gave you so you could service the Homecoming Committee, not so you could run around having some secret love affair."

I freeze, my eyes shooting wide. How could Meli have possibly figured out what I was doing with the Homecoming badges?

I suck in a deep breath before saying, "I'm sorry, Meli, but it's not what you think."

"Someone sent me the link to your little underground café site and said that if I place an order, someone will deliver it under the guise of Homecoming business. Did you really think I wouldn't figure it out?"

And truthfully, I hadn't really thought about Meli finding

out. When Theo asked for her class schedule so we could work without running into her, I was shortsighted enough not to think past that. It just wasn't high enough on my list of priorities, I guess, which I'm definitely not about to tell her now. Instead, I just say, "I'm sorry, Meli. Really. I just—I was desperate. I mean, I'm not having some 'love affair,' okay? I did it to save my parents' shop. It's our only chance."

Her glare softens a little, but she still looks more pissed than I can remember her being throughout the entire course of our friendship. She crosses her arms and turns away from me. "You betrayed my trust, you backstabbing asshole."

"I'm sorry," I say. "I—I'll make it up to you. I promise."

She whirls around, a finger pointed in my direction. "Let me be perfectly clear. If you get caught abusing your Homecoming powers, I will drop you on your ass so fast, you won't even know what hit you. I'll even tell administration you stole the badges. I'm not kidding, Gabi. I've worked too hard on this to lose all of it because you went behind my back to run some shady operation."

The words sting, but I kind of feel like I'm getting off easy. I mean, I knew she'd be pissed when she found out, but she's not reporting me. She's not snatching the badges away and kicking me off the Homecoming Committee and blocking my number. She's just telling me not to get caught. I can manage that.

I nod. "I understand."

Her eyes narrow further and she says, "Also, you owe me."

"Anything."

She stares back at me a moment, and my heart skips a beat. Maybe "anything" was a bad idea.

Finally, she says, "Juniper Mayor was supposed to do a dance on the float. She dropped out because of time constraints, but you can do it, can't you, Gabi?"

"I—you want me to dance? Like, in public?" I say.

She rolls her eyes. "I've seen you dance. You're good. Besides, it's not like we have the time to dig around and find someone better."

And yeah, she has seen me dance, but this is totally different. I mean, sometimes I get into a song or something, but that's not performing in front of actual people.

"I—I can't," I say. "My parents don't even know I do ballet."

She shrugs. "It doesn't have to be ballet. It can be anything. I just need someone to fill the space. You can do a Wonderland cha-cha slide for all I care."

I sigh. We both know I'm not confident enough to lose the last of my dignity doing the cha-cha slide, but I don't know what she expects me to come up with in a week. Plus, it has to be something "straight" enough that my parents won't think too much of it if any of this shit ends up online.

But I also know I'm on thin ice. Meli's right, I betrayed her trust. I got so caught up in Theo and my parents' shop and trying to be a good son that I forgot to be a good friend.

"Okay," I say. "I'll figure something out."

The crease between Meli's brows finally softens as her glare falls away. She slings an arm around my waist and says, "See, I knew you wouldn't let me down."

But that might be too optimistic, since I still have to figure out a dance for the float, and frankly, I get the feeling that it won't be pretty.

TWENTY-THREE
THEO

I'm not the type of person to stress over whether or not someone puts an exclamation mark at the end of a text message, but there's something vaguely concerning when Gabi doesn't. Like, he's not even one of those people who cautiously rations out his exclamation marks. He just throws them all in with reckless abandon in every text, so when I get an *okay* text from him around lunchtime after I ask him to run the most recent order, I can't help but wonder if he's mad at me about something. But it's not like I can ask Justin for his opinion, because I know for a fact that he's mad at me.

Gabi finds me toward the end of lunch, plopping down at the table with the deepest sigh I've ever heard before face-planting on it. "I'm so tired."

I raise an eyebrow. "Was the delivery that bad?"

He groans, shaking his head. "No, it's everything else, I guess."

Which definitely sounds like he's mad at me.

I look up to find Jeff and Joey watching us, but I just opt to ignore them. I'm not sure at what point the soccer team decided to take my word on all things Gabriel Moreno, but after we started hanging out more, I couldn't help but notice the rest of the team became less hostile toward him too. Maybe I was just such a dick that they were scared to go against me.

Gabi pulls out a sandwich and picks at it for a moment before looking up at me, eyes wide.

"Hey, Theo?"

"What?"

"You wouldn't happen to be a good dancer, would you?"

I stare back at him until his face starts turning red before he finally just looks down at his sandwich again. "Why?"

"I—never mind."

We fall into silence for a while before he looks up at me again. "Are you busy tomorrow?"

"Why?" I repeat.

"I thought maybe we could schedule an extra practice for the game. You know, if you're not busy."

"I'm not busy."

He smiles so brightly, it's hard to believe I thought he was mad at me a moment before, but maybe that's just the way he is. It's like nothing ever really keeps him down for long. It's kind of admirable.

"Okay, cool. I can meet you at your place, if you want. I usually help my parents set up the shop on Saturday mornings, so I'll be in the area."

I just nod. "Sure. Are you gonna tell me now why you asked if I can dance?"

Gabi flushes and looks away. "I—I'd rather not talk about it."

Despite our kind-of fight, Justin doesn't bar us from using his kitchen. The problem is just that it feels like a giant block of ice is sitting in the middle of the room, sucking any warmth out of the place and leaving me too distracted to really get any work done. We call it quits early, which is probably for the best since I've been getting home late these past weeks, and my parents hate that.

Gabi offers to stay and clean—whether because he can tell Justin and I aren't getting along or because he feels bad for not having done so before, I don't really know, but I let him.

When I get back to the shop, someone I recognize from school but don't actually know by name is there buying a bun and a milk tea. She flashes me a smile as she heads for the door, and I'm just grateful she doesn't mention anything about our secret bakery operation, though I am kind of curious whether she just lives in the area or actually stopped by because she saw me selling at school.

"Oh, Theo," Dad says as I step past our exiting guest, "how was school? Good?"

I nod. "Yeah, it was fine."

Once the girl clears the shop, Dad flashes me the brightest smile I've seen on his face in years. "Does that girl go to your school?"

"I—why?"

"She said she heard about the shop at school and couldn't get enough of it," Dad says. "Those business cards really worked, huh?"

I completely forgot about the business cards, but they do make for a decent scapegoat, and honestly, my dad's so happy, I can't even bring myself to disagree with what he's saying. Even if the business cards looked like they were made by a six-year-old.

"I'm glad," I say. "So, things with the shop are doing well?"

"It's still a bit slow, but it's getting better," he says. "You just keep telling your friends about it and running deliveries, and I'm sure we'll be overflowing with customers soon."

I smile. "Yeah, I'll keep doing that."

Mom comes downstairs, but it doesn't look like any of Dad's joy has been rubbing off on her at all. Actually, she looks positively miserable, and I can't help remembering what Thomas said, which just kind of sucks the joy right out of me too.

"Everything okay?" I say.

Mom smiles at me, but it's the most ridiculously fake smile I've ever seen. "Yeah, yeah, everything's good. How was school?"

I shrug. "The same as always. I'm helping Gabi practice for the Homecoming game, so I won't be around the shop tomorrow."

My mom just nods like she's not even listening to me.

"Sorry I was late the other day," I say, waiting to see if she'll yell at me, but she doesn't. "What did you want to talk about?"

"Nothing, nothing," she says, waving me off. "Don't worry about it."

My dad starts telling her about the shop's traffic, and she nods along too, but she still feels like a ghost, like maybe she's not even here, and I just feel shittier than I have in a long time. I mean, what kind of shitty-ass son am I that I didn't even notice something was wrong until Thomas pointed it out, and how much shittier must I be that she's still lying to my face, telling me everything's okay?

Saturday morning, Gabi comes by just after nine.

It's October now, and it's pretty chilly out. Gabi's in our soccer uniform, but I'm bundled up in a jacket and sweatpants, since I can't play yet anyway. I'm supposed to go back to the doctor on Wednesday, and then I should be good to play again, but my skin already feels itchy, like I really just need to kick some balls to get this heaviness out of my chest.

We head to campus, walking mostly in silence. Gabi offers to drive, but let's be real. He needs any training he can get, so a nice long walk in decent weather is far from the worst option. I go to the gym to grab a ball, and then I just set Gabi up doing basic drills. It's kind of ridiculous that he's still at such a simple stage, but all things considered, he's definitely improving.

"So, what's bothering you?" he asks.

I tuck my hands into my jacket pockets. "What do you mean?"

Gabi turns to me, his breath a little heavy from practice.

"Well, you said you didn't sleep, and you've just seemed kind of tense. Is it about Justin?"

"No, it's not."

"What did you guys fight about?"

"I said it's not about Justin, okay?" I snap, and Gabi's eyes shoot wide, but he just looks down at his cleats. My instinct is to tell him to just mind his own goddamn business, but I can't. I think a part of me knows that I should talk about it, whatever the hell "it" actually is, and I'm pretty sure that part is the same part that knows there's no one better for me to vent to than Gabi.

But I also hate how vulnerable it makes me. I mean, a month ago, Gabi and I were sworn enemies, and now what? I want to bare my heart to him on the soccer field? Sounds like a pretty terrible plan.

"I'm sorry," he says. "I didn't mean to pry."

I shake my head. "No, it's my fault. Or my problem, I guess. I don't know."

Gabi goes back to lightly kicking the ball, his footwork pathetic, but at least he can actually aim at it now. Finally, I sigh, plopping down onto the grass.

"So, the other day I was talking to my brother, Thomas," I say, "and he just said these things that kind of got under my skin."

Gabi raises an eyebrow. "He was dragging you?"

"I—no, nothing like that. Thomas is just—you know those people who are good at everything, so anytime they say anything, it kind of feels like they're being condescending?"

Gabi laughs, then missteps, tripping over the ball and landing on his ass with a huff. He turns to look at me, his face kind of red, and I don't know if it's from practicing or embarrassment or both. Finally, he says, "So it just runs in the family then?"

"Oh, please, I'm not like that."

"No?" Gabi says, but his voice sounds playful now. "God, Theo, you're amazing at soccer, you're a good cook, you're confident and smart—"

"I have like a C average," I say.

Gabi shrugs. "So what? That doesn't mean you're not smart."

And yeah, I've heard that before. It's one of those backhanded compliments people always hand me after lecturing me for not being organized enough or forgetting something important or focusing on all the wrong things. "If you say it just means I don't apply myself, I'm going to scream."

Gabi lies back against the grass, staring up at the slow-moving clouds across the sky. "No, I wasn't going to say that. I was just going to say that you're a different kind of smart. The better kind."

"Meaning?"

But he doesn't answer. "So, what were you saying about your brother?"

I groan, lying back against the grass next to him. I don't know why he did it until I join him, staring up at the widespread, faded blue, the way the wisps of clouds dance with the thicker, fluffier ones. It feels so . . . infinite? Is that the word?

Like I'm staring into this space so massive, I could follow it forever and never reach the other side. And somehow, that feeling is almost comforting, like nothing I do or say really matters at this point because I'm just a speck, just a tiny little nothing floating in an endless wave of blue.

"I'm just kind of a disappointment, you know?" I say. "I'm always letting my family down. Especially my parents. And the other day, Thomas said this whole thing about how I need to be nicer to my mom because she's going through a lot, and it really pissed me off because it's not like anyone asks me what I'm going through, but I'm also worried he might be right. I think my mom is going through something, but I guess I'm too much of a disappointment to get clued in on any of that."

"So how much of that did Thomas tell you, and how much of that are you projecting?"

I sit up, my eyes flying to Gabi's face. "What?"

But he's still staring at the clouds, his eyes distant. I half expected him to have this evil look on his face, like he was trying to get a rise out of me or something, but I guess that's not his style. And I know that, but it's really hard to believe that people might actually care about me, like they aren't just goading or prodding me to see how I'll eventually combust. God, what is wrong with me?

Finally, Gabi blinks and says, "You keep saying that you're a disappointment and that you're letting everyone down, but did Thomas tell you that or did *you* tell you that?"

I shrug. "Does it matter?"

Gabi chuckles. "I just find it hard to believe that your family would say that."

"Because they're polite?"

"Because no one with any sense would think you're a disappointment."

And it's something about the way he says it, like it's just a fact, some super-obvious truth. Of course I'm not a failure. Of course any family would be lucky to have me. It's weird because in my heart, I know he's wrong, but Gabi sounds so convinced, it's hard to think otherwise.

"So what do I do?" I say.

"Pardon?"

"About my mom. And Thomas," I say. "Well, and everything, I guess."

Gabi sighs, pushing himself up into a seated position. "I don't really know. I mean, I'm not the best person to ask about how not to disappoint one's parents, since mine would probably trade me in for a Pomeranian, but I don't know. I mean, you could always just ask your mom what's going on."

"I did. She says it's nothing, which is what she always says."

"So what about Thomas?"

I raise an eyebrow.

"I mean, he's the one who told you something was up in the first place, right? Did you ask him why? Maybe he'll tell you," Gabi says.

"Maybe, but I don't want to talk to Thomas. It's only guaranteed to make me feel shittier."

Gabi shrugs. "That's fair. I guess the question is just whether you'd rather be out of the loop or waste fifteen minutes talking to your brother. I can't really tell you. I don't have any siblings."

"Don't brag about it."

Gabi smiles, picking himself up off the grass and dusting himself off. He looks over at the soccer ball for a moment as his face reddens. "I—"

"What?" I say.

He sighs. "There's something I should tell you."

"Which is?"

"Meli found out that we've been using the Homecoming badges to make deliveries."

"I—wait, what? Is she going to take them away?"

And it sounds like a ridiculous question, because of course she would, assuming she doesn't get us expelled first.

But Gabi just shakes his head, even though his eyes still look sad.

Finally, he says, "She said she won't stop us, but she also won't protect us if we get caught, which, yeah, I figured as much. It's just—there's one other condition to us getting to use the badges."

"Okay," I say. "What is it?"

"She wants me to dance on the Homecoming float."

"That doesn't sound too bad?"

"I—I guess not. I just—" He stares down at his cleats again. "God, Theo, I'm so nervous. I've never danced in front of an audience before, and my parents don't even know that I dance, and there's just so much—"

"Whoa, calm down, okay?" I say, holding up a hand to him. "Relax. Is this why you asked me if I can dance? You want me to do it for you?"

"I—" He looks at me, eyes wide. Then he looks at me slowly. "No, I wouldn't make you do that. I guess I was just . . . wondering if maybe you'd want to dance with me? So I wouldn't have to do it alone."

God, the look on his face is so sad and vulnerable, it feels like a knife to the gut. I mean, what kind of horrible person must I be to make him feel like that?

I push myself to my feet and step over to him, grabbing hold of his wrist. "What kind of dance were you thinking?"

He looks up at me and smiles. "Nothing too hard, since I only have like a week to put it together. Meli says it doesn't really matter. She just needs someone to fill the space. I—I thought maybe if I had some friends involved, it wouldn't be too conspicuous for my parents."

I sigh. "Okay, fine, I'll dance with you. Consider it a thank-you for everything you've done to help my parents' shop."

And when he smiles at me again, it completely catches me off guard, and I want to kiss him so badly, my lips ache. But then he steps away and turns back to the soccer ball with a look of determination.

"Okay," he says. "I'm going to get this ball into the goal. Watch me."

I laugh. "I doubt it, but good luck."

TWENTY-FOUR
GABI

When I get home late Saturday afternoon, my muscles feel like I've just carried a freight train, and I'm coated in a thin layer of sweat. All I have to do is ask my dad if Theo can come over, but the continuous image of my father seeing us dance together on the float makes me physically nauseous.

So I chicken out and end up calling Vivi.

"You want me to do *what*?" she says when I pitch the idea.

"It's just a short dance," I explain, my voice racing out of me in a jumble. "It won't be hard. I can even make it so that your part is really minimal, but it's really important to Meli, so if you could just do it as a favor. . . ."

"A favor to Meli," Vivi repeats, her voice drawn out a little too long to be casual, "or you?"

I pause. "Um, both of us, I guess?"

Finally, she sighs and says, "Okay, fine, but *minimal*, okay? I have babysitting to do, so I can't just spend all my time learning some dance. Also, like, I'm a shit dancer."

"You'll do great! Don't worry!"

When we hang up, a part of me feels kind of disappointed that this dance isn't one more excuse to spend some alone time with Theo, but I push that thought aside. Even if I can manage to totally straight-wash the dance with Vivi involved, I still have to keep my cool as I talk to my dad.

When I head into the house, my dad sits in the living room, looking over some paperwork that I casually push out of my mind, reminding myself that even if it is the contract, it's not like they're going to sell yet, so I still have time.

He glances up at me with an eyebrow raised, and then, as his eyes rove my uniform and my sloppy condition, a grin spreads across his face.

"Playing soccer, Gabi?" he says.

I shrug, but I know this is basically a holiday for him. To think that his son was out playing soccer *voluntarily*? Christmas could never compare.

But I can only hope this will work in my favor as I casually step toward the stairs and say, "I was just practicing with Theo. He's getting me in shape for the Homecoming game."

My dad's grin widens. "Ah, I knew I liked that boy. You guys gonna win this year?"

"Um, yeah, maybe," I say, even though I know that's definitely not going to happen. "Anyway, is it okay if Theo and Vivi come over tomorrow? We, uh, have an assignment to work on."

The biggest issue is that my parents won't be home, and

they hate leaving me home alone, but at the same time, I also need them not to be home so they can't turn our meetup into something that it's not.

Hence my dilemma.

But instead of giving me that scrutinizing judgment my dad usually gives me when I ask for things I probably shouldn't be asking for, he idly nods before turning his attention back down to his paperwork. "You know the rules, Gabi," he says, "but I'll trust you three can behave yourselves. No secret parties or smoking anything, claro?"

I laugh, because let's be real. I'm the last person who'd be throwing a secret party.

But I also know I'm getting off easy, because if my dad knew what we were actually doing, he'd probably think it was much, much worse.

"Claro que no. Gracias, Papi."

Theo and Vivi come over just after one, which I figured was the perfect time, since it gives us at least three hours before my parents typically come home from the shop on Sundays. Well, Theo shows up just after one, while Vivi's running a bit late.

I mostly cleared the living room before he arrived—pushing the sofas and coffee table out of the way and cleaning up the random papers my dad left lying around. Theo has a box of pastries from his parents' shop that he sets down on the dining table.

"My mom wouldn't let me leave until I took them," he says.

I laugh. "This is good though. Now we have a reward for getting this dance together."

He smiles back at me, but it's short-lived, and his eyes quickly dart around the room. The last time he was here, I was so focused on my parents' opinions of him that I never actually considered whether or not he might be out of his element. He glances down at his shoes for a moment, then awkwardly crosses and uncrosses his arms.

"Are you okay?" I say.

He looks up and shrugs. "Yeah, fine, why?"

"You just seem a little off."

He glances back toward the door for a second before sighing and saying, "You don't have a shoe rack."

I look over to the door, then back at Theo, and laugh. "It's fine. It's not like we don't clean the floors."

"I know that, but—" He glances at my dance shoes and sighs. "You're really just wearing shoes in the house."

"I mean, if I dance in socks, I'll probably fall," I admit.

He shakes his head. "You have feet."

It feels like such a silly thing to get worked up over, but I just say, "You can take your shoes off if you want to."

"It'll just be weird, since you have yours on. Anyway, what's this dance you want to do?"

"Um, about that," I say, awkwardly looking away, "I hope it's okay if I invited another friend to join us. I just thought, in case my parents see—"

"I don't mind."

I turn to Theo to find him looking completely unbothered, which actually kind of disappoints me a little, but I reach for my phone and say, "Thanks. Let me see where she's at."

Vivi shows up a few minutes later, a look of annoyance on her face. "I have to babysit after this, so I can only be here for a couple hours."

"It's fine," I say. "We'll make it fast."

So we start with music. Well, *I* start with music. I acknowledge that Theo and Vivi are really just here out of charity, so I don't want to force them to make any major executive decisions.

I open up my Spotify and cycle through songs—some popular stuff, some club stuff, some Latin stuff. I consider just using some K-pop to get the crowd going, but there's no way the three of us will be able to meet their expectations once BTS comes on. Besides, we still have to keep things somewhat Wonderland-themed, so maybe something instrumental. . . .

"I hope you're not planning on doing anything extra," Theo says.

I laugh. "I mean, my background is in ballet, but there's no way I'd do that on the Homecoming float, so we'll definitely do something simpler. What kind of dance do you do?"

He shrugs. "None, unless you consider occasionally getting into J-pop videos as a kid."

And now I'm just picturing a little Theo hopping around to J-pop in front of his TV.

Vivi rolls her eyes. "You really called us here without a plan?"

Theo says, "If there's nothing for us to do, I brought snacks."

218

"No, wait!" I say. "Come stand here."

So he obediently takes the place beside me as I start brainstorming our steps. Choreographing a dance for myself typically isn't that hard for me, but choreographing one for *three* of us that has enough energy to get people excited but doesn't have us touching or getting too close or looking at each other intimately at all? Yeah, that's a different story.

I try to remember the advice Lady's always giving me. Just don't overthink it.

Ugh, why is not thinking so hard?

Actually, thinking about Lady is giving me another idea. While we never finished choreographing our dance, that doesn't mean I can't use it as inspiration here. Really, I can take most of the core of what we did before, simplify and transcribe it, and then just add an ending, and that would solve everything.

So I gather Theo and Vivi together, thinking of them as Lady and me. Actually, if we're running with the whole Wonderland aesthetic, I can break each part up as different parts of the story, and that means I can give each of us shorter parts so we only have to dance on cue.

Within a couple hours, we have a plan laid out for some simple moves to get us through the few minutes it should take for us to cross the field. The only problem is that the transition from Vivi's part to Theo's feels a little too rushed, like maybe I need to cut one of them a little bit or rework it so that our parts overlap more. . . .

"Okay, sorry," Vivi says, waving a hand in front of my face, "but I gotta go."

"I—"

"I promised my parents I would watch my sisters," Vivi says. Right. I knew that.

"It's fine," Theo says. "We can just figure out the last part and update you when it's done, right?"

And Theo looks way more confident than I feel, so I just nod, and Vivi grabs her things, racing out before I can even tell her we should schedule another day to practice. But whatever, it's no big deal. This is just a favor to Meli anyway. If Vivi's part isn't perfect, we'll just shorten it or something.

"Let's run it through, and then we can take a snack break," I say.

Theo smiles. "Whatever you say, Gabi."

I turn the music on, and we start going through the steps. Since the Junior float will be the third to join the parade, I decide to focus on the climax of the story. I'm first, as the cards come marching in, followed by Vivi's battle with the Queen of Hearts and Theo's run in with the Cheshire Cat as Alice flees. I'm about halfway through my intro when the front door swings open, and I trip over my own feet, stumbling into Theo and knocking him to the floor.

The music keeps playing through the living room, but I can't hear it over the pounding in my ears. My dad stands in the doorway, keys still in his hand as he stares at us.

Theo pushes me off him, awkwardly stumbling to his feet and

dusting himself off. It takes a moment for his eyes to land on my dad, but he seems unbothered as he says, "Hi, Mr. Moreno."

My dad blinks once, eyes slightly narrowed as he says, "What are you boys up to?"

"Just an assignment!" I rush out a little too quickly. Finally, I cough, pulling myself to my feet and saying, "Nothing big. We were just told we have to do this for Homecoming. It's an art project. Vivi's helping, but she had to leave."

My dad stares back at me for a moment like he can't decipher the words I'm using or what planet I just crash-landed from before he lets out a deep, throaty laugh and says, "They have you kids doing all these ridiculous things nowadays, huh? It's worse than the hazing we did in college."

I chuckle nervously because I think that means I'm safe? If he just thinks the whole thing is some sort of academic torture, at least that means he doesn't think I'm gay.

"It's not so bad," Theo says. "I mean, I'm not much of a dancer, but I don't hate it."

My dad laughs again. "Theo, you're a saint. Don't go around saying that, though, or they'll keep pulling you into that stuff."

"What stuff?" Theo says.

My dad just waves him off. "You know, all that gay stuff women are always trying to make us do."

The air feels cold around us, but my dad doesn't seem to notice as he heads toward the kitchen.

Then my blood runs colder as Theo says, "I *am* gay. You know, for the record."

My dad's back goes rigid, but he doesn't move, just standing there in the doorway to the kitchen like somebody hit pause and he can't move again until getting the cue.

Then he turns to look at Theo for a moment, and there's something in his eyes that I haven't seen there in a long time. Disbelief? Disappointment? No, it's more like somebody just told him the sky is green and yeast doesn't rise. It's the same look he had when I first told him that I wanted to do ballet, like all his dreams and expectations were being torn down. Like everything he'd been hoping would come was built on a lie.

Finally, he speaks, his voice low. "¿Perdón? I think I misheard you, Theo."

"No, you didn't," Theo says, though every part of my body wishes he would just go along with it, pretend my dad's hearing really was just slipping. "I said I'm gay. And I'm not ashamed of it either."

Then my dad turns back toward the kitchen and says in a low voice, "Maybe you should be."

Theo turns to me, his eyes narrowed, and I know what he's waiting for. I know he's waiting for me to say that that's absurd. That there's nothing wrong with being gay, and my dad is way out of line.

But when I open my mouth to speak, all that comes out is, "I—"

Because I can't defend him. I know that's what he needs me to do, but I can't.

Because if I do, my dad will know that I'm gay too.

No, worse. My dad will think that being around Theo is what turned me gay.

And he'll never let me see him again.

Theo turns and storms out of the living room, and it takes a whole twenty seconds before my legs finally agree to move so I can chase after him.

I expect to find Theo halfway down the street, but he's not. He's just kicking a small stone down the driveway, a glare on his face.

He whips around the second I exit, like he knew I would follow him, and says, "Are you kidding? You couldn't say anything?"

"I—I'm sorry," I say, because I am, even though I know I did nothing to prove it. "I—I couldn't risk him finding out—"

"God, Gabi," Theo groans, "I don't give a shit what you want to tell your parents or not, but *that*? That wasn't fair! I can't believe you'd just . . . just make me go through that. . . ."

There's a hiccup at the end of his words, like there's something else he wanted to say, and I'm pretty sure I already know what it is.

Alone. I can't believe you'd just make me go through that *alone.*

Because he knows I can't control my parents, but what happened wasn't just about the comment my dad made. It was about the fact that I was the reason Theo was in that situation in the first place, but when push came to shove, I couldn't bring myself to stand with him.

Theo shakes his head, kicking the stone into the street. "Just forget it."

"I—"

But before I can think of any excuse that doesn't just sound hollow, Theo takes off down the street.

TWENTY-FIVE
GABI

Unsurprisingly, Theo doesn't answer any of my texts that evening and into the next morning. I half expect him not to show up for homeroom, but when I get in, he's there, and he just proceeds to ignore me for the rest of the period.

I try to distract myself by focusing on deliveries, but even just keeping track of our stock is hard since Theo isn't talking to me, and as far as I know, he isn't talking to Justin either. I brought my half of our usual supplies, but I slip out of third period to head to the dance room and figure out what we even have available.

Justin and Clara are already there when I enter, Clara's back pressed against the mirror as they make out. They kind of pull away when I get there, but they don't seem to be in any rush as they just casually detach.

"Sup, Gabi?" Justin says, and I just roll my eyes.

"Have you talked to Theo at all?" I say.

He shrugs. "Should I?"

"He's not talking to me right now," I say.

Justin smirks. "Congrats, dude."

I sigh. "Whatever. I just wanted to check our stock. Do you know if he brought anything?"

Justin shrugs again, and it's kind of irritating, since I know he's the only one who has nothing on the line.

"Do you guys need any help?" Clara asks. "I don't mind lending a hand, especially since your little café saved our relationship."

Justin raises an eyebrow. "It did?"

I wince, but Clara's just smiling and nodding. "Please, you think I would've taken you back without that matcha cheesecake?"

He stares at her for a second, and by the time it clicks to him that he should probably just play along, it's already clicked for her that he really has no idea what she's talking about.

Crap.

"You didn't send that matcha cheesecake, did you?" she says.

"Sure I did, babe!" he says, but she's already turning and heading to the door.

"Screw you," she says. "The one time I actually think you're putting in any effort, and it wasn't even you. I should've known better."

"Clara!"

But she just slams the classroom door as she storms out, and before I really register what's happening, Justin turns to me, a glare on his face.

"What the fuck was that?" he snaps.

"I—"

"What matcha cheesecake is she talking about? What did you two do?"

And it's clear to me that he's putting the blame on Theo, and something about that makes me inexplicably angry. I mean, none of this was Theo's fault, and for Justin to just be an asshole to him over nothing is completely unfair.

But I just shake my head and say, "It wasn't Theo, okay? I just saw how miserable you were, and I wanted to help."

"Well, great, now you just made my girlfriend realize she could do better," he snaps.

"Well, *you're* the one who should've done better, and that's not my fault!"

Justin scowls at me for a second, and it finally hits me that I definitely crossed the line with that one. Hell, I've crossed the line with everything. I'm just a professional line-crosser at this point.

And I don't know what I'm expecting, but I still feel kind of disappointed when Justin storms out of the room too without looking back.

It's not like I deserve any better.

By Tuesday morning, I can't think clearly. So many things keep running through my head—my parents, Theo, Justin—and even as I'm reading through our orders, I'm not really reading. I'm more like staring at the screen, hoping the swimming letters and numbers will start to make sense, but failing miserably.

My deadline is at the end of the week, and then what? And there's a traitorous part of my brain saying none of this even matters when I lost . . . well, everything else that matters.

So it's not really a surprise when Theo comes in Tuesday morning and says, "I can't keep working with you on this café stuff anymore, so if you want to run the deliveries by yourself, go ahead."

Before he can walk away, I grab him by the wrist. I'm kind of surprised he doesn't just immediately yank his arm away or slap me or something as I say, "Theo, this whole thing was your idea in the first place. I can't just steal your business."

Theo shakes his head. "School deliveries? That was your idea. Not to mention using the dance room and the website, and well—look, just forget it, okay? I don't want any part in anything you've made, okay?"

"But—"

"I don't need your charity, so fuck off," he snaps, pulling his arm away and heading to homeroom. And really, it's a smart idea if his main goal is to get away from me, because even if we sit next to each other, it's not like I can try to bring the conversation up again without causing a scene.

I sigh, leaning back against the hallway wall, ignoring all the people bustling by and throwing me awkward glances. I don't really care if I look like a caged animal on display or something.

I'm just tired and stressed at the idea of running this whole thing alone, but more than anything, my heart hurts.

Not just because Theo wants nothing to do with me anymore, but just knowing that it's because I hurt him. Or maybe it's knowing that he was right when he said he was better off doing all this without me because I would just mess everything up.

I keep up the deliveries throughout the day, but my heart isn't really in it, and frankly, I don't have the stamina to keep up our three-man operation alone. After lunch, I update the website to show that we're out of stock of everything, even though we still have some stuff left—well, *I* have some stuff left—because I'm too tired to continue on.

I head back to the dance room after lunch to take stock of what's left and count the money. I feel bad keeping all of it when it's only fair for it to go to Theo, but I pocket it anyway because I know there's no way he'd ever accept it.

There's a Homecoming meeting after school, but I skip it. Even if Meli decides to confiscate my badge, it won't matter, since I don't have any hopes of keeping the shop going. And I guess, it'd be kind of a relief to have a reason to give up, like maybe it'd feel a little less like it was my fault that everything fell apart.

I head to the dance room to grab the leftovers so I can get home, and freeze when I find that the door is locked and there's a white notice taped to it that reads:

Classrooms are for faculty and approved student use ONLY. Abuse of student privileges will result in disciplinary action.

The note hits me like a slap across the face as my brain scrambles to figure out what I did wrong.

And then I remember.

I forgot to clean up before last period.

Crap.

TWENTY-SIX
THEO

Tuesday after school, I try to sell a couple of buns, but nobody really cares, since they got more than enough of it during school hours.

A part of me knows this is my fault for telling Gabi he could keep running deliveries, but what else was I supposed to do? I couldn't force myself to keep working with him when every time I see his face, all I can think about is the shit his dad said and the way he just . . . let it happen.

No, I guess it's worse than that. I can't face him because I know that every time I do, I'll think about how, for the first time since I came out, I actually felt like there was somebody who got me, who was in this with me so I didn't have to be completely alone.

And how fucking wrong I'd been about it.

So I don't stay long after school, and I skip soccer practice for the first time in ages, but really, what's the point in sticking around when I can't actually participate in the practice anyway? And I don't want to run into Gabi there or Justin or really, anybody else on the team, since it's their fault for supporting that Fusion Café in the first place.

I was pretty excited about going to the doctor tomorrow and getting approval to play again, but now I just don't really know. I mean, it'll be nice to get things back to normal, but there are just so many things going to shit right now that it's hard to see the positives in anything.

But one thing I'm absolutely sure about is that there's no way I'm going to be able to save my parents by selling at school anymore.

When I get home, I head straight up to my room, crouching down on the floor and sliding the shoebox out from under my bed. I hate the way my heart contracts as I open it, looking at all the stolen tips I've been saving up for college.

It really was absurd for me to think that the one thing standing in the way of me and a successful future was the lack of a college fund. My grades suck, and I suck, and even if I got as far away from Vermont as possible, it wouldn't be enough to fix all the broken parts of me that make me ruin everything I touch.

I sigh, running a hand over my face and gulping down air. I'm sick of feeling helpless, but more than that, I'm sick of feeling guilty. I'm sick of feeling like everyone is better off without me.

I'm careful as I make my way back downstairs, making sure nobody's around before I sneak back into the office and find the tip can. I don't know how I'll explain the sudden surge of tips for the day, but I'm sure my parents won't mind. I feel like giving them back the money I took is the least I can do, and maybe it'll help at least a little bit.

But even if it doesn't, at least it's one less thing to feel guilty about.

Once I've stuffed the money into the little tin and returned it to its rightful spot on the desk, I step back out into the shop and freeze. My parents aren't around, but Thomas stands behind the counter, wiping down the display case. He looks up as I exit and raises an eyebrow.

"What are you up to?" Thomas says.

"Nothing," I snap, but I'm sure the sudden burst of anger gives me away.

Thomas sighs and says, "Whatever, just don't go causing any trouble, okay?"

"Right, because that's all I'm good for," I say. "Theo the troublemaker. Theo the son who ruins everything and just makes everyone's lives harder."

Thomas's eyes shoot wide as he stares back at me like some kind of rabid dog who just broke free of my leash, and I guess he's not wrong about that. I almost feel bad that all my pent-up anger is getting thrown at my perfect brother, but then again, I also kind of don't. I mean, at least half of this is his fault anyway for bailing on us and expecting us to just put the pieces back together.

Thomas places the rag down on the counter and says, "Are you okay?"

I just shake my head. "It doesn't matter."

Thomas chuckles, and I kind of want to punch him for it, but he just leans against the counter and says, "You just caused a whole scene and now you're pretending you don't want attention?"

That's pretty dramatic, since we're the only people here. But when I try to say that, all that comes out is "Is wanting attention really that bad?"

Thomas stares at me for a moment before slowly looking down at the counter. "Mom and Dad aren't ignoring you, okay? They just have a lot going on."

"I know. They have better things to worry about." And my tone sounds bitter as hell as I say it, but I can't pretend I'm not resentful. The only problem is I'm not entirely sure who I'm resentful of. My parents, I guess, for making me their lowest priority. For praising Thomas, who's never around, while not giving a shit about anything I do for them.

Thomas shakes his head, turning to look at me. "Theo, what do you expect? They have to deal with Uncle Greg and the shop and—well, the point is they have more pressing stuff to worry about. You're sixteen. You can take care of yourself."

"So I'm old enough that I can take care of myself, but not old enough for them to trust me with anything," I say. "They still keep all their secrets, and they still think I'm incapable—"

"They don't think you're incapable."

"Of course they do!" I shout. "They wouldn't even let me run deliveries by myself. They'd rather let their enemy's son handle things than me."

"You sprained your wrist!" Thomas snaps. "They were worried about you, okay? They're just trying to protect you. Don't be so hard on them."

"Hard on *them*? What about them being hard on me? Do you think it's easy constantly trying to live up to their expectations? Do you think it's easy to follow in your footsteps? Between school and soccer and college and the shop—I don't even know what they want from me! I can't do it all! I'm not you!"

The shop falls quiet, and all that fills the space between us is the sound of my heavy breathing. There's a weight on my chest from having snapped, and if my parents were here, I'd probably get grounded for life, but I can't apologize for what I said. Hell, I can't even bring myself to storm out of the shop and up to my room. I just want to collapse right there on the shop floor, no matter how dirty it is, and cry myself into a coma.

Thomas stares straight at me a moment before sighing and saying, "Are you mad at *them* or me?"

And then I feel a tear slide down my face, and I quickly brush it away. The last thing I need is the humiliation of crying in front of my brother.

But of course, he's right. Perfect Thomas, always there with the solution.

I *am* mad at him. I *hate* him. No, I'm mad because I *can't* hate him.

Because even after he bailed on us and left me to carry the

weight of all our family problems, even after he left me to fill a role I have no idea how to fill, I'm mad because I can't even hate him for it. I just feel so useless knowing I can't fill the gap that he left. I can't do *shit*. All I can do is stand here in this shop, wishing my older brother would fix things like he always used to.

Thomas looks down at his feet as he says, "Mom's been stressed because she's been fighting with the family again. They want us to visit for New Year, but—"

The room falls silent again, and I'm afraid that even breathing the wrong way will cause some massive explosion.

Then Thomas says, "But A-ma says you have to stop being gay first."

And then tears are rushing down my face, and I'm trying to wipe them away as fast as I can, but fuck. *Fuck*. Like, I knew my family hated me. I knew they wanted nothing to do with me the moment I came out, but this is different. This is like a whole new level.

"What did Mom say?" I say, my voice cracking as I speak.

"What do you—"

"When A-ma said that. What did Mom say?"

And I kind of don't want to hear it, but I need to. I need to know if my mom said that she felt the same way, that she didn't want to be seen around her gay son. I need to know if she even called me her son at all anymore.

Thomas just shakes his head and says, "Obviously she defended you, asshole. Why do you think she's been so stressed?

She's been fighting the family on this for weeks now."

And I don't know why, but that just makes me cry harder.

Thomas steps around the counter, reaching out like he's gonna hug me or something, but we don't do that. I can't remember the last time anyone in my family hugged me. It's just not our style.

Finally, I say, "I'm sorry. I never meant to cause her trouble."

Thomas shakes his head again. "Relax, okay? It's not your fault. You know how the family is. They're just—well, they're assholes, but if you think Mom and Dad won't defend you no matter what, you're wrong, okay?" And after a moment, he adds, "And I will too."

I wipe the tears from my eyes, even though they still feel swollen and sore. But really, that's probably the single nicest thing Thomas has ever said to me, and part of me wants to run away in embarrassment, but the other part of me is just really fucking grateful that he said it.

And then something in me aches as I think about the fact that Gabi's never had that.

"Theo," Thomas says, placing a hand on my shoulder, "I'm sorry. About everything. I'm the oldest. I should've been here helping, and instead I left all of it on you, and I'm sorry."

I shrug, since I can't find the words to say how much I need to hear that.

Thomas smiles. "I should've made more of an effort to come around the shop. And, well, check in, in general. The truth is, I saw my chance to run away and do my own thing, and it was really freeing, but it was also really selfish. You're my brother, and I should be around if you need me."

I shake my head. "Like I'd ever need you."

But he clearly sees through that, because he just laughs as he turns and heads back to the counter. "You know, you've actually done a hell of a lot more good than you realize."

I raise an eyebrow. "Oh? How so?"

"Well, for one thing," he says, "your delivery operation helped the shop out a lot. Uncle Greg's still being an ass, but I overheard Mom saying we brought in way more than expected this past month. It was a really smart idea. I never would've thought of it."

And I wait for him to follow that up with some backhanded compliment about how I could've been doing so much more this whole time if I'd just tried harder, but he doesn't. He just looks back at me like he's actually impressed with me.

Then he says, "And I know it was hard for you to come out and deal with all the backlash, but to be honest, it actually gave me the courage to start questioning my own identity a bit."

My eyes shoot wide and I splutter as I say, "What?! You?!"

Thomas rolls his eyes. "Yeah, but keep it between us for now, okay? I'm still figuring things out, and you know how the family is."

And I can't even process the idea of my older brother telling me he only has the courage to do something because *I* did it first, but something in my chest feels warm, like maybe thinking I wasn't alone was less ridiculous than I thought.

"I—thank you," I say. "I mean, for telling me all that."

Thomas smiles. "You're welcome. But for real, this is our secret, okay?"

I roll my eyes. "I'm not gonna out you. What kind of asshole do you take me for?"

TWENTY-SEVEN
GABI

Tuesday evening, I get an email through the student portal telling me to report to the principal's office Wednesday morning before homeroom. It kinda sucks that they couldn't just explain everything in the email, but given that I'm the delinquent in this situation, I acknowledge it's not my place to push my luck.

When I get to her office fifteen minutes before homeroom, Mrs. Perkins just motions for me to sit and says, "We're waiting for someone."

True to her word, when Melissa gets to the principal's office to answer for my crimes—selling stuff on school property, misusing classroom space, and disrupting class under the guise of Homecoming businesses as evidenced by the FAQs on our website—she listens patiently to the accusations before deadass looking me straight in the eye and saying, "Gabi did that?! I can't believe it!"

But apparently the principal can believe it just fine, because she completely buys into Meli's performance about how it's such a great betrayal to have your best friend break school rules behind your back and whatever.

Mrs. Perkins turns to me and says, "Lady told us she entrusted the room to you for Homecoming purposes, and she had no idea you were violating school rules. So what do you have to say for yourself, Gabi?"

"I—I'm really sorry. I was desperate, and I just—I'm sorry."

And I expect her to tell me that she hears a thousand and one sob stories a day, and she's perfectly content with expelling me, but she just leans back in her seat and heaves a deep sigh. "Everyone's looking forward to the big game, and I don't want this to interfere with the festivities, so you'll serve a week of in-school suspension, starting next week. And, of course, your parents will be informed."

A bubble of dread surfaces in my mind as I think about having to justify my rule-breaking to my parents, but then I realize how mild that is compared to what could've happened. "I—wait, are you serious?"

She raises an eyebrow. "Do you have a problem with it?"

I shake my head rapidly. "No, no, that's fine. I'll serve my sentence."

"This better not happen again, you hear me?"

I nod. "I promise."

I get up and head for the door before she speaks again.

"And one more thing."

I pause, slowly turning back to face her.

"It looks like this was a pretty elaborate scheme. Did you really do it all on your own, or did you have help?"

And I swallow. "No, no help. It was just me."

She stares back at me for a moment, like she's not sure she believes me, before finally nodding and looking away.

Meli and I are dismissed with five minutes to get to homeroom, but the second we're out in the hallway, I no longer care about getting to class on time.

I know Meli told me this was exactly what would happen if I screwed up, and it's pretty clear that it was *my* fault for screwing up, but I'm still angry. Maybe not so much at Meli or Theo or Justin, but maybe more at my dad. Or maybe more at myself.

Either way, I stop Meli in the hallway, and she turns to me with a disgusted look that churns my stomach.

"What?" I say.

"Don't fuck with me, Gabi. I'm sick of your shit."

"*My* shit?" I snap. "You've been a really terrible friend lately. Even besides throwing me to the wolves just now—"

"*I've* been a crappy friend?" she says. "Please! You put the whole Homecoming Committee in jeopardy because of your selfish little stunt. And that's before we even get into what a shit friend you've been to me personally."

"What are you even talking about?"

"Oh, so you're just gonna stand there and pretend you weren't shit-talking me with Vivi?" she says. The words hit me like a slap across the face, and I don't know what my expression looks like, but it's obviously enough to convince her she's right. "Yeah, Meli's so uptight. Meli's ruining everything! At least I didn't put all our work at risk to go chase some guy."

"I wasn't chasing a guy," I say, the words blowing through my teeth, but it doesn't matter. She knows how low that comment was, and she did it on purpose. To hurt me.

She rolls her eyes. "Whatever. I have a lot of work to do after all the trouble you've caused."

I can't bring myself to say anything else as she turns and heads to homeroom.

Getting through the day is . . . hard. And not just because I have to spend most of it just trying to avoid Theo and Justin and Meli, and really, everyone on the Homecoming Committee, since I have to assume Meli already told them that I'm a traitor. It's just hard to focus on anything besides the pain in my chest, and the anger coursing through me.

And as the day stretches on and finally ends, and I slowly make my way back to the student parking lot, I finally settle on a truth I've been avoiding for as long as possible.

The person I'm angriest at is myself.

I slam the car door shut behind me, throwing my head flat against the steering wheel. I accidentally smack against the horn, a loud beep tearing through the parking lot and all eyes turning to me.

And God, I deserve it. I deserve to be put on display, to be called out for all the things I did wrong in my own selfishness.

I betrayed Meli's trust because I was scared of losing the shop. I hurt Theo because I was scared of my parents finding out I'm gay. I screwed up Justin's relationship because I was scared our sales would suffer if he was distracted by Clara.

I manage to keep from crying until I'm pulling up into the driveway. Then I let it all out, clutching my seat belt as tears race down my cheeks, knowing that I have to get through all these twisting emotions before I face my dad, because he'll never allow it.

Once the tears stop, I take a deep breath as I go through the motions. Unbuckle my seat belt. Breath. Turn off the car. Breath. Open the door. Breath.

Finally, my book bag is slung over my shoulder and my feet carry me to the front door.

My parents sit in the living room, which just reminds me once again that everything is wrong. They shouldn't both be home so early. Someone should be at the shop.

But the shop sells this weekend, so of course they don't care about that.

And just like that, I'm crying again.

I rush to wipe the tears away, but my parents stare back at me with wide eyes.

"Gabi?" my mom says, but my dad's eyes narrow as she stands up and walks over to me, taking my hands in hers. "What is it, mijo?"

I pull away from her, ready to race to my room and not look

back, but I can't bring myself to move. I want to run, but I can't. I don't think I'll be able to survive the weight of the guilt if I run again.

Finally, I suck in a breath and say, "Theo's not a bad guy."

My mom scrutinizes me for a moment before turning to my dad. I'm sure he told her about what happened, but I don't doubt he framed it as Theo being predatory or aggressive or some other terrible thing he associates with gay people.

But I kind of hate the way she turns to look at him, like this is purely his fault. Yeah, he was the one who completely pushed Theo away, but it's not like his homophobia began with the cruel words he threw at Theo. Hatred isn't just in the things a person says. It's in the way they stay silent when someone else spews hate, the way they nod along or entertain the ideas at all.

My dad may be the more vocal of the two, but it's not like I don't feel the same chill down my spine when I see how readily my mom agrees to his shit. And then there're the little things. The way she never defended my right to do ballet. The way she never told me it's okay to cry when my dad isn't around.

The way she still hasn't said anything about Theo.

She thinks that by letting my dad be the face of their joint disgust, she's somehow not responsible, but it almost hurts more this way, knowing that she hates me just as much as he does but doesn't even have the guts to acknowledge it.

Finally, my dad sighs and says, "He's gay, Gabi."

"So what?" I shout, and I don't think I've ever screamed

louder. My throat already feels raw from just those two words, but I can't stop. "So that's it? You thought he was perfect and now you just hate him? Because of who he's attracted to? Because you think it's somehow wrong or contagious to live differently than you do?"

"Gabi," my mom says, but I step back, putting as much distance between us as I can without leaving the room.

"You really hate gay people that much?" I say, tears pouring down my face. "After everything Theo has done for me, you'd really rather shove him away and treat him like crap than accept that he's gay?"

My parents are silent, and I know something's about to go down, since they haven't called me out for my language yet.

My dad crosses his arms and says, "You really want to associate with a boy like that? What do you think people will say?"

"I don't care!"

"¡Cállate! You don't know what you're saying," my dad snaps. "You know what they do to boys like that, Gabi? We're just trying to protect you. If you spend time with people like that, people are going to start thinking you're gay too. You want to go to college? You want a good job? The odds are already stacked against you, mijo. You're gonna close a lot of doors if you keep doing these things."

I shake my head. "You want me to deal with bigotry by being bigoted?" I say. "I don't care what people think about me. I care about—" I pause, sucking in a breath before I say too much. "Theo's my friend. How can you ask me to turn my

246

back on him to protect myself? Is that really the type of son you want to raise?"

My dad squeezes his eyes shut. I half expect him to stomp over to me and slap me across the face, not that he's ever done anything like that before, but I also can't remember ever seeing him this upset or ever talking back to him like this.

Finally, he sighs, looks at me, and says, "Gabi, I've seen boys like you beaten bloody just because somebody thought they might be gay. You know how many guys I knew in school who barely made it to graduation? Living like that—do you think I could ever ask that for you?"

"Papi—"

He waves his hand to cut me off. "I'm sorry about Theo, but he's not my son. It's not my job to protect him, and I can't stop him from getting hurt. I just want what's best for you."

"You thought Theo was good for me a week ago," I say.

He sighs again and says the last words I ever expected to hear out of his mouth: "You're right."

I stare back at him as a few thoughts seem to war across his face.

Then he says, "I'm sorry things turned out this way, Gabi. Standing by your friends is important, but your safety is important too."

And I don't know what to say, because that wasn't what I'd expected. All this time, I'd assumed my parents were disgusted by the idea of me being gay because they thought queerness was a sin on the world. I'd never considered that they might think the world was the problem.

And I know it doesn't make them less wrong. It doesn't change the ways they've hurt me or Theo. But sometimes people do terrible things when they're scared, and I can't pretend I don't understand that much.

The room falls into an awkward silence. Finally, my dad looks up at me and says, "I'll let you decide what you do."

My eyes shoot wide. "Wait, really?"

"I don't think it's safe for you to be around people like that, and I'd rather you weren't, but I guess there's only so much I can do to stop you."

My mom chimes in with, "Just be careful, okay, mijo? We don't want you to lose everything."

It's definitely not acceptance, but it's at least a step forward.

And I know I'm pushing my luck, but I say, "What about the shop?"

"Gabi—" my mom starts.

"It's doing better, right?" I say. "With Theo and me running deliveries? We made a lot. I know you said that the offer was too good to refuse, but we're already doing so much better, and if you just give us more time, I'm sure—"

My mom places a hand on my shoulder and I stop talking. There's a sadness in her eyes that feels overwhelming as she says, "Cariño, we're not keeping the shop. That was never an option."

"B-but you said we just weren't making enough—"

"Between school and everything going on—it's not worth

it, mijo. It takes a lot of time and energy to run the shop, and once I become a nurse, your papi's not gonna run it by himself."

"I can help!" I say. "I mean it. I can help."

My dad just shakes his head. "It's already been decided, Gabi. You asked us to keep it open until Homecoming, and we agreed because we wanted to give you some time to find closure. But that's all. We're going to sell."

Everything aches as I finally head back to my room, but even after I close the door, I'm too tired to cry, so I just lie on my bed, stare up at my ceiling, and hope for the pain to stop.

The only benefit of lying collapsed on my bed for an entire evening with nothing to do and no one to talk to is that it actually gives my brain time to think through next steps.

The first thing I need to do is talk to Vivi, so Thursday morning, I find her at her locker just before homeroom. She's got this deep frown on her face that melts away when she sees me, and I feel kind of bad that I'm here to start trouble, but I just say, "Why did you tell Meli what I said about her?"

She stares back at me for a second, like she's processing what I said, before wincing and closing her locker. "How'd you find out?"

"How would I *not* find out? Of course she gave me shit for it."

Vivi sighs and tucks a strand of brown hair behind her ear. "Okay, look, I know it sounds bad, but it wasn't like I just . . . went up to her and was like, 'Gabi thinks you're being a bitch.'

It just kind of . . . slipped out, I guess."

"You told her I called her a *bitch*? Why?"

"I told you it just slipped out!" She shakes her head, turning away from me for a second before turning back. "Okay, let's be real here. Meli's been a raging nightmare lately, not that she wasn't always kind of a nightmare. And then I snapped after she said—"

Vivi's complexion is only a little lighter than mine, but her face turns red as she says, "Well, never mind."

I raise an eyebrow. "What did she say?"

"I don't want to talk about it."

"Vivi!"

"All right!"

She looks around the hallway for a second before grabbing my wrist and pulling me toward the water fountain. It's tucked away from all the open classroom doors, like she thinks a couple extra feet will make all the difference to our privacy.

Finally, she drops her voice low and says, "I told Meli something over the summer, and she kind of threw it back in my face."

"What did you tell her?" I ask, keeping my voice low too.

"I told her that I kind of have a crush on this guy, and she told me to just get over it because it wasn't like he'd ever like me back," she says. "And I mean, even if he won't, it was still a really cruel thing to say, and I know she only said it because she wanted me to focus more on Homecoming, but who *does* that? So I guess I just wanted to hurt her too, you know? Make her feel bad for saying something so shitty."

"Okay? Why are you being so hush-hush about this? What's the big deal?"

And then she looks up at me with these wide eyes, and suddenly everything clicks.

"Wait, *me*?" I say, my voice still low but definitely panicked. "You have a crush on *me*?"

Vivi rolls her eyes. "Duh. I thought that was obvious. I mean, we get along great, and we have so much in common, and I guess the other day on your porch, it felt like we really connected, so that's all I could really think about during the meeting—"

But I can barely process anything she's saying. Hell, it feels like I'm underwater and she's shouting at me from the shoreline, but all I can hear is the flow of waves against my eardrums.

"I—I'm gay," I blurt out, and Vivi freezes, eyes wide as she stares back at me.

Finally, she shakes her head and sighs. "If you don't like me back, you can just say that. You don't have to make up some excuse about—"

"I'm not making up an excuse," I say, but it sounds like a bad joke. My parents have spent my whole life drilling into me that I need to do everything possible to make sure nobody reads me as gay, and now I'm here trying to convince my friend it's true because I was too good at it. "I'm really gay. Meli already knows. That's probably why she told you that."

"Oh," Vivi says, and the disappointment in her voice feels like a palpable thing.

The bell rings, and I turn to find the hallway has completely cleared out, but I can't bring myself to just leave Vivi standing there next to the water fountain. I was kind of mad at her since my fight with Meli, but standing here now, I just feel really bad for her.

We can't help who we like. I know that better than anyone.

But God, why did it have to be *me*?

Finally, I laugh awkwardly and say, "I've spent the past few years trying really hard to hide the fact that I was gay, but I kind of assumed I was doing a terrible job."

Vivi smiles sadly back at me and says, "I never would've guessed you were gay. You nailed the straight-passing thing."

And ordinarily, I think that would have felt like a relief, to know that nobody was onto me and I really was covertly gay, but now it stings. It makes my skin feel itchy and my stomach feel weighed down.

Maybe it's knowing how proudly Theo wears his gayness and wishing I could be like that too. Maybe it's what he said about all the good parts of being gay and some cruel, self-flagellating part of my brain feeling like I'm not entitled to those as long as I'm buried in the closet.

Or maybe it's just finally admitting to myself that being gay isn't a bad thing. It's not even a neutral thing. It's a *great* thing, something I deserve to be proud of the same way I'm proud to call myself Puerto Rican. It's just as much a part of me as my own culture, as my parents' shop, as dance and my friends, and every other thing I've come to associate with being Gabi.

I don't want to look straight. I don't want to hurt my girl friends by telling them I could never be interested in them. I don't want to pretend to hate dance or love soccer.

I just want to be happy in my own skin.

Vivi stares at me, and I realize that my lightbulb moment must be showing through on my face.

"Um, sorry," I say.

She raises an eyebrow. "Everything okay?"

But it's not. Not yet, anyway. There's still so much I have to make right, and so much I'm still uncertain about. And then there's the fact that we're both late to homeroom and I'm already on thin ice with administration as it is.

"Thank you for being honest with me," I say.

She laughs. "Seriously? You're the one who just came out to me. What I did was nothing."

"We don't really have to compare them, right?" I say, because I know it was hard for her, even if it didn't have the same impact as it did for me. That doesn't mean she has to act like opening up didn't mean anything.

"I guess so," she says. "And Gabi?"

I pause, an eyebrow raised.

"I—I know I promised to dance with you on the Homecoming float, but I think it's better I didn't," she says, her voice low.

She laughs before looking up at me. "You're into Theo, huh?"

My eyes shoot wide. "I—"

"I didn't see it before, but now I guess it seems kind of obvious. You two would be good together."

I shake my head, because I don't really know how else to process that thought. "I mean, yeah, I'm into Theo, but that doesn't mean you shouldn't be on the float."

"Well, it's that and . . ." Her voice drops again. "I think I need some space. From you. To get over my feelings, I mean."

"Oh."

And the reason she's pushing me away is nothing like the reason my parents were, but it stings just the same.

"I'm sorry," she says.

"I-it's fine. I get it," I say. I turn to leave, then pause. "Since you can't do the float, do you think you could help me out with something else instead? I'll give you the space you need, but there's something I need to do."

She smiles. "Sure."

And just like that, my plan moves on to stage two.

I get an email from Lady asking me to meet her after school, which is pretty much perfect, since I was hoping to talk to her anyway. She meets me outside the dance room, a stern look on her face, which seems completely out of place given her usual personality.

"Gabi, what the hell happened?" she says as I approach.

And I don't know what she was actually told, but I just laugh awkwardly and say, "I, um, was trying to help my parents' shop, but I guess I got carried away."

She stares back at me for a moment before sighing and shaking her head. "When you asked to use the classroom, I didn't

254

think you'd be getting into this much trouble."

"I'm sorry," I say. "Really. I know I betrayed everyone's trust."

"I'm not your parent," she says, "so I'm not gonna yell at you. I just hope you won't get into anything like that again. You could've gotten expelled."

I nod. "I know. Actually, I'm pretty sure the only reason they're giving me a pass at all is because of Homecoming, which I kind of wanted to talk to you about."

She raises an eyebrow but doesn't say anything else.

"I'm supposed to do a dance on the float, and long story short, I was supposed to be doing it with two friends, but it looks like I'll be going solo now."

"So what do you need?" she asks.

"To somehow figure out how to condense a three-character dance so I can do it myself."

Lady watches me warily for a moment before heaving a deep sigh. "Gabi, don't you think you've asked enough from me as it is?"

"I—" I pause, my face falling. "Yeah, I have. And I know you're right. I just don't really know what else to do. I agreed to do the dance for my friend because she's in charge of the Homecoming Committee, but the truth is . . . after this, I'm losing everything. My parents are closing our shop, and all my friends are over me, and I know I'm never really going to be able to dance again, so to just give up now . . . I want to make this last dance count, you know? I understand if you can't help, though. I can figure something else out."

The air is silent as I stand there staring down at my shoes. Looking at Lady feels too daunting, but I also feel bad that after everything, I'm here asking her to give me more of her time.

Finally, she crosses her arms and says, "The reason I agreed to teach you how to dance in the first place was because I could see how much it meant to you. There are plenty of people with skill out there, but there aren't a lot of people who show up as wide-eyed and passionate about dance as you did. People like you are the reason I wanted to start teaching."

I look up, my mouth slowly stretching into a smile as I meet Lady's eyes. "Does that mean you'll help?"

She nods. "Sure. *However*—"

And I freeze.

"—I know your passion is a huge part of who you are, Gabi, but there are some things you just can't control. They're officially hiring a new dance teacher next week, and that means I'll be leaving the school permanently. I need you to promise that you'll stay out of trouble and let things run their course, okay?"

My heart feels heavy, but I nod anyway. I know I've done enough meddling for one lifetime. When this is all over, I'll accept that I can't control everything, no matter how much it hurts me to say goodbye. I have to.

Lady spares me a soft smile and says, "Good. Oh, and one more thing. There are a lot of things you can't control, but dancing doesn't have to be one of them, okay? You can keep going, even without me. You've gotten pretty damn good at it."

And I nod again because I want to believe her, but I know

that's not going to happen. Dancing won't be the same without Lady, and even if it could be, even if I did have complete control over my dreams and future, I don't have any control over my parents, so that door closed a long time ago.

TWENTY-EIGHT
THEO

Wednesday after school, I get the all clear to get back into soccer, and while I hoped it'd make me all excited and competitive, I actually just feel tired. Even after all the time and energy I put into trying to help Gabi up his game, I know it won't be enough to change him. And with only a couple days left until the big game, I'm kind of just bouncing on my toes waiting for it to all be over.

Thursday, I head to practice and try to go with the flow, like the most important game of the season isn't the next day and I'm not expected to carry the weight of the whole team. Gabi doesn't even show up, so I guess that shows how invested he is in trying not to embarrass us.

Coach sets us up to scrimmage, and I know I should be feeling pretty confident, since Gabi's not around to trip me up, and everyone's probably realized by now just how vital to the team I really am. But really, I feel pretty out of it. Unpracticed, for sure, but also just out of my element. Justin meets my eyes from across the field, but then immediately turns away to stare at the side of the goal, and I guess that basically puts my feelings into action.

Practicing, winning, whatever the point was when I first hit the field at the beginning of the season—none of it really feels important anymore. I'm not here to impress anyone. Not my parents, who have other things to worry about, or colleges that I've already accepted I can't get into. And that joy that I felt while training Gabi is gone too. I can't even pretend I'm here to enjoy the game with my friends.

Even feeling pretty crappy, I'm still the best player on the field, and as I easily tear past the defensive line and score another point against my fake rivals, I'm not sure if it makes me feel better or worse.

Coach finally groans, blowing his whistle and calling us all in.

"It's okay," he says, but we all know it's not, and really, starting off the big speech like that just kind of makes it even more clear how screwed we are. "Look, tomorrow—well, don't get too worked up over it, alright? The point of Homecoming is to bring the school together, and everyone'll be hyped to be there, whether we win or lose."

"Still kind of wish we could win, though," Jeff grumbles, and the whole team joins in with low moans and aggravated sighs.

Coach dismisses us, and I hear someone say something

about "heading to that Fusion Café" as compensation for our shitty practice, but I just ignore it. It's funny how a month ago, that would've sent me into a rage, but now it just makes me feel kind of empty.

Who cares if they support the Fusion Café anyway? Once the Morenos go out of business, my parents will be down one rival, so things should mostly go back to the way they were before the Fusion Café opened at all.

And I hate how disappointed that makes me feel, and I hate how much I hate the thought of going back to the way things used to be.

I went through all this just to keep my parents from losing the shop, to keep them on their feet so they wouldn't fall apart when I left Vermont for college, but now that everything seems to be on track to turn out the way I wanted, I can't understand why I ever wanted that at all.

"Theo?"

I was so caught up in being mopey that I didn't even notice Justin coming up behind me until he's standing a couple feet to my right, awkwardly staring past me like he can't bear to actually look at my face.

"Uh," he says, "can we talk?"

The rest of the team has cleared off the field, and I catch sight of Coach a little ways away, lugging the water cooler back to the building. I don't really have any excuse to bail, but I guess I could make up something about needing to get home to help my parents or something.

But the truth is, the walk home has really sucked lately, and not just because I'd gotten comfortable having Gabi drive me. Things just aren't the same without Justin, and I really felt that running through practice today. I don't want to go into tomorrow's game feeling the same way.

I look at him, but I don't say anything. He glances up at me, and I guess he sees something on my face as a cue to start talking, because he says, "How's your wrist?"

I shrug. "Fine."

Then we're quiet again. Really, I guess the strangest part about my friendship with Justin is the fact that we get along at all, given neither of us can apologize to save our lives. We usually just end up shoving anything aside and pretending it never happened.

I glance down at the browning grass as I try to work up the energy to say . . . well, I'm not even sure what, but just something to make us feel less terrible.

Then Justin says, "Look, I'm really sorry about blowing up at you. And about everything, I guess."

I raise an eyebrow, but Justin's not looking at me. "You were right. I'm the one who's always making everything about me."

He shakes his head. "No, you weren't. I mean, it's not like you took over or anything. You just had a lot going on, and I guess I just never really have anything going on."

"You had Clara," I say, though I have noticed that they haven't been together the last couple of days. I don't think I'm really allowed to ask about that. "I'm sorry I didn't acknowledge that."

"It's not a big deal," he says. "Clara and I—well, you were right, I guess. I mean, I'm into her, but I'm not *that* into her. And I guess she's not really that into me, either. I just started feeling like I needed to get close to her because of you and Gabi."

My eyes shoot wide, my face feeling warm. "Me and *Gabi*? Why would—what does that have to do with you and Clara?"

Justin laughs. "Okay, don't get mad at me or anything, but it seems like you're really into him," he says. "I mean, I've never seen you get all weird around a guy like that before."

And I don't know what to say because obviously he's right, but I also can't tell him that Gabi's gay, and it's weird thinking that all this time, Justin was seeing the way we interacted and piecing together that we had something going on.

Because that means it wasn't just in my head. We really did have *something* going on.

But now we don't.

"Anyway," Justin says, "I'm sorry about making things awkward. I guess I just got a little jealous or worried you were gonna fall in love with Gabi and forget about me or something."

"I did fall in love with Gabi, but that doesn't mean I forgot about you."

And we both just kind of stand there in stunned silence for a moment, because I know neither of us really knows how to respond to that. It was actually pretty shitty of me to just throw it out into the world like that.

But it's true, and I know that's why my heart has felt so heavy all this time. And I also know it's why what his dad said

262

hurt so much. I eat homophobia for breakfast. It's whatever. My own family doesn't even want me around because I'm too gay, and I can deal with that. No big deal.

But I know how much Gabi cares about his family, and I know that he'll never feel comfortable being around me as long as they can't stomach the two of us being together.

And that means it doesn't matter how I feel about him or if he even feels the same way, because no matter what, his parents will never accept him as long as I'm in the picture.

The silence stretches out between us for too long before Justin finally says, "Did you tell him how you feel?"

I shake my head.

"He'd be a fool not to return your feelings," Justin says. "I mean, you're Theo fucking Mori."

And he says it like that should be something impressive, but it feels like the opposite. How could Gabi ever feel the same way about me when I'm Theo fucking Mori, the son of his parents' enemy, the kid who can barely pass a math class or get into college.

The guy Gabi's parents absolutely despise.

How could he ever fall in love with a guy like that?

Justin and I walk home together for the first time in a while, and it's pretty quiet, but it's kind of nice just knowing that he doesn't hate me.

Before we go our separate ways, he says, "Don't stress about the game tomorrow. It doesn't really matter."

I flash him a smile, but I think it comes out more like a grimace. It's kind of hard to work up the energy when I'm already this messed up.

When I get to the shop, there's an elderly couple on their way out and a woman in her midtwenties waiting for her drink at the counter. My dad catches sight of me as he reaches to grab her a straw and pass her the plastic cup.

"Oh, Theo," he says, waving me in like I'm a vampire who's never gonna enter without a proper invitation.

My mom's standing in the corner counting boxes of straws, but once the customer leaves, she pushes the stack of boxes away and turns toward me.

"Did something happen?" I ask, because anytime I get this much attention from them, it generally means I'm in trouble.

"Thomas said he talked to you the other day," my mom says.

"Oh."

I should've expected Thomas to rat me out, but considering he'd entrusted me with a secret of his own, I thought maybe we were on the same page. No such luck.

"So, am I in trouble or something?" I say.

My dad doesn't meet my eyes, but my mom sighs and steps around the counter. She leads me over to one of the tables and waits until I'm seated before saying, "About your a-ma," she starts.

I just shrug. "Whatever. It doesn't matter."

My mom stares back at me blankly until my dad cuts in, "Let her finish, Theo."

So I do.

My mom folds her hands together, which is weird because she never does that. Hell, she used to always tell me to stop fidgeting or squirming, so this is especially weird for her. Finally, she says, "I told her, and the rest of the family, that we won't be visiting for New Year. She said family should be together for it, but I told her we can't do that."

"Mom," I say, but she's staring down at the table, "if you want to go, you can go. I'm not gonna be mad if you, Dad, and Thomas want to. I know you miss them, and I'll be seventeen by February. It's not like I can't be home alone."

She finally looks up at me, but there are tears in her eyes, and my stomach lurches. I hate knowing that all this is because of me, that she's hurting because of me, because I couldn't be the son she deserves. And I hate that I want to cry too, but I can't. My throat hurts, but my eyes feel dry, like my body knows I don't deserve to cry when all this is my fault.

"Theo," she says, her voice cracking as she speaks, "your a-ma is right. Family should be together for New Year, which is why I could never just leave you behind."

I shake my head. "I'm sorry," I say, my voice low. "I—I'm sorry for causing you so much trouble. I'm sorry for pulling you away from your family. This is my fault, and I really won't be mad if you want to go. I understand."

Tears start pouring down my mom's face, and God, I've never felt so guilty. What kind of shitty-ass son am I that I did this to her?

But then she wipes them away and says, "Theo, enough. You're my son. Anyone who can't accept that isn't family. That's not how family works."

And I don't know what happened, but suddenly my eyes aren't dry anymore. Tears starts falling, and I rush to wipe them away with my sleeve, but I'm not fast enough.

I feel a hand on my shoulder and look up to find my dad standing over me, a smile on his face.

"Come now, Theo, you didn't think we'd choose your a-ma's bao over you, did you?"

I laugh, but my voice still cracks when I say, "It's good bao."

My mom reaches for my hand across the table, and it feels warm, comforting. She runs her thumb over the back of my hand. "Thomas told us you were blaming yourself, and I—" She pauses, takes in a deep breath, and then says words I didn't even know were in her vocabulary. "I'm so sorry, Theo. None of this is your fault. Not the store, not your a-ma, none of it, okay?"

My dad squeezes my shoulder and says, "And we're proud of you. I know we don't tell you that enough, but you've done so much to help this shop, and we're grateful for that. We're lucky to have such amazing boys. We know that."

My mom nods along, and I only realize I'm shaking as I see her squeeze my hand tighter to steady me.

No, I'm not just shaking. I'm sobbing, my whole body rocking with each ragged breath.

My dad rubs my back, but neither of them speak as I just

sit there in the middle of the shop sobbing like somebody just died.

Because I can't even put into words how good it feels to hear them say that. That they're proud of me. That they're lucky to have me.

That all this time, Gabi was right, and all the hatred I'd thought they'd felt toward me was just in my head.

Because they're proud to have me as a son. They're proud.

And they don't say that they love me, but I don't need them to. I can feel it in the way my dad holds my shoulder. I can see it in the tears in my mom's eyes.

All this time I was so afraid that they thought I was a disappointment, a failure. That they would do anything to get away and leave me behind.

But the only person trying to get away from me was myself.

And now, all that weight washes away, like a part of me has died, but it was the part that I never knew was dragging me down. Like some sort of leech, sucking away any hope or love or validation I received.

And now that it's gone, it's like I'm finally free.

Friday morning, I'm almost late for school, and it was all because I wasn't sure if I should bother bringing my outfit for the dance. After all, I'd promised Gabi I would do it with him, but since we're not talking, that kind of implies I wouldn't need it, right? But then if I don't bring it and he's relying on me . . .

So I leave late and skip going to my locker just so I can make it to homeroom in time. Classes are supposed to run normally until noon, when we all head out to the field for the Homecoming rally, but homeroom is buzzing with this energy, like no one can sit still with everything that's still set to happen today.

It's only after the bell rings signaling the start of homeroom and everyone's rushing to get back to their desks that it clicks that Gabi isn't here. I get a sudden surge of fear and guilt as I realize I actually have no idea what's going on in his life right now, and something terrible might have happened. After all, Gabi's not the type to show up late, and it's not like he'd skip school today with Homecoming.

And then that fear is followed by a surge of sadness as I remember that I'm not really in a place to ask him about those things anymore.

When the bell rings, and we all shuffle out of the classroom to head to first period, I finally head to my locker to grab my stuff. I'm halfway down the hallway when I freeze, my eyes landing on a small group of people surrounding my locker and lines of paper and text I can't make out from this distance.

My stomach drops as I think about what it might be. I'm not typically the type to get targeted by bullies, and today seems like a weird day for them to start, but crap, who else would deface my locker like that?

So I start walking again, my hands shaking at my sides as I speed up to get there as fast as possible.

The crowd steps away as I get close, mumbling in low voices

but at least having the decency to let me get to my own locker.

And then I freeze again. There's construction paper all over my locker with little designs of buns and boba tea. They trickle down to the locker below mine, which is full of paper cut-outs of coffee and pastelitos. But I'm sure the thing that has everyone staring is the little spread that rests just between the two lockers: a bun next to a cup of coffee, with hearts all around them and a little thought bubble that reads *I miss your buns*.

"Theo?"

I'm already laughing before I even turn around. Gabi's standing a few feet behind me, a single red rose in his hand and his face flushed.

I just smirk and say, "Is that supposed to be a gay joke, asshole?"

He winces and says, "I meant it literally, but I think everyone's reading more into it than I intended."

And I laugh harder, because that's such a ridiculously Gabi thing to do.

He stares down at the floor as he says, "I—I'm sorry. Really sorry. About everything. And I—well, if you can forgive me and you want to, I was wondering if maybe you'd go to the Homecoming dance with me?"

He's still staring down at his shoes as he awkwardly holds out the rose.

There are still all sorts of eyes on us throughout the hallway, but I box them out as I step closer to him, pushing his hand down. He looks up at me then, his eyes kind of sad.

I say, "You realize you basically just outed yourself to the whole school, right?"

"I—yeah, I know," he says. "I know it's kind of extra, but I just—I'm tired of being afraid. And I guess I'm tired of pretending to be something I'm not."

I smile. "Did you tell your parents?"

He shakes his head. "No, but I will. I haven't figured out exactly what to say, but I want them to know."

"Is it safe?"

He glances down at his feet for a second before looking up at me and nodding.

I take the rose from him, holding it up to my face. "Okay, well, you need to tell them before the dance. There's no way they aren't going to start piecing things together if they find out you went with your gay friend."

He nods, a small smile spreading across his face. "I will. I promise."

"Then I'll go to the dance with you," I say. "Just don't make it weird."

He laughs, and suddenly the hallway breaks out into applause and cheers, which I have to admit is a bit much even for me.

Gabi winces and says, "Sorry about all that."

"*You're* apologizing to *me*? I'm surprised you managed to survive the attention."

He smiles. "I don't care. I just care about you." Then he blinks, his eyes going wide. "Oh no, was that awkward?"

I smile back, placing a finger to his lips. "No, no, that was actually very smooth."

The bell rings, and it hits me that I still haven't actually gone to my locker. The hallway starts to clear out and Gabi says, "I have to get to class before I get called into the principal's office again."

"*Again?*" I say.

He laughs. "I'll explain later. I—are you still down to dance on the float?"

I nod.

"Okay, cool, I, um . . ." He turns, looking at the near-empty hallway. With a sigh, he turns back to me and says, "I'll text you the details. Also, I'll pull you out of class at eleven thirty, okay?"

I nod again, but he's already turning and sprinting down the hallway. If he can run like that during the game, maybe we'll actually stand a chance.

TWENTY-NINE
GABI

I can't believe I actually did it. I can't believe I somehow found the nerve to actually ask out Theo Mori.

I've still got a whole bunch of things to worry about regarding Homecoming and coming out to my parents and the game and the float and the dance. . . .

But God, I can barely feel my feet as I enter first period and only manage to escape a detention because the class is so chaotic anyway that nobody really notices I'm late.

Theo Mori.

Like holy crap.

I give myself another few minutes to freak out in my head before trying to shift my thoughts over to what happens next. Theo says he's still down to do the dance, which means I have to grab him from class and catch him up on the changes. Since nothing actually needs to change about his part, it shouldn't be too hard for him to follow, but I'm getting a little antsy about it anyway, especially since I'm also taking Vivi's part. Or maybe I'm just antsy about the performance in general and everything that comes after.

Breathe, Gabi. One thing at a time.

The float is just for the student body to kick off the pep rally, so it's not like my parents will be involved at all. I won't have to deal with them until after school.

So I just have to find a way to keep my cool until then.

I leave class at eleven to meet up with the rest of the Homecoming Committee. Meli has admin stuff to take care of, so she's mercifully not around as we get the float ready to head to the field. Just before eleven thirty, I go back to class to grab Theo. He gives me an apprehensive look as we walk down the hallway, a bag of clothes slung over his shoulder.

"You okay?" he says.

"Why wouldn't I be?"

"Because I know you, and you get nervous about everything."

I laugh, but yeah, my hands are shaking. "Are you not nervous?"

He shrugs. "I mean, worst-case scenario, we make fools of ourselves in front of a bunch of people who don't matter and everyone gets over it in a week, so not really, no."

And yeah, I envy his confidence a lot, and I think that's part of why I wanted him to here with me so badly. Everything feels a little less daunting with him by my side.

I slip my hand into his and am a little surprised that he lets me, just gently squeezing mine back as we head to the locker room to change.

"The music and everything will be the same for you. I'll basically just be taking over Vivi's part," I explain from inside one of the bathroom stalls. I feel almost guilty about it, but I still don't feel comfortable changing in front of anyone.

"That's fine," Theo says from the other side of the door.

"We can run through it really quick, since it's only a couple minutes long."

"That's fine."

I step out of the stall to find Theo dressed as planned—black pants and a red muscle tee to go along with the Alice in Wonderland theme. And it's such a simple look, which will really only be tied together when he puts on the heart and spade headband I made, but he looks so good in it that I'm kind of starstruck, and I realize I've spent so long trying not to admire guys that it's taking everything I have not to just stand and gape at him now.

Theo laughs and says, "Pick your jaw up off the floor. We have work to do."

I blink. "Oh, I—sorry."

He grabs my hand and gently pulls me forward. "Let's get this run-through over with so we can get to the fun stuff."

I smile and nod.

Ten minutes later, we head out to the field, waiting for the all clear before we climb up into the float. The actual parade won't start for another fifteen minutes, but we'll wait here so we're good to go the second they start leading us out.

Theo sits next to me, and I fiddle awkwardly with some loose strings at the edge of my shirt. My outfit is the opposite of Theo's—black top, red bottom—and I settled on hacking up an old T-shirt to get the right cut. I should've cleaned up all the loose strings at the edge, but it makes me feel a little badass to have them there, even now they're basically just a fidget toy.

To calm myself down, I run through the moves over and over again in my head. The truth is, when I first thought about how to go about it, I was focused on trying to make it good. That was why I asked for Lady's help at the end to keep me from overthinking it. Ultimately, we still kept the concept of the disjointed eeriness of the Wonderland theme with separate dances, but we reorganized it so I could do each part individually. Now, with Theo taking up his part again, we'll be able to do our parts separately and meet together at the end, a perfect metaphor for the way everything in Wonderland is so chaotically different but somehow still manages to meld together into one world.

But now I kind of wish I'd just had us jump in place. At least then I wouldn't have to worry about messing the whole thing up.

Theo takes my hand in his and squeezes it gently. "You'll be fine, okay?" he says. "This isn't soccer. You're actually good at this."

I roll my eyes. "I don't know about that."

275

"You love dancing. That passion'll come through, and everyone'll love it. Promise."

And I don't know if I really believe him, but he's so confident, it starts to rub off on me too.

We hear the first float jerk into motion and quickly skitter into our crouched positions. I count down from ten, my heart pounding in my chest.

The music starts up and the lights on our float turn on. I rise first, slowly turning to face the audience, blood pounding in my ears. I try to rearrange my face so my abject horror doesn't show through, but I can't tell if I'm doing a semi-decent job.

Instead, I focus on the beat, the thrum of the music and the colorful lights raining down on me. I can feel the beat in my muscles, in my hips and feet as I move. When Theo joins me, he becomes the centerpiece. I freeze like a paused scene at the corner of the float until my next cue brings me to life and I whip around him. We're two pieces of an old music box brought to life, the way things in Wonderland so often are.

Finally, I twirl into him, and he grabs my arm, pulling me close. And just like that we halt in our final pose, the two of us pressed together while our heads face away, two pieces clearly connected but opposed in every way.

I can just make out the distant rumble of applause from the crowd, and Theo laughs even though we're supposed to be frozen, like the music box has returned to rest once more.

"Did we actually just pull that off?" he says, voice low.

I smile. "You're the one who said it would be fine!"

"I lied."

I blink as his words hit me. Maybe it should be disappointing that he had no faith in us either, but even if his confidence was a ruse, I can't deny that it's the one thing that kept me on my feet.

The float finally stops moving as we reach the end of the field, and we're able to jump off it.

"You wanna join the pep rally?" Theo asks.

I nod. "Can we change first?"

He smiles. "Yes, please."

"Gabi!"

We turn in unison as Meli comes up to us, a serious look on her face.

Theo winces and says, "I'll let you talk. I'm gonna go change."

And I kind of want to tell him not to go, but I knew I'd have to face Meli eventually, so I just nod and watch him go, feeling a little sad.

"You two seem to really be getting along," Meli says.

I turn back to her, but my throat feels dry. I mean, I'm not really sure whether she stopped me because she wants to talk or just yell at me some more, and I've got so much running through my head right now, I doubt I can handle the second.

She stares back at me for a moment before heaving a sigh and saying, "Gabi—"

"I'm sorry, Meli," I say.

She waves me off with an eye roll. "Stop, okay? I didn't come here to yell at you. I—well, I came to explain what happened with Vivi."

"You talked to her?" I say.

She shrugs. "She said she was worried about you, which made me kind of worried too. Look, I only told her that you weren't interested because she was all heart eyes over you, and it seems pretty unfair, since you're obviously never gonna like her back. I didn't think she'd be all vindictive about it, and I didn't think it'd pressure you to come out."

"It didn't," I say. "I mean, I didn't tell her because I was pressured to. I told her because I wanted to."

Meli blinks back at me like she barely recognizes me, and I guess that makes sense, since I barely recognize me either.

"Meli," I say, "I'm sorry about abusing the badges. And I'm sorry about putting my needs ahead of everything else, especially when Homecoming meant so much to you."

"You know it doesn't," she says, shaking her head. "I just—I got caught up in it and was stressed out, and I'm sorry I took it all out on you. I should've been helping you with your parents' shop, not giving you shit for being into Theo Mori. Are you guys like . . . a thing now?"

"I—I guess I don't really know," I say, pushing down the part of me that's thinking how much it really, really hopes we are. "We're going to the Homecoming dance together, but we haven't really talked about anything else."

Meli laughs. "God, you're so into him."

My face feels warm as I say, "Yeah, I kind of am."

"Well, I'm happy for you," she says. "I'm sorry for not being more supportive. I should've been here for you, but I was too caught up in my own shit. It won't happen again, I promise. I'm always on your team."

And knowing Meli, she'll probably get caught up in something else down the road even if she says she won't, but if our friendship can get past everything that's happened over the past month, I feel pretty confident we can get through whatever comes next.

The field blurs past me in a sea of green, the uniforms of our rivals nearly identical to the grass beneath my feet. I don't know how many seconds are left in the game, but it's not many. We're down 3–1 with no real chance of recovery, but the team is still racing onward, so I'm doing my best to keep up.

The thing is, we knew we were screwed about thirty seconds into the game, when the enemy put all their defense into stopping Theo. If we had another competent player, that would've been a death sentence for them, but as it stands, Theo's only been able to score one point, and that's the most we could have really hoped for.

I come to a stop, taking a quick look around. The game's as good as over. The defense has Theo's path to the goal completely blocked off, and there's no way he's going to get past them.

Then I glance at the goal, watching as the goalie moves to the far left of the goal to be ready if Theo tries to shoot.

And then it occurs to me.

I'm completely open.

And so is the goal.

"Theo!" I shout before I can remember that I don't actually play sports, and this can't end well for me.

Theo glances over and does some quick calculation before locking eyes with me and kicking the ball. It soars in my direction, landing just a couple feet away. It takes the defense a moment to acknowledge where the ball even went. The goalie still hasn't noticed me.

There's no time to hesitate.

I take a deep breath . . .

. . . and I charge.

The toe of my cleat smacks right into it, the ball shooting forward like a bullet.

And straight into the net.

A dull roar pounds through my ears as the team surrounds me, everyone screaming and pounding my back or punching my arm. I can just make out one of our opponents saying, "I don't get it. They still lost, didn't they?" But I don't care.

Then Theo's there, and he's squeezing me so tightly I can barely breathe.

"You hit the ball!" he screams.

And somehow that sounds like the highest praise I've ever heard.

The team chants my name as they hoist me up and carry me back to the sidelines, where Coach waits for us with tears in his eyes.

"I've never been more proud to be your coach," he says as we get back, and the team cheers.

Once I'm back on solid ground, Theo steps up next to me and bumps his shoulder into mine.

Coach gives us the usual closing speech, where he tells us to keep our heads held high, though this time he actually sounds like he means it for once, and then we all line up to congratulate the other team before we head out.

Once we clear the line and head back to our side of the field, I step up next to Theo again, but he's looking past me, eyes wide.

I turn and catch sight of my parents walking over to us, and I instinctively take a step away from Theo. It's ridiculous because I need to be honest with them soon, but God, there's no way I can do it here.

"You were amazing, mijo!" my mom says, kissing me on the cheek.

I smile a little self-consciously. Theo shuffles awkwardly beside me, and I'm torn between telling him he can skip out if he doesn't want to be there, and just telling my parents to leave him alone.

Then my dad sighs and says, "Theo?"

Theo's back goes rigid like he's bracing to be slapped.

But my dad just says, "Thank you for coaching Gabi. He's gotten a lot better with your help."

"Papi," I say, and he gives me a look before shaking his head.

"And I'm sorry about the other day," my dad says. "You're

obviously a good friend to Gabi, and we're happy he has you."

Theo looks super uncomfortable, but he nods and says, "Thank you" anyway.

Jeff comes barreling over to us and says, "Gabi, Theo, you guys coming to celebrate with us or what?"

Theo rolls his eyes. "Celebrate what? We still lost."

I smile, glancing from my parents back to where the team gathers a few yards away. Then I look to Theo, who's looking back at me, and say, "I, um, actually have something I need to take care of. You know, for the thing tomorrow."

He gives me a knowing look before wincing and saying, "Text me later?"

I nod.

Theo heads back with Jeff, and I turn to my parents, letting them know I'm ready to head home.

Then I suck in a deep breath and attempt to prepare myself for what I know comes next.

I have the car ride home to myself, since my parents had to drive to campus separately. The greenery rushes by as I dive deep into suburbia and turn onto our street. My head was mostly clear on the drive back, but now that I'm pulling into the driveway, my heart pounds in my chest as the reality of the moment settles in around me.

This is it.

When I clear the front door, I find my parents in the kitchen, music playing as they pop a pan of I'm not sure what into the oven.

"What are you doing?" I ask.

My mom looks up and smiles. "We wanted to have something ready for you when you got back, to celebrate. Just give the rum cake some time to bake."

It's a sweet gesture, but considering we lost the game and we're about to lose the shop and I'm about to lose their respect . . . well, I guess it doesn't mean a whole lot.

"I need to talk to you guys," I say.

My dad reaches for his phone, turning the music down. "What is it, Gabi?" he says.

I sigh, but I know the longer I drag this out, the harder it's going to be. I squeeze my hands into fists and say, "I'm gay."

Cold creeps over me, and it feels like all the air in the room has gone instantly stale. Even the soft beat of Celia Cruz in the background just sounds hollow and tinny to my ears.

The awkward emptiness stretches over us for too long before my dad finally says, "Gabi," in the most exhausted tone I've ever heard.

And then the words rush out of me. "I know what you're going to say, but this isn't about Theo, okay? He didn't turn me gay. And I'm not just saying that because he's gay or because anything else. I've known for a long time, but I never knew how to tell you, and I'm sorry, but I—"

"Gabi," my mom says, and her voice sounds gentler than my dad's, so I let my eyes fly to her. That was a mistake, of course, because she looks sadder than I've ever seen her.

My dad shakes his head and says, "We knew something was up with the way you reacted about Theo."

And it's basically my worst nightmare come to life, even if it doesn't hold that weight anymore. Everything still feels hollow, though.

"Gabi," my dad says again, his voice low, "we're going to need some time to think about this."

And I want to scream, *What is there to think about?* Because what *is* there to think about? It took them no time at all to decide they wanted to sell their life's work, but deciding whether they can accept their own son is going to take time?

But I don't scream anything. I came here expecting them to yell and scream and throw things. I expected them to say that I wasn't their son, that I was just some freak who'd taken his place and done nothing but broken their heart.

So I guess this is better. Good, even.

Even if it feels like my heart has been ripped right out of my chest.

THIRTY
THEO

After the big game, we all head out for maple creemees, which is kind of a relief because I was worried they'd want to go to the Fusion Café. Everyone's cheering like we just won the lottery, even though we didn't even win the game, but it's fine, and the cold of the ice cream helps keep me in the moment.

Because if I let my mind stray, all I'm going to be able to think about is Gabi.

"You good?" Justin asks, sitting down next to me on the wooden bench.

We ended up at a little local shop full of a trillion different maple syrups and other maple snacks. Now we're out back, where they have a bunch of picnic benches and a wooden swing bench turned toward the mountains. It's one of those cutesy, romantic places I'd never have taken any real interest in before, but now I'm thinking about whether I should bring Gabi back here.

You know, if his parents don't kill him first.

"Am I that obvious?" I say.

Justin laughs, deep-throating his ice cream cone. Then he says, "It's a shame Gabi couldn't come, considering he was basically the star of the game."

"He has to deal with his parents," I say, and I guess there's something in my tone, because Justin winces.

"Sorry for being a dick to him," Justin says. "I mean about the homophobia thing. I didn't realize he was gay."

I laugh. "Yeah, I guess I didn't either. Funny how compulsory heterosexuality works."

"The way those words just flew out of your mouth, but you failed our last English exam," Justin chokes.

"I know relevant words! I don't care about soft butts and breaking windows, okay?"

Justin rolls his eyes. "*Romeo and Juliet* is all about young love and crossing enemy lines. That should be *particularly* relevant to you right now, huh?"

But I'm gonna pass on that one. I may not have followed like 90 percent of the play, but I do remember the ending, so if we're Rome-Theo and Gabliet, I should be even more worried about Gabi than I thought.

Like he's reading my thoughts, Justin goes, "I mean, not that that shit would happen to you guys. I'm sure it's fine."

I roll my eyes.

My phone vibrates, and I slip it out to find a text from Gabi saying, **Can you talk?**

I quickly type back, I'm out with the team, but I can head home now. Are you okay?

I'm fine! No worries! Have fun with the guys. We can talk later :)

But besides the way that smiley faces always feel beyond passive-aggressive to me, something about his message just isn't sitting right with me.

I turn to Justin and say, "I'm gonna head home. If anyone asks, tell them my parents called."

"When the strict Asian parents stereotype actually pays off," Justin says.

I just roll my eyes again.

I catch a rideshare back home so I don't have to waste time walking. My mom's the only one there when I enter, and she just smiles at me and says, "You did good today."

I pause, an eyebrow raised. "In what?"

"Your game," she says. "You and your friend did good. We were impressed."

"Wait, you saw the game?" I say, mouth gaping.

She nods. "Of course we saw your game, Theo."

"Who are you, and what have you done with my mom?"

Her eyes narrow. "Theo, show some respect. We taught you better than that."

I smile. "Okay, closer."

She shakes her head as my humor is completely lost on her, which is just par for the course, I guess. "You have some time to help with an order?"

"I—I can't," I say. She looks up at me, and I just sigh. "I'm sorry, I just have to check on Gabi."

She stares back at me for a moment like she's going to lecture me about putting somebody else before our family, but she just shakes her head again and says, "You have more scheming to do?"

"I—what?"

"You think we wouldn't find out about your selling at school?"

I freeze for a moment as the realization washes over me. I pause, my body half turned toward the hallway, then slowly turn back to face my mom. "I—I can explain."

She raises an eyebrow in that always judgmental way only parents really can.

"Look, I'm sorry," I say. "I mean, about lying and stuff. I'm not really sorry about the sales, because they helped, right? I mean, Uncle Greg obviously noticed the difference, even if he's still a dick about it."

"Theo!"

"Sorry!" I say, rushing to cover my tracks. "I just—Gabi and I were just worried about the shops is all. And I guess it doesn't really matter anymore, since Gabi's parents are going to sell anyway, but we were just trying to help."

"And you did help," Mom says, which completely catches me off guard until she follows it up with, "But you better not lie to us again. And you can't just give our secret recipes away to the enemy!"

288

"I'm sorry," I say again, though it's pretty much empty at this point.

Finally, she nods, turning away. "Go check on your friend."

I race up to my room, pulling out my phone and hitting the FaceTime button before I've even thrown myself back against my bed. A couple seconds later, Gabi answers. He's sitting in his room on the floor, legs crossed, eyes red.

"Theo?" he says. "I thought you said you were out."

"I was. Now I'm not. What happened?" I say.

Gabi sighs, wiping the back of his hand across his face. "I came out to my parents. It was—well, I guess it could've been worse, but it wasn't great. It's not like they were super supportive or anything."

I hate how sad he looks, and I hate knowing it was his parents who did that to him. It's just so completely unfair.

But more than anything, I hate that we're talking through phone screens, and I can't just reach out and hug him and make him feel better.

"I'm really sorry, Gabi," I say, but it feels hollow. Like what good do words like that even do?

But he just smiles and says, "Thanks. To be honest, I'm kind of relieved. I mean, they didn't take it super well, but it's not like they disowned me or anything. And at least this means we can go to the dance together tomorrow, right?"

And I hate the way his voice cracks on that last word, like he's worried I'm going to change my mind and tell him to go take a hike.

"Of course," I say, maybe a little too forcefully, but his smile looks a little less sad than it did a moment before. "You know, I still don't know what to wear. I mean, I wasn't really planning on going, so . . ."

"Oh," he says. "Do you not want to go?"

"No, asshole," I snap. "I mean, I want to go. I'm just saying you should help me pick something to wear."

"Oh! Sure, I'd love to."

And it's a simple thing, and I don't know how much time it'll really occupy, but hopefully it'll distract him long enough that he can forget about his parents, at least for a while.

THIRTY-ONE
GABI

Saturday, I manage to avoid my parents all morning and spend the afternoon getting ready for the dance. I know it's the last real day I can spend at the shop, since they'll be selling Sunday morning, but I can't bring myself to face them, not after everything that's happened.

It's just after six thirty when I drive to Theo's. We spent the night before coordinating our outfits as well as we could with what was already in our closets, and we basically settled on white button-downs and black slacks since that was all we had. Still, I have to admit the distraction helped more than I thought it would, and even avoiding my parents all morning hasn't felt so bad knowing that I get to see Theo now.

I walk up to the shop to find that there's a closed sign on the window, which is odd since the Moris usually don't close till nine on weekends. The door's unlocked, though, so I push it open and step inside to find Theo's mom behind the counter. She flashes me a huge smile and says, "Oh, Gabi, you look so nice!"

Heat rises in my face as I stammer back a quick, "Th-thank you."

"Theo's almost ready," she says. "Just give him a minute."

I nod. She places a box of pastries on the counter and pushes them toward me. "For your parents."

I smile, though I know I won't actually be giving them to my parents. Maybe Theo and I can eat them in the car on the way back.

Finally, I hear footsteps and turn to find Theo emerging from the hallway, his dad right behind him. And while we'd coordinated our outfits together the night before, I'm surprised to find Theo in a dark suit jacket now, a dark blue tie around his neck.

I only realize I'm gawking when Theo rolls his eyes and says, "Stop staring, asshole."

"I—um, sorry."

"*Theo*," his dad says, but he's smiling too broadly to feel like he really means it. And then I notice he's holding something, which he quickly holds out to me. A suit jacket. "Theo said you two didn't have any. I think this will fit you."

I stare back at him for a moment before my polite nature takes over. "Thank you, Mr. Mori, but I don't want to take your—"

"Nonsense," he says, pushing it toward me again. "We need you two to look your best so June and I can take pictures. Put it on."

So I agree, casually slipping it over my shoulders and buttoning it at the front. It's a little loose, but it doesn't look too bad.

"Let me help you with the tie," Theo's dad says, holding out a light blue tie to me.

I nod because I don't know how else to respond. He wraps the tie around my neck, quickly going through the loops like clockwork, and before I know it, he's stepping back to admire his handiwork.

And I feel a tear on my cheek that I quickly brush away.

Theo's next to me now, his voice low as he says, "You okay?"

I just nod because I know if I try to say anything else, I'm going to start crying harder.

"Okay, let's get some pictures!" Theo's mom says, coming around the counter with her phone in hand. God, I hope my eyes aren't red.

Theo slides his hand into mine and flashes me a smile. "Just humor them, okay? They'll never let us leave otherwise."

I nod and smile, but the truth is, I'm glad somebody cares enough to get pictures of us tonight. Even if it's not my own parents here seeing us off, I'm glad somebody cares.

Theo slings his arm around my waist, and we smile awkwardly as his parents snap I don't even know how many pictures. Finally, they wave us off and his dad says, "Have fun! Be home by eleven."

Theo grabs my wrist, pulling me out of the shop the second we're permitted to leave.

We climb into my car, and he laughs as he leans back against the seat. "I'm sorry for all the chaos," he says, reaching for his seat belt. "They're just like that sometimes."

I don't realize I'm crying again until I feel the tears and wipe them away, but Theo's already noticed. He reaches across the center console and takes my hand, a look of concern in his eyes, and it's weird to think that that worry is for me.

"What is it? Are you okay?" Theo says.

I nod, but it's hard to be convincing when I'm still crying. I start the car, but I don't pull away from the curb. Finally, with a deep breath, I say, "I'm sorry. It's just—I guess it was kind of nice."

"Being bombarded by my parents?" he says with a smile.

I nod again. "I guess I always knew I'd never get that, you know? The way they do it in movies where you meet your date, and the parents swarm for pictures and everyone's talking about needing to share those pictures with your grandkids and stuff? I always knew my parents would never want anything to do with that. So I guess it feels nice knowing that your parents do. I know they're not my parents, but—"

Theo presses a finger to my lips and flashes me a smile, but something in his eyes looks kind of sad, and now I feel bad for doing that to him. "It's okay," he says. "I get it. I mean, to be honest, I'm a little surprised my parents are going so hard too. They never really showed a lot of interest in my love life before, but I guess they're trying to be more supportive now since things with my grandmother have been . . . well, not good."

"I'm sorry," I say.

He shakes his head. "Don't be. I just mean maybe your parents will come around eventually. And even if they don't, it's not like you have to be miserable. There are a lot of people who love you and want to see you happy, okay?"

And, God, I can't even begin to explain how much those words mean to me. I don't know how Theo manages to always find the perfect thing to say, but I quickly swipe the tears away from my face and say, "We should go. I've been looking forward to this dance."

He smiles. "Me too."

The hall the school rented for the dance is a bit farther than campus, but the trip is kind of nice. When we hit the dance hall, I wait for everyone's eyes to turn to us in stunned silence, a continuation of the applause from yesterday intermingled with complete shock that not only is there another gay kid at school, but now the two enemy gay kids are dating and the world is about to implode.

But nobody in the large Wonderland-themed room so much as glances our way as we enter, the speakers pumping out music and chaperones hovering around, making sure nobody's doing anything too mature.

"Ah, school dances," Theo says, running a hand through his hair. "Good in theory, so, so awkward in practice."

I smile. "Do you want to leave?"

"No," he says, turning to me and taking my hand. "We should hang out for a while. I'll go ask Justin what they're planning in terms of an 'after-party.'"

Theo drags me through the room, and I half stumble after him. We're all washed in red lighting, and the crowd is dense enough that I know I'll lose track of him entirely if I let go.

Justin's in the corner with a couple of the guys from the soccer team, and I'm a little surprised Clara is nowhere to be found, but I guess their last breakup was for good.

"The couple of the hour finally makes their appearance," Justin says, and Theo shoves him.

"Shut up," Theo says. "You're lucky I came at all. You know how much I hate these things."

"You can stop playing cool, Theo," Justin says. "Everyone knows you're as corny as the rest."

Theo shoves Justin again, and he just laughs, but then I blurt out, "Justin, I'm sorry," and the humor dies.

Justin turns to me with an eyebrow raised, but I don't know what to say. I'm not sure why I opened my mouth at all when everyone seemed perfectly content to just ignore my existence a moment before.

Justin steps over to me, slinging an arm around my shoulder and casually walking me a few feet away from the crowd. He turns me toward him, pulling away and saying, "What are you on about?"

I sigh and say, "I'm sorry about meddling in your relationship. I—I should've minded my own business. I'm sorry."

"Don't worry about it," he says, flashing me a smile. "We're cool."

"Wait, really?"

"Yeah, of course." He takes a step closer to me, squeezing my shoulder and dropping his voice just low enough that I can hear him, but I doubt anyone else can. "But listen, if you ever hurt Theo like that again, you won't live long enough to regret it. Got it?"

I nod stiffly.

He smiles, letting go of my shoulder. "Then no hard feelings."

Theo sidles up next to me, shooting Justin a glare. "Whatever he said, just ignore it," he says.

Justin rolls his eyes. "I'm just airing all your dirty laundry, Mori."

Theo turns to me and says, "You wanna dance?"

I nod, and Theo leads me over to the dance floor. Even after our performance on the float, it feels weird to dance in public with all these eyes on me. I wonder if it's something I'll ever grow out of.

Theo says, "Justin didn't say anything weird to you, did he? I swear I have to leash him or something."

I just smile and shake my head. "He's just being protective of you. I get it."

Theo looks vaguely mortified, but considering how bad he is at realizing how much people care about him, I guess that shouldn't be a surprise.

When Theo finally recovers, he leans in closer to me and says, "Hey, I just wanted to tell you that I'm proud of you. I mean, for coming out to your parents. I know it must have been hard."

"I never would've done it without you," I say, and Theo's eyes widen.

"I didn't mean to pressure you at all—"

"No, you didn't. I just meant—well, there was something you said to me a while back about the good parts of being gay. I never realized there *were* good parts. I thought it was all running and hiding. I never would've realized how much happiness there is in it if not for you."

Then Theo's got his hands on my face, and our lips are pressed together, and I feel like my whole face is on fire.

He's holding me so gently, and my arms circle his waist, and I feel like my whole body is melting into him, like I'm being completely carried away.

And it's only for a moment before Theo's pulling away, and I see Justin standing there saying something about getting food or something, but all I can think about is the feeling of Theo's skin against mine.

Theo turns back to me, slipping his hand into mine, and says, "Do you wanna go grab food with the guys?"

And it's such a casual request that shouldn't really mean a whole lot, but it feels like Theo's welcoming me into his world, a world that I thought I'd never stand a chance in. A world I'd been so convinced wanted nothing to do with me.

But it feels like I've never belonged anywhere more than I belong right here.

❧❧❧

We pile into three cars, stop to grab some burgers, and head to campus, but the whole thing is locked down, so we end up staying in the parking lot. It's like the world's worst picnic as we pull out any blankets we can find thrown in our trunks and behind our seats and toss them over the car hoods we turned inward toward each other. Jeff turns on his car radio, and it's like we've got our own little party filled with cheap food and cheaper jokes.

Theo and I go back and forth passing a shake between us, but before I know it, I've got a line of ice cream trailing down my wrist. Theo leans forward, his tongue swiping it up as my face warms.

"What—"

But he just smirks at me and says, "I mean, it wasn't gonna lick itself."

And my brain struggles to piece together how we went from that day in his kitchen when I couldn't even function for fear of being outed to this easy understanding between us. I don't know how he went from being Theo Mori, the son of my parents' rival to just Theo, my best friend, the one person I know I never have to second-guess myself around.

"You're amazing," I say, and his eyes widen slightly like I've completely caught him off guard.

"Yeah, okay," he says.

And I just laugh because I know I can't just convince him to unlearn every bad thought he has about himself in a night, but we've got all the time in the world.

❧❧❧

Before I know it, I'm dozing off on Theo's shoulder, only getting woken up twenty minutes to eleven as he tells me we have to go before we both get beat.

Once Theo's safely dropped off at home, I drive back to my house, quietly creep up the stairs, and slip into bed still in my dress shirt.

The next morning, a loud pounding on my door wakes me up just before my dad throws it open, shouting, "Gabi, get up!"

I jerk back, falling out of bed and smacking into the floor.

My dad stares down at me with a stern look on his face. "Ay, Gabi, you're not hungover, are you?" he says.

I shake my head, wiping my eyes. "No, we didn't drink," I assure him. "I'm just sleepy. What time is it?"

"Just after seven."

I groan.

"Vamos, Gabi, we have important things to do."

I groan. "You can sell the shop without me. I don't need to be there."

"We're not selling the shop. At least, not yet."

My eyes shoot wide. "Wait, what?"

My dad waves me off. "Get up, get dressed. We have something to show you."

And I'm not sure how I feel about the tone of his voice, but I oblige anyway, quickly changing into fresh clothes and getting a brush through my hair before rushing downstairs. My parents wait by the door like they're barely managing to wait for me.

"What's going on?" I say.

"We'll explain in the car," my mom says, ushering me out the door.

The car ride begins in silence, but I easily recognize the route back to the shop. I lean back in my seat, waiting for my parents to explain, but when they don't say anything, I say, "So?"

My dad sighs. "We know how important the shop is to you."

But that's all he says.

My mom turns back to look at me and says, "Gabi, we thought selling the shop would be the best because it's a lot to take care of, and we could use the extra money, but seeing how hard you and Theo worked to keep it alive . . . You really meant it when you said you wanted to take over someday, huh, mijo?"

"Of course I did," I say.

The car comes to a stop, and I look out the window, expecting to be parked in front of the shop.

But we're not.

We're parked in front of the Moris'.

"What's going on?" I say.

My parents get out of the car, and I scramble to follow them, trying to keep up as they head into the Moris' shop, which currently sits closed.

Theo waits in the corner of the shop, lounging lazily at one of the tables, his parents standing nearby. I catch his eye, and he shoots me a sly grin like he's got some information that I don't.

"Did you tell him?" my dad says, and I'm not sure who he's talking to until Theo's mom nods.

"What is going on?" I repeat.

"Gabi," my mom says, "we thought we could get more money from selling the shop than keeping it open, but seeing how successful you and Theo were, we realized that may not be true. Considering how hard you two worked, it seemed like a waste not to even give it a shot."

"Give *what* a shot?" I repeat, my heart thudding in my chest.

My dad sighs. "A joint venture."

Theo's dad laughs. "We spoke last night while you boys were out. There was obviously some magic in the way you two ran things, but we think we can do just as well if we combine our shops."

I stare back blankly. "Wait, you're serious?"

My mom nods. "With the Moris' help, it'll save us a lot of time, and I can still get my degree. And the Moris have struggled with their landlord some, but we already own our space, so it only makes sense for them to come work with us."

Theo leans forward in his seat, flashing me a smirk. "I don't know how they're gonna make this work, considering all they do is shit on each other."

"Theo!" his mom snaps.

His dad shakes his head. "We may have had some respectful differences, but I don't see why we can't work past that now."

Theo rolls his eyes. "Yeah, mm-hmm."

Theo's mom slaps his shoulder.

But all I can think about is the fact that this means the shop isn't over. It's staying open.

It'll be different, but it'll still be ours.

No, more than that, it'll be like working with Theo forever.

That *Beauty and the Beast* style daydream of us dancing through the kitchen together pops into my head again, and I quickly force it away. Yeah, our relationship will probably never be at quite that level, but I'm still happier than I can put into words.

"There's still stuff to work out," my mom says, "and it'll be a test to make sure we can make it work, but we wanted you two to know. And we wanted to thank you for everything you did to help."

Theo's mom nods. "Yes, but don't lie to us again or you're grounded, got it?"

Theo and I exchange smiles, even though what I really want to do is kiss him. But it's fine. We'll have more than enough time to do that in the future.

So we just say, "Got it."

We stay a little longer to talk out some shop logistics and get another box full of pastries from Theo's parents before heading out. On the drive home, my dad reaches up and adjusts the radio volume down to near silence and says, "Gabi?"

And I don't know what to do at that moment except clutch my seat belt as I say, "Hmm?" and wait.

After the good news of the day, I knew I should probably be braced for something terrible to balance it all out, but God, did it have to be trapped in the car on the way home?

My dad sighs and says, "How was the dance?"

I stare down at my shoes. "Fine."

"Did you get any pictures?"

I nod before I remember that he's driving and can't actually see me. "Yeah, we did."

"Send them to me?"

I look up slowly, but of course, he's still eyeing the road. I know I shouldn't push my luck, but when I open my mouth to say okay, all that comes out is "Why? Why do you care?"

The car falls silent again, and I consider opening the door and rolling out into open traffic.

Then my dad speaks again, his voice low as he says, "Lo siento, Gabi."

"For?"

He shakes his head for a moment, then says, "For not supporting you. I—the last thing I ever wanted—"

"Was for me to be gay?" I say.

The car swerves, and I grip the seat belt tighter as we pull over to the side of the road. Cars whiz past us on the street, and I try to calm my breathing as I wait for my dad to blow up or something. I've never seen him mad enough to stop the car before, but now, now I have no idea what to expect.

Finally, he looks up at me through the rearview mirror and I freeze.

Because he doesn't look angry at all.

Instead, he has tears in his eyes as he says, "The last thing I ever wanted was to hurt you. Lo siento, mijo. I thought—"

My mom takes his hand, but she's still looking down at her purse on the floor. "*We* thought," she says, "we were protecting you. We thought we could protect you, but what you really needed protection from was us and—we're so sorry."

They're both crying now, and I reach up to wipe the tears from my own eyes. I don't know how to tell them that no matter how sorry they are now, it doesn't erase the last sixteen years, the doubt and self-hatred and pain that I've carried for so long because of the way they treated me. I don't know how to tell them how much it hurts that they tried to change me, even if they did it all to protect me.

But God, does it feel good to hear that they're sorry. To hear that they aren't disgusted by me. To hear that they want to make things right.

My dad wipes a hand across his face and says, "Theo—well, you really like him, huh?"

I shake my head. "I love him."

My dad stiffens in his seat for a moment before taking in a breath and wiping his eyes again. "Right. He's a good kid. I'm glad you found someone who makes you happy."

And I never thought I'd hear my dad say words like that, so much so that I'm having trouble believing I really *did* hear him correctly until my mom says, "And we'd like to get to know him better too, if that's okay with you? Maybe have him over for dinner sometime?"

"You can't be homophobic to him," I say, and they both wince.

Finally, my dad says, "Of course. It might take us some time, mijo, but I swear we'll do better."

And I smile because for the first time in a long time, I really feel like they mean it. Because it feels like, finally, we can start putting the pieces back together.

THIRTY-TWO
THEO

O nce Gabi and his parents leave the shop, my parents immediately stick me with cleaning duty. I take a selfie of me scrubbing the sink and text it to Gabi with a couple of devastated emojis, and then I hit send, wondering what the hell has happened to me that I'm now one of *those* people who texts selfies to his boyfriend.

Oh God.

Now I'm one of those people with a boyfriend.

And even worse than that, I don't absolutely hate it.

Who even am I?

The door swings open, and Uncle Greg enters with that irritated look on his face. Before I can tell him to go fuck himself, my mom comes back into the shop carrying a box of plastic cups with a stack of papers held on top of it with her chin.

"What do you think you're doing?" Uncle Greg snaps. "What do you mean, 'working somewhere else'? Where else you think you can work?"

Mom sets the box down on the counter. "We're going to be working with the Morenos starting next week, so you can convert the shop into whatever you want."

Uncle Greg's face pales. "I—convert the shop? Why would I do that when you love it so much? You can stay."

"No, no, you had those plans for that spa and everything. You should do it, Greg. I don't want to hold you back."

I can barely process the thin layer of sass to her voice, like who the hell is this? Mom would *never* talk back to Uncle Greg.

But Uncle Greg looks like he can barely believe it either. "I—June, listen, with Theo running deliveries, I think you're making enough now. I can let you stay."

"Actually, Theo's the reason we decided to move on. Turns out his business model worked better than ours, so we have no reason to stay."

And Uncle Greg shoots me the dirtiest look ever, which kind of feels like a badge of honor, all things considered. Then he says, "I couldn't get the funding for the spa, so the shop has to stay for now."

Mom smiles. "Then you can run it."

Uncle Greg stares back absolutely speechless before grunting, spinning on his heel, and storming out of the shop.

I turn to Mom and say, "That was amazing!"

My mom just shakes her head, but I can see a small smile tugging at her lips. "I guess it was a long time coming. Here."

She passes me the top page off the box, a series of fonts jotted down, showing the new shop name in all sorts of different letterings.

"What's this?" I ask.

"We agreed that since you and Gabi came up with the new name, you should have final approval on the signs. Any thoughts?"

And when we first suggested it, it just seemed like the obvious answer, given it was the culmination of everything we'd come up with together and the bestselling item on our menu, but as I look down at the fonts now, Café Con Lychee scrawled out in so many different styles, it all feels kind of unreal. I can still barely believe it's all happening.

I can't say I'm all that picky about the fonts, but I point to one anyway. If Gabi has any complaints, I'm more than happy to let him win that battle.

About an hour later, Thomas shows up, and I just throw a dirty rag at him and shout, "We're closed!"

He catches the rag and rolls his eyes. "You treat all the customers this badly?"

I shrug. "Just the ugly ones."

Thomas smirks, leaning on the counter, and says, "Mom told me they're thinking about merging the shop with the Morenos'. Your doing, I'm assuming?"

"Guess so," I say, turning back to wipe down the display case even though it's already clean. I'm not in the mood for a "You Really Had to Go and Meddle Again" lecture from Thomas.

But he just says, "Something going on there?"

"What's that supposed to mean?"

"With you and Gabriel Moreno?"

And it's weird to think that a couple months ago, that name

would've gotten my heart racing too, but for a completely different reason.

I opt for indifference as I make slow swipes across the display case. "We're dating now."

Thomas laughs, and I turn to toss another rag at him, but he just holds his hands up in surrender. "Congrats. I'm happy for you."

"Really? 'Cause it sounds like you're laughing at me," I say.

He smirks. "I mean, I *am* laughing at you, but just because you hated him like three months ago."

I roll my eyes. "I didn't *hate* him," I say. "We just had"—I think back on what my dad said earlier—"respectful differences."

Thomas shrugs. "Yeah, okay, sure. Whatever you say. Really, the main reason I stopped by was to give you this."

He pulls a folded sheet of paper out of his pocket and passes it over to me. I eye it warily before taking it, an eyebrow raised. "What the hell is this?" I say.

I start unfolding it and freeze.

"An invitation to a drag show," he says, eyes on the floor. "My friends kind of pressured me, but I agreed to it, so you should come. Bear witness to my drag debut."

"You're doing *drag*," I say, because this is the last thing I ever expected my "straight," parent-pleasing older brother to be doing, especially not *voluntarily*.

He winces. "Yeah, and I'm inviting you confidentially, so don't be a dick about it."

"I—sorry."

"It's chill. I know it's kind of weird, but I thought you might want to check it out," he says. "And you can bring Gabi too. He might like it."

I smile. "Yeah, I think he'll like it. Thanks for inviting us."

Thomas just waves me off, like this is the least consequential thing in the world, but I know it must have been a big step for him. Especially when he still doesn't feel ready to say anything to our parents.

And it's funny because three months ago, if someone had said *Thomas* would be inviting me to a drag show and I'd be eagerly attending with Gabriel Moreno, I'd have asked them where they'd gotten their drugs and told them to share, but now . . .

Well, I guess I can't even remember why I was so eager to get out of Vermont when everyone I love is right here.

ACKNOWLEDGMENTS

Just like the perfect sweets, there's a finely tuned recipe behind every book. For *Café Con Lychee*, it looks something like this:

Start with one agent who believes in the project and keeps it from falling apart. Thank you, Claire, for being the base I needed to keep this story alive.

Next, add a publication team to make the story rise. Thank you to my editor, Alex, for helping this book reach its potential, and thank you to my copyeditor, proofreader, and every other member of the HarperCollins team that put countless hours into making this book the book it is today.

Add two friends to help maintain the kitchen. Thank you Kelsey and Soni for being my support system through this entire journey, for being that extra pair of hands when I needed them, and for keeping me from cracking under the heat.

Sprinkle in a little community for taste. Thank you to all the friends and supporters who've made this publishing journey a little less lonely: Jonny, Aiden, Becky, Rod, Torie, Tee, Blake, Gabhi, Gee, Amanda, Molly, Lilly, Gabriel, Claudie, RoAnna, Mia, Ocean, Anniek, Blue, Colton, CW, Leah, and everyone else who's shown up for me and my books.

And the most important ingredient is a hearty dash of readers. Thank you for continuing to read, engage with, and put your entire selves into my stories. Thank you for taking these words that grew from my heart and giving them a place in yours.

The team who helped make
CAFÉ CON LYCHEE possible are:

Laura Harshberger, Senior Production Editor

Mark Rifkin, Executive Managing Editor

Erin Fitzsimmons, Art Director

James Neel, Production Associate

Kristen Eckhardt, Senior Production Manager

Alexandra Cooper, Executive Editor

Allison Weintraub, Assistant Editor

Lauren Levite, Senior Publicist

Shannon Cox, Marketing Associate

Thank you for picking up *Café Con Lychee*,
and we hope you enjoy it!

Quill Tree Books
An Imprint of HarperCollinsPublishers